Driven By Desire

'Where's Robyn?' asked Rachel.

'Inside, being attended to by two women,' came the reply.

Adrian's casual tone made her turn around. 'You mean swinging?'

He chuckled softly. 'Is that what the English call it? We come for good food, wine and conversation. Then, after coffee, we explore our sensuality. This time Robyn wanted to extend her experience. And I came out here to extend mine.'

'I don't mix business with pleasure,' Rachel said sternly, but Adrian was already working his hand under her skirt. Inside his trousers, his cock was bursting out of his very small briefs.

Author's Other Titles:

Wolf at the Door
Stormy Haven

Driven By Desire
Savannah Smythe

BLACK LACE

Black Lace books contain sexual fantasies.
In real life, always practise safe sex.

First published in 2003 by
Black Lace
Thames Wharf Studios
Rainville Road
London W6 9HA

Design by Smith & Gilmour, London
Printed and bound by Mackays of Chatham PLC

ISBN 0 352 33799 0

1

'How dare he do this to me! The fucking cowardly, sleazy fucking bastard!'

It had taken twenty years for Rachel Wright to learn how to curse like a King's Cross call girl but, six months after her husband had run out on her, leaving her with an empty bank account, a loan shark with a grudge and a business going down the pan, she was a fast learner.

'Do you know how he chatted me up?' she fumed to her closest friend as they attacked pasta at her favourite Italian restaurant on the King's Road. 'I got into his cab and at the other end, after I'd paid him of course, he announced he was going to take me out for a drink. I asked what made him think I'd want to go with him, and he said it because he was my Mr Wright. How cheesy is that? And I still fell for it.' Like she had fallen for his story that he had bought his way out of the army, when in fact he had been thrown out, as was revealed years later, for misusing the explosives he had been trained to handle. And the excuses he had given for hiring a succession of useless blonde secretaries who only ever lasted up to six months at a time.

'At eighteen I would have fallen for it, too.' Sharma, who was used to being used as Rachel's sounding board, threw the object of Rachel's rage on the table in disgust. 'What goes around, comes around, honey. Jerry's too much of a schmuck to live the high life for long. When he comes down, it'll be with a crash. You'll see.'

Rachel hoped she was right. The photograph gurned mockingly up at her. She turned it over so she did not have to see her soon-to-be ex-husband's dumb grin. It had arrived that morning, postmarked from Brazil. It showed Jerry, looking like a boiled lobster, raising a cocktail glass with a plethora of fruit and paper parasols, a smug grin on his face. Next to him, pushing her gravity-defying breasts proprietarily into his face, was their former receptionist. Framed with bouncy, bleached blonde hair, her tanned face was serious as she sucked a straw dipped into a piña colada with the concentration of a straight-A student.

Rachel almost felt sorry for Jerry for being such a cliché, but knew if she said so she would look like the typical sour-faced wife thrown on the scrapheap. That was unfair, for at 38 she had grown unusually beautiful. Her mahogany brown hair was sleek and glossy, complementing vivid blue eyes framed with strong brows and pale skin that freckled in the sun. She had always maintained herself well, even more so now she was getting older, but it still didn't stop her husband walking out on her, the stupid, blind bastard.

'I'd love to believe you,' Rachel said, picking up the photograph and shredding it into a hundred pieces. 'I just wish he didn't think it was funny to rub my nose in it.'

Sharma waved her words away with one large, beringed hand.

'Forget that arsehole, he's putting me off my food. Tell me about this new client of yours. Is he cute?'

'Adrian Grodin? Very cute and very married. They're flying in from Paris in two weeks' time for some do in Hertfordshire. Big house, big party, blah, blah, blah. How the other half live and all that.' She said it with only a tinge of envy. Really she wasn't into all that social stuff. Just being in her (rented) terraced Victorian cottage in Henley and having a job to go to was enough for now, thank you very much.

'Oh Lord, did you say Grodin? He's the artist that

married into the Valmez family last year.' Sharma was an avid collector of society gossip, and always seemed to have information to hand on just about everybody, especially those who chose to appear in tabloid chat magazines. It was her one vice, she said proudly.

'Who are the Valmez family?' Rachel asked blankly.

Sharma settled into village gossip mode, heaving her ample breasts up under her silk sari and plumping them on the table like a busybody leaning over a neighbour's fence. It was an in-joke of theirs whenever they had spicy titbits of information to impart. 'Well,' she said conspiratorially. 'Lots of raised eyebrows in Paris because old man Valmez is very protective, even though Robyn is in her forties. She's been married twice before, doing the Stephanie of Monaco thing with totally unsuitable men. Lion tamers and street cleaners, you know the deal. Adrian Grodin had nothing but a big schlong and marginal talent, but this time Daddy gives the blessing. Huge wedding, lots of piccies in *Paris Match*, and always at the best parties. Apparently she's a real bitch and since marrying Grodin has become totally insufferable. So it sounds like you're in for a lovely time.'

'Oh, super,' Rachel said archly, thinking that she had enough to worry about already. The pretentious mansion she had shared with Jerry had just been sold, but she was still five figures in the red with the bank manager breathing like a mad bull down her neck. 'Have you seen any of his paintings?'

Sharma thought for a moment. 'Yes, there was an article in the Saturday *Telegraph* ages ago, just after they were married. I didn't rate them much. He specialises in nudes –'

'Of course,' Rachel chipped in.

'Yes, but they're hideous. He was blathering on about the aesthetic beauty of the female form, but in my opinion he could make Uma Thurman look ugly. They're all sallow and bony or really over the top in the tits-and-arse department. And he uses yellows with skin tones. Not good.' Sharma was strictly a primary, in-your-face-colour girl.

'It hasn't done him any harm though, has it?' Rachel suddenly remembered something totally unrelated. 'Oh yes, I've got a bone to pick with you, Sharma McKenzie. Mr Grodin wants me to wear The Hat.' Sharma had bought the chauffeur's cap for her as a joke, but it had been requested by one or two of her clients, usually when they were slightly tipsy and having a laugh on the way home from some social function. None of them had asked her to wear it in the middle of Terminal Two.

'Sounds like he's a bit kinky. What is he like in the flesh, as it were?' Sharma's intrigue had been piqued by Rachel's description of their first meeting. She had been waiting at Arrivals, holding her smart laminated card with her client's name on it, sticking out like a sore thumb as usual among the massed ranks of male cabbies and chauffeurs. Some were smartly dressed, but most of them just looked crumpled and overweight. They in turn had been slightly derisory, some openly hostile, when she had first shown up in her smart black suit and high-heeled shoes. She had been given a good few cards by passing businessmen, some with messages on, and not all of them very gentlemanly. She didn't mind that. It came with the job.

Adrian Grodin had easily been the most stunning man coming through the double doors, walking as if in slow motion, dressed in the sort of carelessly tailored cream suit that only a well-heeled European could get away with. His short, floppy hair shone like spun gold. In one hand he carried an undoubtedly real crocodile-skin attaché case. The other held a leather Vuitton overnight bag. He looked like an angel among the uniform grey and dark blue suits scurrying like ants all around him.

He headed straight for her, although she knew he

wasn't her client for that day. As he drew close he seemed to envelop her in an invisible cloud of Etienne Aigner cologne, so much so that later she could still smell him on her, as if they had already become lovers. He produced a small cream card, embossed with his name and a French telephone number, and had slipped it into her blouse before she had a chance to take it from him.

'Yours, please,' he said in a thick French accent. For a moment she had been stunned; by his beauty, by the fact that he had spoken directly to her and by the depth of his liquid golden eyes. She fumbled in her top pocket to draw out one of her business cards and slipped it between the first and second buttons of his cream silk shirt. In that moment they were connected, and she knew without doubt that sooner or later he would have some kind of impact on her life.

'Probably one of the most beautiful men I've ever met,' Rachel said simply. 'And a bit of a rake, I'd guess. I might have to watch my virtue.'

Sharma sipped at her Chablis, leaving a perfect lip mark of Renegade Red on the wineglass. 'If it's on offer maybe you should fuck him. Get into practice again.'

'What about his wife?' Rachel said, laughing.

Sharma shrugged. 'They're French, aren't they? They don't mind that sort of thing.'

'Sharma McKenzie, I never thought I'd hear you say anything so dumb! That's like me saying because you're Pakistani you brought Matt up on curry, or that Col being Scottish makes him a tight wad! And I know damned well that isn't true.' Colin was Sharma's dashing consultant gynaecologist husband. He, like Sharma and everything else in her seemingly charmed life, was big and beautiful.

'Fair comment. Maybe it was wishful thinking on your behalf. When was the last time you had a good shag, anyway?'

'Don't, it's too embarrassing. I can't believe I was with that meathead for twenty years. The last time we did it was over a year ago.' Rachel looked around and then lowered her voice. 'He only knew two positions. On my back and doggy style on his birthday.'

Sharma snorted with laughter. Her laugh was loud and ringing, attracting stares from other tables. For almost five minutes they could do nothing but giggle. Rachel could never stay gloomy for long; it wasn't in her nature.

Later on, they were just saying goodbye in Sharma's bespoke country kitchen when her son Matt loped in. He went straight to the walk-in fridge, saying 'Hi, Rachel' over his shoulder. Being Sharma's son he had always been charming and articulate, towering over Rachel even when she first knew him as a gawky fifteen-year-old. Now nearly eighteen, he had clear skin the colour of coffee cream, deep chocolate-brown eyes and thick brows that gave him an intense, moody look that would no doubt go down a treat with the girls at Oxford, where he was inevitably headed that autumn, a year early because of his superior intellect. In the meantime Rachel was growing aware of his hungry looks whenever he thought she could not see him. Now, seeing her, his face had a very attractive rosy hue.

'Has he got a girlfriend yet?' she asked when he was safely up in his room in front of his beloved Power Mac.

'I wish. They're queuing at the door, but he's not interested.'

'You don't think . . .?'

'Gay? Definitely not. You should see what he hides under his bed.' Sharma paused by the front door. 'Tell you what, I'll get a table at Quagliano's tomorrow night. My treat, but in return I've got a favour to ask you.'

'Anything. I owe you big time, remember?' Rachel gave her a warm hug and left, wondering what she could possibly do for Sharma to make up for the financial and emotional support she had given her recently.

When Matthew McKenzie answered the door a week later his heart skipped a beat. Rachel was there, holding a bottle of Rioja. Black leather trousers, high-heeled black boots and a short jacket over a white silk blouse, the buttons of which stretched deliciously over her generous breasts. She gave him a friendly smile as he let her in.

'Sharma not home from Stratford yet?'

'No.' He felt trembly and a little weak. She had been the focus of many a wet dream in the past, but never as she looked now, sexy as hell in the snug black leather. 'She called and said to tell you she'd be a bit late.' He wondered what to say next. 'Do you want a cup of tea?' he said eventually.

She held up the bottle of wine. 'Show me a corkscrew. We'll start this without her.'

Matt mentally kicked himself. A gorgeous, sexy woman was standing three feet away and all he offered her was a cup of tea. He should have asked if she wanted gin and tonic, whisky, something sophisticated. Grateful for something to do, he went to fetch the corkscrew. When the telephone rang he ran back in.

'Oh, hi, Mum.' He listened with growing disbelief. Her client couldn't decide on cream silk or cerise satin so she was staying the night in Stratford to help her make up her mind. He shot a nervous, guilty look at Rachel. His father was also away until the weekend, which meant he was on his own with the woman he had spent the last few months fantasising about. And she seemed in no hurry to leave. He passed the phone over to Rachel and listened to her side of the conversation.

'It's really no bother. Matt will look after me.' An incredibly sexy wink in his direction. 'If you trust me with him.'

Then: 'I'll be gentle with him. See you on Friday.' She cradled the receiver and smiled at Matt. 'Oh well, I guess you and I will have to drink that wine. Unless you have something else to do?'

'No!' Matt said, too quickly. 'I mean, I've some work for college but it'll keep.' He looked at the corkscrew and realised uneasily that, despite his father's tuition, in his shaken state he was bound to make a hash of it.

'You want me to do that?' Rachel took the corkscrew from him and expertly opened the bottle. The cork came out with a soft pop. Matt put two glasses on the breakfast bar and she poured.

'It's too bad about dinner,' she said lightly. 'Have you eaten yet?'

'I, er, just had a pizza.' He sipped nervously at his wine. He could not have eaten a thing anyway. His stomach was tied up in a tight knot, which hardened as she slipped off her jacket. Her breasts pushed against the white silk, the fat nubs of her nipples unmistakable through a bra slightly darker in colour. He involuntarily licked his lips as he watched them. He had been hard the moment he had first smelled her perfume, and he knew it would not go away again until she had gone, and he could have a wank as he had so many times before.

She seemed not to notice his transfixed gaze, stretching easily and pushing her wondrous breasts further out at him. 'Do you mind if we go in the other room? These stools make my bum ache.'

'Sure. I just have to check the computer. I'm printing off the Net.'

'You're on line? I've never surfed the Net before. Do you mind if I have a look? See what all the fuss is about?'

Matt had a mild panic attack, before remembering that by some miracle his mother had tidied his room that morning. What had possessed her to do it was beyond him. She usually left that kind of irksome task for their cleaner. But the posters covering most of the walls suddenly seemed kind of dumb, the sort of thing a kid would have, and the thought of having Rachel Wright sitting on his bed made him feel both hot and cold at the same time.

'Come on up,' he said, and hoped it did not sound too reluctant.

The room was large, set out like a bedsit with a working space in one corner, and a television and sound system in another. The bed was wide, wrought iron and covered with working papers and compact discs. Every inch of wall space was covered with posters for films, Britpop bands and intelligent pin-up beauties, Sandra Bullock and Gwyneth Paltrow being his current flavour of the month.

At his desk he collated papers and shoved them back in the file to clear a space. He turned as she was inspecting his CD collection.

'I'll put one on if you like,' he said.

'Great.' She handed him Coldplay's *Parachutes*. It was a good choice, he thought as he put the music on. She leaned over his chair to look at the screen.

'You can sit down.' He motioned to the chair.

'I'm fine. I'm on my bum all day.' She did not move. He had no choice but to sit and almost feel the weight of her breasts on his shoulder. The music was soft but distinguishable, the light restful and intimate as it always was when he was working. His fingers rattled over the keys, seeking the best search engine and waiting for it to appear.

'OK. It's so easy. See these items here?' He pointed. 'Choose one and click on it.' He chose 'Media and Entertainment'. 'And it gives you all these choices here.' He used the mouse to find a listing on the latest film releases for April, and their critiques by various film magazines.

'The possibilities are endless. All you have to do is know how to use the mouse and not panic.'

'OK, so if you go to here –' she covered his hand with her own and moved the mouse to a long box at the top of the screen '– and type in whatever you like, you'll get every listing on the subject known to man?'

'That's right.' His voice wobbled. Her hand was warm and soft on his. Her perfume was light and flowery, unthreatening yet incredibly sexy. His raging erection had returned tenfold, and he prayed she could not see it, straining against his unforgiving Levis.

She clicked and typed 'Harvey Keitel'. Immediately an array of different subjects scrolled before her. She clicked on one of the options and started to read what was there.

'He's a great actor. Did you see him in *Pulp Fiction*?' she asked. 'Oh, I guess not. You're not allowed to watch "18" movies for another three months, are you?' She grinned at him.

He shrugged nonchalantly. 'I've seen a few already. It's no big deal.'

'I bet. It's crazy, isn't it? You can have sex at sixteen, but can't go to a movie and watch it on screen for another two years.'

Matt tried to reply but the words dried in his throat. She was in profile, leaning over his chair to read the screen. The top button on her blouse had slid out of its hole so that he could see one creamy breast, cupped in a gauzy, dusky-pink brassiere. The nylon was translucent enough to reveal dark areola and a pert pink nipple. As she shifted, her leather trousers creaked softly. He took a gulp of his wine and felt it kick in, from the warmth in his stomach to the buzz in his head. He was terrified of the temptation that plump nipple offered to him. Half of him wanted to grab her and screw her to the floor and the other really wanted the bathroom.

'Sorry,' she said after a while. 'It's addictive stuff, isn't it?' She looked round at him and he hastily shifted his gaze to her face. Her mouth was so close he had no choice but to press a kiss upon it. It seemed to happen quite naturally. His lips were warm and dry and hers were moist and open, the tip of her tongue brushing against his. Totally mortified, he jerked away. Thoughts of his mother raced through his head. To even think about kissing one of her friends in her own house ... he could not even imagine the ruckus. He would be grounded for months. He opened his mouth to apologise but this time she kissed him, tenderly, but with her tongue seeking his. He whimpered softly, unable to move. She moved away, smiling.

'You want to do that again?'

Dumbly, he nodded. She bent her head and, shyly, he began to return the kiss, tasting the wine and drinking her in. She found his hand and placed it on her breast. This time he grew more confident as he felt the weight of her breast in his hand. He kneaded it tentatively as she kissed him more deeply, responding to his own growing confidence, her tongue reaching to the back of his throat while he tried to match her but failed, too engrossed in what was happening to him. Mouths still locked, she drew him to his feet and they stumbled to the bed, scrambling on to it and sending CDs sliding to the floor. Feverishly he dry-humped her, unable to hold back any more.

'Stop!' She pushed him away and stood up, breathing heavily. He sat up as well, almost overcome with the urge to cry.

'Mrs Wright ... I mean, Rachel. I'm sorry. I didn't –'

She put her finger to his lips. 'You've never had a woman, have you?'

All his proud male instincts instantly rose to the surface. 'Of course I have!'

'No. I mean a woman. Someone who knows what to do.'

He was breathing heavily, leaning back on the bed, watching her with total disbelief. She undid what was left of the buttons on her blouse and slipped it from her shoulders, dropping it to the floor. The sight of her standing in just her bra and the tight leather trousers gave him back the hard on he had lost when she had pulled away from him. Her breasts thrust out at him, the nipples as hard as bullets. As her gaze dropped to the bulge in his jeans, she passed her tongue slowly over her lips. She cupped each breast in her hands and stroked the nipples, watching his expression turn hazy.

'Do you want to touch me, Matt?' Her hips moved slowly, a gentle circling that accentuated her small waist and tight backside. Before he could move she dropped to her knees before him. He felt overcome, terrified that he might shoot his wad right there and then. She picked up one hand and began to suck the middle finger. The warm, pulling sensation was almost too much.

'Don't do that!' he blurted, then felt incredibly stupid.

'It's all right,' she said firmly. 'You won't come until I say you can. Understood?'

He nodded. 'It's just that you look so . . .' He fought for the word and could not find it. 'Hot,' he said at last. Hot? What sort of fucking word was that to describe a woman who had occupied every fantasy of his for the last six months? He couldn't remember how it started. In the two years since his mother had been friends with her he had always liked her, but maybe it happened when her husband had walked out. At first he had felt sorry for her, then uncomprehending that a man would want to leave an attractive woman like her. Then he realised that she was now available. After that it had snowballed, and he had been jacking off most nights since, conjuring a similar scenario to what was happening now. But even in his wildest fantasies he had not dared for something like this.

'Just lie back and enjoy it,' she was saying, unbuttoning his shirt and pulling it away from his jeans. His body was smooth and elastic, with tiny dark nipples and a faint line of angel hair descending from a neat navel. He drew in his stomach as she moved closer. Her warm tongue touched each nipple in turn, then drew a wet line to his navel, where the dark hairs made a swirling pattern with the moisture she left on them. His balls felt full to bursting, pressing uncomfortably against the tough denim. His mouth dropped open in an involuntary gasp as her tongue wended its way back up his body to his throat. Her restrained breasts brushed against his chest as she licked his jaw, the soft skin behind his ear, each collarbone. Tiny 'uh' sounds emitted from his throat. Though he bit his lip he could not stop them. The smell of warm woman in leather drifted past his nose. She sat back again, watching his stunned expression, then she placed his hands on her breasts. Immediately he kneaded them, his eagerness almost painful. She stopped him.

'Take it really, really slow.' She showed him, using his fingertips to graze the hard points under the soft lace until he really understood. She hooked her thumbs into the cups of her bra and let her breasts spill out over the top. The tightness of the material held them up and together, the raspberry-pink nipples inviting him to taste and suck. The first time he did it was her turn to gasp. At the sound it seemed as if something snapped within him. He plunged his face into the warm mounds, running his tongue around each stiff nub. Now she was the one who was reacting, her hips undulating, her lips half open and feathering tiny sighs against his hair. He felt for her trouser zip and pulled it down, thrusting his hand between her legs. His fingers burrowed deeper into the black leather, finding her panties and working past them to the wet warmth he was instinctively seeking. Years of sneakily reading his mum's copies of *Cosmo* helped him find his way. Her cleft was molten, her panties already soaked. She managed to work her hand down between their writhing bodies and grasped at his balls. Her unexpectedly firm grip shocked him into looking at her face.

'Listen to me,' she said, a little breathlessly. 'If you want to learn how to please a woman, you do it my way.'

With an effort he reined himself in. It would have been so easy to push her back on the bed and plunge straight into her, but he would have lasted about five seconds. He let her get up and watched her as she pushed the black leather trousers down over her thighs, kicking them off together with the black boots. When she stood up again his breath caught. The tiny thong panties were the same dusky rose as her bra. They sat high on her hips, making her long legs seem even longer, and dipped low in front so only her sex was covered. But only just. As she parted her legs slightly so he could better appreciate her, he could see the plump outline of her labia, swelling against the damp scrap of lace. She slid her fingers into her panties and moistened them with her juices, then pulled them out and held out her hand to him.

'You want to know what a real woman tastes like?'

He greedily sucked her fingers into his mouth. She tasted divine, delicately musky, with a hint of hot leather. When she pressed his face between her legs he nuzzled the plump pad of flesh before pulling the panties to one side and pushing his tongue into her slit. She obviously wasn't prepared for that, as she steadied herself with her hands in his hair. The panties thwarted him from exploring further, so he pulled the moist piece of material downwards. She backed towards the bed and lay down so he could examine her fully. The dark hair covering her sex was soft and springy, quivering with each breath he bestowed upon it. The outer lips were plump, coyly hiding her inner folds. She reached down and spread them, opening herself up for him. She reminded him of some of the women he saw in the magazines under his bed, with their long fingernails stroking and teasing the mysterious folds of flesh. She gasped again as he ran his tongue around each inner fold, nudging her fingers out of the way. He knew the nut of flesh protruding at the top was her clitoris, so daringly he stuck out his tongue and fluttered at it. Immediately she groaned, opening herself out to him even more. Emboldened, he did it again, then strummed against it gently. Overwhelmed, she pushed against him, demanding him with her body to continue. He played with it, revelling in her hot little cries. A sudden, violent jolt made her body buck violently but he kept up the pressure, feeling her inner muscles contract and flood his face with feminine honey. He felt like shouting with triumph. He had actually given this luscious goddess an orgasm!

'You've done that before,' she said, when she could speak.

'I've been watching Mum and Dad's videos. Shit, it really does work!'

'Nine times out of ten it hits the spot. You're a good pupil, Matt. I think you deserve your reward.' She was stroking his hair, but not in a motherly way. She had the look of a woman well satisfied but still hungry. It made his cock swell again, reminding him he was still in his jeans. Without warning she pushed him on to his back. She straddled him and rubbed her velvet breasts over his chest, effectively wiping the smug look off his face. She shuffled back and carefully unzipped his Levis. As she did a massive bulge in white designer trunks reared through the opening, swollen even more by pride.

'Sit up,' she said.

He did so, feeling suddenly uncomfortable under her intense stare. Maybe he wasn't as big as she was used to after all. But the new position accentuated the shape of his balls in the soft cotton and the rearing beast above them. She made him stand up. He folded his arms across his chest in a show of bravado, while she ran her hands over his tight buttocks and up his back. At her command he removed his underwear, and when he lay down again she examined him properly for the first time.

He was big for his age, even considering his height. His cock arced with readiness, each throb a compliment to Rachel's ripe curves. As she swept her tongue around his balls he groaned uninhibitedly. She was better than even his wildest fantasies. He still could not believe she was here, stark naked, lavishing attention on his cock. The desperate feeling was growing again and he tried to fight it. He wanted to show her what else he could do, how hard he could fuck, but her mouth was so warm and her skin was so soft. His balls tightened as he neared exploding point, helpless before her scalding tongue and wondrous body.

She sensed the building tension and drew back just in time, letting him sink down to a controllable level of pleasure before climbing on top of him. Her moist folds wrapped around his cock as she displayed her breasts to him, toying with the fat nipples. He had his hands on her hips, squeezing her soft flesh, his body lifting occasionally to tell her he wanted to be inside her. She would not let him, continuing to tease him with her body.

But frustration and renewed confidence made him strong enough to sit up and throw her on to her back. By now he had enough control to savour the journey deep into her pussy. His eyes closed involuntarily as he felt her tight grip, and as her inner muscles massaged his whole length he sobbed with joy, but he wasn't going to lose it yet. Her fingers dug into his buttocks, opening them up, pushing them together, pushing him deeper and deeper inside her.

'Do you want me?' he asked, arrogantly extending the torture.

'What do you think?' She was challenging him.

'All of me?' He held back a little, making her whimper with her own frustration.

'All of you,' she said tightly. 'I want all of you.'

'Beg me. Say, "I want your cock, Matt." '

He could tell she was reluctant. After all, she had come with the intention of teaching him, he knew that now, but the power had shifted, and she was now his slave. His resistance to her was building, despite the punishment her tight pussy was inflicting on his cock. The longer he drew out her torment, the longer he would be able to fuck her with some of the stamina he imagined his father had when he fucked his mother.

'Say it,' he said again.

She looked up at him with luminous dark eyes, the tip of her pink tongue moistening her top lip.

'I want your cock, Matt.'

At her words he let go, plunging into her with all his weight behind each thrust. He was like a wild thing, teeth gritted, eyes blank as he fulfilled the hot dream he had been tormented by for months. If they never saw each other again, he would always remember the way her beautiful body surrendered to him and the tremulous pout on her lips as she said with complete truthfulness, 'I want your cock, Matt.'

But he wasn't satisfied with just the once. She had lit a flame in him and he wasn't prepared to snuff it out just yet.

2

It had been a stroke of luck that made Jerry indulge Rachel's wish to set up a chauffeur company of her own. He had given her an old S Class Mercedes and told her to get on with it, thinking that she would go back to coffee mornings and manicures when the first tax return needed filling in. The cabbie's licence had been a rubber stamp formality, and she had plenty of experience of handling large cars, as she had stepped in on occasions when one of Jerry's drivers was ill. The reception she had received from male clients encouraged her to form Interlude. She was determined to do it on her own, without Jerry's help. She procured a loan from the bank and bought herself a few smart black suits, then sent a flyer to every CEO in Hertfordshire, offering her services. Jerry was amused, but not for long, when it became apparent that her business was gaining the kind of clients that he was aspiring to and just not getting. While he was sitting outside pubs on a Friday night, she was winging to Heathrow with millionaires. It just wasn't right.

Then he had bailed out, leaving her with enough debt to put her straight back to square one. Now all Rachel had was a burgeoning overdraft and Reginald Tagger, a loan shark known for his brutal collection methods, who was still after the £20,000 that Jerry had owed him in gambling debts. Only unbeknown to her, Jerry, the little darling, had forged her signature, so the loan agreement appeared to be in her name.

Six months passed before she realised that, by leaving her, Jerry had freed her from her old self. Their marriage had been stale for years, but she had been too dulled by it to consider upping the ante. Now she was transforming into a new Rachel, teetering on the edge of self-discovery, fearful of what she might find underneath the middle-class mediocrity of who she had been for the last 38 years. Seducing Matt a couple of weeks earlier had only been the start. She had initially been appalled at Sharma's suggestion, but it had only taken a bottle of Shiraz and one of Sharma's superlative lamb curries to convince her. That alone had shown her how far she had come in such a short time.

The day that Rachel was due to pick up Adrian and Robyn Grodin from Heathrow was also the day she realised that life could be a lot worse. Up until now she had been so busy clearing away the detritus of her collapsed marriage and learning to survive that she had had no time to actually register the fact that she was alive. That day, with Heart FM on the radio and the sun shining down on to the black tarmac necklace of the M25, she could think of her bank manager and say for once, and very briefly, to hell with him.

She knew that Robyn Grodin would be bad news as soon as she saw the ill-tempered pout on her scarlet mouth. It seemed obvious that Adrian had not prepared his wife for an attractive brunette in stiletto heels to drive them to their party that night. It was also – more subtly – obvious that Robyn had a good few years on her husband, who Rachel guessed was in his early forties. Robyn had probably already seen fifty but, like most affluent French women, had looked after herself from the cradle up. She was very tiny and very chic, with breasts like bee stings and a concave stomach in a black woollen mini-dress, together with fierce Laboutin black boots with scarlet soles. Her dark brown hair capped her head in a gamine crop, with two perfectly teased tendrils below each earlobe. Pale foundation emphasised her dark eyes and crimson mouth, which perfectly matched a quilted crimson Chanel bag. She looked as hard as Adrian was gentle, but Rachel suspected that they cultivated the contrast for their own amusement.

Robyn spoke in rapid French that sounded like machine-gun fire, ignoring Rachel completely. As far as she was concerned, Rachel was nothing more than a servant and not worth the effort of being pleasant to. Rachel bore it with smooth detachment. She was used to frazzled tempers, and she was hardly in a position yet to get offended by her client's behaviour. In her own high heels she topped Robyn by several inches, and for once it made her self-conscious. She felt like a lumberjack next to the petite woman waiting impatiently by the car door, sucking fiercely on a slender cheroot. Rachel lugged a small Vuitton weekend bag, denser than the average black hole from the weight of it, into the boot and opened the door for her.

Inside was a prominent sign, understandable in all languages including French, saying that for the consideration of other travellers, smoking was not permitted. Robyn blatantly ignored it, coolly staring at Rachel to dare her to ask her to dispose of the cheroot. Rachel weighed up the situation and turned to Adrian, putting as much patronising politeness into her voice as she could muster.

'Would you explain to your wife for me that my next client suffers from asthma, so I would be grateful if she could refrain from smoking in the car, as the sign suggests?'

Adrian spoke in French to Robyn. Whatever he said was a great deal more than Rachel had asked for, and at the end of it Robyn's lips were tight with irritation. She blew a particularly long, noxious cloud of smoke into the interior of the car and flipped the half-smoked cheroot into the gutter by Rachel's feet. Then she flared her dainty nostrils at Rachel's considerably more curvaceous figure and gave a little humph of disgust before slamming the door shut.

Adrian spoke. His thick French accent was as seductive as his gentle golden eyes.

'You will get used to her,' he said.

'Was that an apology or a threat?' The words were out before she could stop them. 'I'm sorry, Mr Grodin –'

'Don't be. She's a difficult woman.' He smiled wryly. 'We've been married a year, and already I know.' He let Rachel past to open the door for him.

Rachel drove them to the Savoy and waited for two hours while they dressed for the party. When they appeared again Robyn looked exquisite, but Rachel would never have given her the satisfaction of shooting down any compliment. Adrian wore a white tuxedo and burgundy bow tie and cummerbund, his blond hair smoothed straight back in the style of a 1920s fop. Robyn wore a pale lavender silk flapper dress, so gauzy it was practically see-through, with pearly flower sequins to preserve her modesty. The handkerchief-point hem accentuated her shoes, which were of the period, square toed and only flattering to those with the refined bones of a Parisian model, which she had, of course. The dainty heels tapped sharply on the pavement as Rachel escorted them to the car. Once inside, Adrian explained to Rachel that the theme of the party was the 1920s, which she had already guessed, and that he and Robyn had been practising their charleston. He made it sound like a hilarious game of Twister, which didn't seem to relate to the ill-tempered woman at his side. Robyn eventually told him in French to be quiet, and the partition was slammed shut.

Chauffeuring was supposed to be all about driving, but mostly it was about waiting. As the evening was warm,

Rachel ate her supper of smoked chicken and rocket leaf salad outside, knowing that, even given her nationality, Mrs Grodin was unlikely to appreciate the smell of garlic wafting through the car on the journey home. She washed down her meal with mineral water and tidied up. It took organisation to do her job and maintain a healthy diet, but she managed better than some of her peers. Then it was the usual thing: a stroll round the grounds, a chat with some of the other waiting chauffeurs — those who would speak to her — a pee break and back to the car for another hour of reading and waiting.

She perched on the bonnet of the car in the fast-fading light, admiring the last burned-orange clouds hanging over the large lake and thinking affectionate thoughts of Matt. She hadn't seen him since the night she had seduced him; she was giving him a chance to get over any residual embarrassment. She realised now that Sharma, the sly minx, had not only suggested it for his benefit, but for Rachel's. Killing two birds with one stone and all that. Rachel laughed softly to herself and once again thought that life was pretty good considering she was on the outside of that beautiful house and not inside, rubbing shoulders with the elite.

Light and music floated from the house like streamers on a distant fan, together with the occasional burst of laughter. As midnight approached, Rachel was snoozing in the car, forced inside by the freshening temperature, when a knock at the door woke her. It was Robyn Grodin.

'Didn't you see us?' she snapped in perfect English.

'I'm sorry, Mrs Grodin.' Rachel opened the door for her, instantly awake again. Falling asleep on the job was something she just didn't do as a rule. Absolutely bloody typical it should happen tonight.

Adrian Grodin merely looked amused. There was the usual polite chat about enjoying the evening and then the partition window was shut again, cutting Rachel off from the occupants of the back seat.

She listened to Nina Simone and the journey passed. She hit negligible traffic until they got into London where, unbelievably, a burst water main was causing a large build-up. Stuck in the resulting jam, she opened the partition slightly to warn them of what was happening.

Of course, it had to happen sooner or later. Another first for her career, catching a couple *in flagrante delicto*. Fortunately, Robyn was unaware that Rachel had spotted what they were doing, as she seemed totally absorbed in nibbling at her husband's scrotum. Adrian's eyes were closed. He had undone his shirt and his trousers were pushed down past his thighs. Rearing above Robyn's still neatly coiffed head was his cock, long and fat, jumping against his bare stomach. Rachel felt that stab of hunger she had experienced when seeing Matt's lean young body in all its naked glory for the first time. Her throat had gone absolutely dry, watching Adrian languorously submitting himself to his wife's attentions. Rachel swallowed, trying to encourage some saliva back into her parched mouth, when Adrian's eyes slowly opened. He saw her and smiled beatifically, his cock rising and slapping back against his taut belly. Then he ran his tongue over his lips, at the same time pushing his hips out in the most lewdly erotic gesture Rachel had ever seen. It was a message sent directly to her own pussy, over his wife's unknowing head. Robyn responded to it, closing her lips over his cock and engulfing it to the hilt, totally unaware that she was in the middle of something dangerously close to infidelity being committed by her husband. His hips continued to move, fucking her mouth, but Rachel knew that in his head it was not his wife who was being fucked. She should have closed the partition, but she was mesmerised by his sensuous play-acting. Still blissfully unaware of her audience, Robyn climbed on to her husband's lap and pulled up her delicate dress. No panties. Had she ever been wearing any, Rachel mused. Then she noticed that Adrian Grodin had no pubic hair whatsoever. His balls and groin were completely denuded. Before she had a chance to register it completely, he steered his cock between his wife's plump, hairless pussy lips. He held her in a tight embrace, looking over her shoulder at Rachel. She felt his melting amber gaze but could not concentrate on anything but his cock, pumping up into his wife, and his jiggling, hairless balls. Robyn was screeching in ecstasy, rubbing her angry little breasts all over his bare chest. Rachel thought of a disparaging saying: 'All cats are the same in the dark.' It was unkind, but it seemed that sometimes sex could be a great leveller. She realised she was smiling when Adrian's look suddenly became desperate. He gave a snarl of pleasure, still watching Rachel, thrusting hard up into his wife's frantically wriggling body.

A loud horn made Rachel jump violently and turn back round. The car behind her was flashing its lights. The traffic in front of her had disappeared. She hurriedly pushed the gear stick into 'drive' and moved off, thoroughly shaken by what had happened. Between her legs she felt so moist and swollen it was as if he had actually penetrated her. It took a huge effort to drag her focus back to being professional and getting on with the job.

When she left them at the hotel, Adrian pressed a fat wad of notes into her hand.

'You did an excellent job. We'll use you again.'

'Nobody *uses* me, Mr Grodin,' she replied, steadily holding his look.

He nodded, smiled and obediently followed his wife into the hotel.

* * *

The next day she was at Arrivals to pick up her next client, a regular from Basingstoke who she got on well with. Such good timing was rare, but on this occasion it just so happened that he was coming in from the States half an hour after the Grodins' check-in time. She had a coffee and joined the others at Arrivals with her smart laminated placard, which she had had made up for each one of her regular clients. It stood out next to the scruffy bits of cardboard around her with names scribbled on in marker pen. She stood there, silently bearing their hostility, others that she had chatted to in the past not approaching her for fear of being accused of consorting with the enemy. It was one part of her job that she didn't enjoy that much, especially when she was feeling premenstrual and insecure.

Her client came. They exchanged pleasantries and walked back to the car park, where he waited while she went to bring the car round. As she approached it, she saw two people standing close by, staring at it. At first she did not think anything of it until she saw what they were staring at.

Someone had sprayed across the huge silver bonnet, in bright-red aerosol, the word 'WHORE'.

3

'He was a real gentleman about it,' Rachel said to Sharma later, 'but if it happens again I could be put out of business. The bank manager almost accused me of doing it myself to get the insurance money!'

She had offered her client a refund, which he had refused. He had even directed her to a garage to get the damage fixed for a minimal fee. Even so, it had been hideously embarrassing and only added to her overdraft, making the man at the bank even more tight-lipped than ever. She had not slept that night, wondering who hated her enough to do that. Other clients would not be so understanding, she was damned sure of it. She had already lost one deal because the car had not been ready in time. Even though it had hardly been her fault, it smacked of inefficiency on her part.

Sharma looked at Rachel's hollow, sleep-deprived eyes. 'You need feeding up. Get this down you.' She thrust a mug of seriously obese latte into her hands. 'And now I want to hear about Mr and Mrs Grodin. How did it go?'

'Pretty eventful.' Rachel told her what she had seen. They had settled at the kitchen table with their coffee. Sharma sucked froth off her spoon.

'I don't know of any man of sound mind who would willingly have his balls waxed. Shaved? No, not that either. Did you notice if he had razor burn?'

'I didn't actually get that close,' Rachel said, primly.

They concentrated on their coffee for a few moments.

'I'm a big-hairy-balls woman myself,' Sharma continued.

'I can't help thinking of them all vulnerable and skinny like newborn puppies without a bit of fuzz.'

'Not big and supple and leathery like a Hermes shoulder bag?' Rachel suggested. 'And you don't get hair stuck in your teeth.'

Sharma choked on her coffee and burned her tongue. 'Do you mind if we talk about something less dangerous? Well, almost. Matt's had a serious attack of hormones. He's nearly ripped my head off twice today.' She started moving around the kitchen again, inherently unable to keep sitting still for more than five minutes. 'You want to go and do a bit of detective work while I make a call?'

'Sure.' Rachel shook off her own troubles and went upstairs. They had not talked much about the favour. Sharma was content to know that it had gone well. And she had added that Matt had been in an insufferably good mood for all of the following week.

But not any more. His door was closed, but Rachel could almost smell the bad atmosphere radiating from behind that solid rectangle of pine. Thinking wryly that she knew how to seduce a teenage boy but had no idea how to get into his psyche, she took a deep breath and knocked softly.

'Hey, big guy. It's me, Rachel.'

No answer. Gently, she opened the door. He was lying in bed, speakers covering his ears, his eyes closed. From the slow movement she could see further down it was pretty obvious what was going on. She watched for a moment, wondering whether she should just creep out again and save him the embarrassment of knowing she had seen him. But the awakened, naughty side of her made her close the door quietly and go over to the bed. She slipped her hand under the duvet and squeezed the hand that was wrapped around his cock, clamping her other hand over his mouth to muffle his cry of shock.

His lower body jolted and his eyes flew open. She put

her finger to her lips as his breath came thick and fast. He was fighting mixed feelings of anger, embarrassment and delight at her seemingly magical appearance at his bedside.

'Your mother sent me up here to see why you've been like a bear with a sore arse all day. What's up?'

He sat up and shrugged moodily, suddenly looking like the teenager he was.

'Nothing,' he said sullenly.

She sat next to him on the bed, very close, and nudged him gently. 'This isn't like you, Matt. Can't you tell me at least?'

He laughed humourlessly. 'Maybe I'm young and stupid, but I thought that after you sleep with someone you at least ring them afterwards. You haven't been here for two weeks! I just feel –'

'I know,' Rachel said quickly, understanding perfectly but unsure how she should handle it without sounding patronising. This was a complication she hadn't expected. She bet that Sharma hadn't thought of it either. She chose her next words carefully.

'We had great, beautiful sex, Matt. It was something I'll remember all my life and I hope you do too, but I'm not your girlfriend, OK? Don't start going down that route because it isn't going to happen.'

He seemed to think for a very long time. She could almost hear the battle going on in his head. Reality versus fantasy, and what it was he really wanted.

'So what about this?' He flipped back the duvet and pointed to his penis, still half erect. 'What am I supposed to do about it when every time I close my eyes I see us on this bed. I can't get rid of it, Rachel. I want you all the time.' Even as he was speaking she saw his cock begin to shift and grow. She couldn't take her eyes off it. He leaned back on his elbows and let it unfurl straight up his belly, staring at her with confident, insolent eyes. 'You want it right now, don't you? You want my cock as you begged me for it the first time.'

How he could read her mind so readily was a shock to her. The temptation to suck him into her mouth and give him the pleasure he was yearning for was so tempting, but Sharma was downstairs, and could walk in at any moment. How she would react at seeing her best friend giving her son a blow job was anyone's guess. She tore her eyes away from that searing compliment to her charms and stared levelly at his face instead.

'Sharma's concerned. She isn't expecting an apology, but it would be a good idea.'

'And what about you? What are you expecting?'

It was a question no seventeen-year-old boy had a right to ask, and the half-smile she had put on his face seemed twenty years more mature than the face it belonged to. She left the room without answering him. On the way downstairs she considered warning Sharma that things could be getting complicated, but decided against it. This was something she would handle herself. Sharma had taken on enough of her problems already.

Two days later she took the Mercedes to the local tyre fitters for a check over. She loved her big bad Benz, but it was beginning to cost her a hell of a lot of cash. Dreading the fortune she was about to be charged, she swept into the forecourt and had another shock. Matt was standing there, watching her speculatively, wiping his filthy hands on grubby blue overalls. She smiled radiantly at him, although her heart had suddenly started thumping wildly. It was that burning look he had that seemed to vaporise her clothes and leave her standing naked in her kitten heels that did it.

'I didn't know you worked here,' she said.

'He isn't. He's gawping at you,' the oldest mechanic said, but his terse voice was kind. It was easy to like Matt.

'I'm only here for the holidays aren't I, Jim?' he said. 'Something wrong with the motor?'

She bit her lip to stop laughing. He would always sound educated, however much he tried to fit in with the blue-collar boys. She told them about the two front tyres, which were showing their age. Jim said they would get the car on the lift and have a look.

'Matt, take this young lady and see whether we have any of these in stock,' he said, winking at him. Matt smirked, full of bravado.

'Come with me, Mrs Wright. I'll sort you out.'

'I really hope it isn't going to be expensive,' she said as he prodded at the keys with short, dirt-impacted finger-nails. She walked around the counter so she could see the computer and the information on it. It was dangerous because she could sense his arousal from across the room. All swaggering bravado had gone. His breath was uneven and his hands trembled slightly as they fumbled over the keyboard, and she felt all that lust for his young flesh come rushing back. The smell of rubber was intoxicating too, hanging thickly in the air like an invisible curtain. Together they looked at her options as they came up on the computer screen.

'Those are your best bet, and we have them in stock,' he said, tapping at the screen. His voice wavered slightly. Her heart sank. Another five hundred to add to the overdraft. Oh well, business was business, and Rome wasn't built overnight.

A mechanic lumbered in. 'Uh, those tyres only have a few miles left in 'em, ma'am. You want us to do them now?'

'Yes, please.'

Matt stood up. 'I can sort out payment for you, Mrs Wright. Come this way.'

Rachel followed Matt through the workshop. The back office was tiny and filled with receipts, invoices and brochures. The walls were white and grubby, the windows unfettered and too high for anyone to see in or out. A curling girlie calendar hung on the wall, and two cups of old coffee sat on the brown Formica desk. It was an unattractive, stark environment.

'Everyone uses it,' he muttered, disposing of the scummy coffee. She shut the door as he wiped his hands on a useless tissue. She suddenly felt very nervous, but he no longer did. Without hesitation he pressed his lips to hers, being very careful not to soil her clothes with his oily hands. She licked her lips to savour the kiss.

'Matt, I don't think –'

'Good, because I'm not thinking either.' He kissed her again, barely restrained passion shimmering from every pore. She could smell it on him, musky and so hot he seemed to be surrounded by a heat haze. He took her hand and placed it over his crotch. He was rigid with excitement.

'Please, Rachel. I've been going crazy thinking about you.'

'But . . .' This was hardly the time to explain that she had only slept with him as a favour to his mother, and to be honest she needed something to take her mind off her ever-present financial crisis. 'If they catch us you'll get sacked,' she whispered.

He shook his head rapidly. 'They won't catch us. I'm about to lose it, big time.' As she rubbed her hand up and down the ridge in his overalls his eyes closed with pleasure. His wanton need had made her wet as well. Her sex was suddenly heavy and full, moistening her panties in response to his overwhelming desire. She stepped back and inched her tight chino skirt up her thighs, thankful that she had put on a small white cotton thong that morning.

His eyes bulged at the first sight of that small, plump triangle, his jaw tightening with the effort it took to keep control. She could hear the sawing of his breath, but he had lost the ability to move, so she took the initiative and reached out for the buttons on his overalls. She undid them very slowly, down to where they ended at his crotch. He let her slip them from his arms and they fell down to the floor, landing in a blue pool around his ankles. Underneath he wore tight black Levis and a surprisingly clean white T-shirt.

He nudged papers out of the way and leaned back against the desk, holding on to the edge. The outline of his erect cock was clearly visible under the tight material and her clitoris twitched in response. His raw attractiveness had lit a primitive fire in her that she did not want to control. When she took his jeans zipper and pulled it slowly down, his cock distended his black trunks, nudging his zip open even wider to make way. It was hefty and thick, almost out of proportion to his slender body and hard, flat stomach. The dark red tip pushed out to the top of his briefs, resting just below his navel. She ran her fingernail along the tense outline and he thrust involuntarily towards her, still keeping hold of the desk. His breathing was the only thing she could hear in the small room. She bent down and, with a flickering tongue, washed out his navel, blowing on the wet skin. Dark hairs flattened and swirled into patterns as she licked him. Her bottom stuck out as she bent down so he could see her thong panties disappearing under the cotton skirt.

'Oh God, let me fuck you,' he said. His voice was strangled with desire. She watched his cock, bouncing with every breath she played across it. Her mouth watered and she smiled at him. His jaw was clenched with anticipation. The atmosphere in the stuffy office had suddenly warmed up, and right then all she wanted was him, inside her, pumping like the young animal he was. She turned around and braced herself on the desk, pulling her panties to one side. Her sex was open and ready as he entered her with one deep, hard thrust. His filthy hands were on her hips, leaving dirty smudges on her lily-white skin. He withdrew, not all the way, but tantalisingly close, before plunging into her again. She had taught him well. He was considering her pleasure as well as his own.

But it was no good, he was too full of need to stop himself. He began thrusting at her with solid force, grunting deep in his throat to stop himself alerting the world outside. She bit her lip and pushed back, needing him and more besides, but relishing his ferocious attack. He came with a pulse that rocked her lower body to the core, her hot little cries intensifying his pleasure and adding to her own. Her climax was far less intense, but as satisfying as a bar of Swiss chocolate at coffee time. She sighed deeply with pleasure as he withdrew and zipped himself back up. He handed her some tissues to wipe herself.

'I wish I could offer you a discount for that, Mrs Wright,' he said, as respectful as ever. There was a tentative knock on the door. It was almost as if they had been waiting outside for them to finish, but that could have been her guilty imagination.

'Your car's done, ma'am,' Jim said. He did not meet her eyes, so she was pretty sure he knew what had been happening, though not quite believing it.

'Thank you,' she said smoothly. 'Will Mastercard do?'

4

A week later she came to the short-stay car park at Heathrow to find that all her brand-new tyres had been slashed. This time she had no choice. She lost the client, his business and another seven hundred pounds for the tyres. That night, for the first time since Jerry had walked out on her, she cried herself to sleep.

The next day, she went to the bank to see the Mole. That wasn't his name, but he had round wire glasses, a little pink nose and mean little lips, as well as hands that were never still. He had taken over very recently from her old bank manager, who had been a lot more sympathetic. But he had died suddenly of a heart attack and now she was at the mercy of a new broom, determined to make his stock look good. The overdraft was getting out of control, he said. She had three months to prove that Interlude was a viable proposition, or he would call in the loan. There was no negotiation. His decision, he said triumphantly, relishing the control he had over her life, was final.

That night she went through her finances with a fine-tooth comb to see what could be done. At least when Cab-U-Like, Jerry's cheesily monikered taxi firm, had gone into receivership, most of the major creditors had been paid off. That left her own overdraft and Reginald Tagger. Pretty soon he would call in the note on his £20,000. At first she had been able to put him off, because it was obvious that she had nothing to give him. Now she wondered if he had anything to do with her latest problems. She was streetwise enough to know the score. Soon he would call round, offering his protection for a fee. She was beginning to get jumpy every time there was a knock on the door.

There was no way she could pay him. Her earnings from Interlude just about paid her rent and kept her fed, but right now there was no chance to raise any capital so that she could expand Interlude and bring in more money to pay off her debts. In her despair she began to understand why Jerry had done what he had done.

Don't even think about going there, she scolded herself sharply. Jerry was a coward, but you're not. Fight it and win. The line of a song kept coming to mind. Desperation makes you strong. Thank you, Spandau Ballet. She wrote those four empowering words on a piece of card and pinned it up on her fridge at home. And she repeated the mantra on the way to Heathrow to pick up Adrian and Robyn Grodin. She drove around and around until she found a spot directly opposite a security camera. She also alerted the security staff, but guessed they wouldn't do much unless they caught the culprit in the act. Reluctantly she left the car alone and went to Arrivals. She had begun to dread the place. Every face seemed like a potential enemy. News of her trouble had spread through the cabbies at Arrivals. They looked at her as if they couldn't believe she was still there. 'Was it one of you bastards?' she wanted to scream at them, but they wouldn't say, and no one would tell. The barrier between her and them was almost visible.

The next morning, Saturday, was a perfect English summer's day, and she woke up not wondering who was going to bang on the door that day, which was a mistake. She took Adrian and Robyn back to Heathrow, stopped for a coffee at the Starbucks there and went back home to vacuum the car and give it a polish. She was just about tall enough to reach into the middle of the roof to buff up the last smudges. As she was reaching over she sensed someone behind her. It was Reginald Tagger.

She only knew because there was no one else who would come and visit her on a Saturday morning in a big black Mercedes, driven by Mike Tyson's double. Tagger was even bigger, built like the proverbial brick shithouse, a fat gold cobra link chain around his chin, because God had not thought to give him a neck. He looked like a bullfrog, all bulging eyes and rubbery wet lips, quite repulsive. She looked for the baseball bat. He didn't have it, but she was sure that it wouldn't be too far away.

'I hear you're having some trouble,' he said, pleasantly enough. 'Lots of vandals around these days. Don't think twice about slashing a lady's tyres.'

She nodded wearily. Her instincts about his involvement had been right on the money. 'I am. Twenty thousand in the red, another twenty owed to you and just enough money coming in to keep this car on the road. If you want money from me, I can't do it. If you smash up my car, you'll get fuck all anyway. Everyone loses.' She kept polishing, not meeting his eyes. He was giving her close scrutiny, from her snugly clad backside in denim shorts to her long legs and battered Nike sneakers.

'I could use a good driver.' He looked back at the heavy-set man behind the wheel of the shiny Mercedes. 'He's a prick. Doesn't know how to park the thing. I've seen you in action and you're pretty good.' She felt his hand on her backside, fondling her buttocks. 'I think we could make a pretty good team.'

She shifted away from the invading hand. 'I appreciate what you're saying, Mr Tagger, but I work for myself . . .'

She found herself pushed up against the car, held there by one porky, sausage-fingered hand. The other was in her face, his finger stiff and angry.

'I don't think you appreciate it at all, Mrs Wright. You

owe me, and right now you know as well as I do that you can't pay it back. I'm offering you a way out, so be a grateful bitch and take the opportunity to thank me while you still can. You've got two months. After that, you're on my payroll, like it or not.'

He stepped away from her and picked up the bucket of grubby water. He threw it all over her beautiful clean car and strode back to his own. With a screech of wheels he was gone.

'Terrific,' she muttered, but she felt sick. It hadn't been a surprise, but she had hoped for a few more weeks. Now she had a month before he came back for her body as well as her soul. The thought of having to get naked with him made her gag.

She was still shaken when Sharma came round an hour later.

'Look, you knew this was going to happen, didn't you? And Colin's already negotiated a deal with his bank to lend you the money with minimal interest, remember? Do it and get him off your back.'

Rachel shook her head. 'No.'

'What do you mean, no? You don't have any choice!'

'I mean it won't make any difference. He isn't going to leave me alone. He's made it quite clear what he wants.' She hugged her coffee mug for comfort. He wanted her to whore herself to him and be in his power until he tired of her. Then he would throw her away like trash. 'This one is going to run and run, Sharma. He doesn't give a shit about the money. It's the kick he gets from grinding people into the ground.'

'You don't know that for sure. Let's deal with the problem we know about and worry about others when they arise.' She draped a heavy arm around Rachel's hunched shoulders and held her tight. 'Come for supper tonight. We've got company, but there's always room for one more.'

Rachel shook her head. 'Thanks, but I'll be OK. I think I might go to the gym and sweat it out.'

Rachel was glad that Sharma didn't press her. She wanted to convey that, although she was very grateful for Sharma's help, she didn't depend on it. But her visit had made Rachel feel a lot stronger inside. One problem at a time, she reminded herself, and only worry about them as and when they come up. Which they were doing with depressing regularity.

Early that evening she drove to the health club. It was very classy, attached to a hotel, and was the last thing she had paid for before Jerry's departure; as refunds weren't an option, she had decided to make good use of it while she could.

On her way she was aware of the red Porsche 911 in her rear-view mirror. It was hanging well back, which was unusual. Was it one of Tagger's men, trying to intimidate her? Probably not, because no one on his payroll was allowed to drive a better car than him. But it was odd. Men in those motors usually liked to overtake everything in sight or, if they knew the S Class Mercedes driver was a woman, do a bit of ducking and diving, for some primeval, pointless reason. Every time she looked up he was there, the bold paintwork gleaming in the early evening sun. She checked out the driver and decided he looked promising. Dark suit and dark hair, probably mid-forties. White collar. This is where I go all blonde and superficial, she thought resignedly. I have loan sharks banging on the door, the bank about to pull the plug on my business and I can still think about sex. Things can't be that bad just yet.

Idly, she began to think bad thoughts. What if Mr Porsche was going to the health club? What if he hit on her and wanted a different kind of work-out? Would she say no and be incredibly responsible about it, like the old Rachel? Or would she give a Gallic shrug and murmur 'c'est la vie' into his ear before leaping on top of him? Probably the latter, she decided, and blamed her wanton behaviour on stress.

But when she reached the turn-off to her health club and he followed her in she felt almost sick with anticipation. He swung into the space next to her and climbed out. Just over six foot, she judged, and slim. The suit was expensive, like his black lace-up shoes and attaché case. Aware she was staring, she scooped up her sports bag and lingered over locking the door. To her total disappointment he did not even look at her. Instead, he ran up the stone steps to the adjacent hotel entrance, leaving her to turn in the other direction to the health club.

In the changing room she felt completely flattened, although she could not put her finger on why. Half-tempted to just go home, she forced herself to undress and squeeze into her bitter-orange thong leotard, adjusting the skimpy black shorts over her thighs. Her skin was pale but even, and the piped trimming on the leotard accentuated the swell of her breasts and the narrowness of her waist. She pulled the tab on the black zip, watching how it confined her breasts as the material closed over them, creating a deep, shadowed cleavage. Suddenly she felt hot again, and hoped there would be a man in the gym she could indulge in a little flirtation with. She tied the laces on her Reeboks, and with a final critical glance, stepped out into the fray.

He was there in reception, chatting to the pretty brunette behind the desk. He had changed into a pair of grey jogging bottoms and a burgundy hooded sweatshirt. He looked up as she approached and gave her a flickering glance before turning into the men's changing area. Her heartbeat quickened.

She retrieved her card and exchanged small talk with the young, lithe gym instructor. He was blond and outgoing and knew every woman member's name. Consequently he was popular and never short of fawning admirers. It made her laugh, the feeble questions they asked just to grab his attention. He flashed Rachel a genuine Colgate smile because she was one of the few women he took seriously.

She had been on the treadmill for three minutes, warming up, when her executive friend reappeared in small, dark-blue shorts and a white singlet. He sat on one of the bikes and began prodding at the buttons. For half an hour they both did the rounds, Rachel observing how his muscles worked under his tight, tanned skin, he watching (she hoped) the sweat patches form on her back and under her breasts. The more she worked and watched him the hotter she became. At the back of his neck his hair was short and slick, the sweat trickling down and settling in damp grey patches on the white cotton. He was obviously very fit, and very intense in his concentration. His eyes were blank, all energy turned inwards. Out of the blue came the clearest image of him in the shower, covered in soapsuds. She knew exactly how he would look. Long, lean thighs, a meaty cock and silky dark hair spreading across his broad chest. Her sex felt hot and moist and could not be ignored. She could almost feel moisture slowly seeping through the two thick layers of Lycra to darken the orange material drawn tight between her legs.

At that moment, he looked up and saw her looking at him. The lust on her face was obviously transparent and he acknowledged it with a small smile. Suddenly desperately thirsty, she stopped the Stairmaster and went to get a drink from the water dispenser. The flush on her face subsided with the cool water, until he took the paper cup from her and drank the remainder, watching her blush deepen again.

'Do I come up to the mark?' His voice was deep, well educated and amused. His slow smile had reached his eyes, which were as blue as the Mediterranean. She coughed to clear her throat.

'I haven't seen you here before. Are you new?'

He looked down at his finely tuned body. 'Does it look like it?'

She flushed again, before realising that most men would probably have taken the question at face value. But something told her he was not like most men.

'No, you have a great body. What I meant was, are you new to this club?'

'Is this like, do you come here often?'

'Oh, for heaven's sake!' She stalked away from him and climbed back on the stepper, away from his mocking eyes and insolent expression. He climbed on the one next to hers and started to work.

'Do you always answer a question with a question?' she asked. He opened his mouth to speak, thought better of his answer and grinned again.

'No. In fact, I'm staying at the hotel. On business.' He blatantly appraised her body with lazy eyes, and this time he was not smiling. The desire on his face was potent and immediate. 'Can I buy you dinner?'

'Is that what you really want to do?' Her full lips curved into a smile as she stared straight ahead to the television screens.

'You won't believe this, but I've never picked up a woman in the gym before.'

'Is that what you're doing?'

'Do you always answer a question with a question?'

She looked at him then, and they laughed together. 'Touché. Dinner sounds good.' Her fingers found the deep pulse on her neck. It was racing more than usual. They walked to the changing rooms. His hand stayed her arm.

'Do they have a steam room here?'

'Sure. Next to the –' But he was already guiding her towards the pool. The night was now dark and the water was back lit, glowing an ethereal green. A lone swimmer carved a swathe to the far end. They walked past into a smaller changing area leading to the steam room, the sauna and the Jacuzzi. Soft saxophone music drifted through the ceiling. There was no one else in sight. A pile of neatly folded, fluffy white towels lay by the door. He took one and handed it to her. She took it reluctantly. After all, she had only known him five minutes, and now he was expecting her to sit with him in an enclosed, quiet space, wearing only a small towel.

'Do I have a choice?'

'Not if you want dinner.'

The determination in his voice made her shiver, despite the intense warmth surrounding them. Silently she locked herself into a cubicle. As she stripped off the leotard and tights she could smell her own musky aroma. She lingered over her thong panties, trying to decide whether or not to keep them on. In the end she removed them as well. If he really wanted to try it on, they would hardly be an effective barrier. When she came out with the towel wrapped firmly around her body, he was nowhere to be seen. The small window into the steam room was covered in moisture, blurring her vision. As she pushed the door she realised she did not even know his name.

To her relief he was wrapped modestly in his own towel, sitting on one of the wooden benches. There were three levels, the highest being the hottest. He sat in the middle, perspiration dripping freely down his face and body.

'I thought you had bottled out,' he said.

'Why should I?'

'There you go again, answering with a question.' He stuck out his hand. 'I'm David. And you are?'

'Rachel.' She took the proffered hand. It was large and

firm, like ... Her gaze dropped to his lap. Her eyes snapped back up again, but he had seen.

'Good. Now we know each other's name we can dispense with the formalities.' He went to remove the towel but her hand on his stopped him.

'No! Not yet.' It was too quick. His thumb stroked hers as if he could read her mind.

'I'm sorry. It's just that watching you working out and imagining the sweat pooling between your breasts and making your sex all sticky has given me the biggest hard on and now it's beginning to hurt.' Gently he placed her hand over the towel-covered bulge and leaned back against the wall, watching her reaction. Her hands were small and his cock, what she could feel of it, was very long. She panicked and turned to go, but he caught her wrist.

'Where are you going?'

'You obviously took me for someone who knew what they were doing. I've never done this before in my life. I don't even know why I'm here.'

'Would you like to find out?'

His soft voice lured her into looking at him. Suddenly she felt like a virginal teenager again. She nodded mutely, aware that a golden opportunity had just fallen into her lap. Or, more appropriately, into his.

'Someone might come in,' she whispered.

He smiled. 'They might.' He sat back again and placed her hand on the bulge under the towel, pressing and rubbing gently against it. She could feel his erection growing again, and remembered her vision of him in the shower earlier on. Her clitoris started to beat its own rhythmic tattoo as he let the towel fall to the white-tiled floor. His cock was just as she had imagined it. Long and dull red, the glans like a ripe plum. She ran her finger along its length, feeling it quiver under her touch. He parted his legs, letting his balls fall between them. They too were heavy, pulling at his scrotum, and covered with the same soft, springy hair that matted over his chest. She lifted them gently, fondling their delicacy. He was watching with heavy-lidded eyes, leaning back against the wall. The steam drifted around them both, making her skin slippery to the touch. He lifted his hand again, as if it were made of lead, and stroked the back of her neck.

'Kiss it.'

After token hesitation she brushed her lips against the veined shaft, letting her tongue flicker over the thin skin. It tasted of musk.

'Yes, like that. That's good. Now ... use your tongue around the head.' She drifted upwards, tentatively flickering the pointed tip of her tongue against the teardrop-shaped hole and tasting salt.

'That's great. Run the length of your tongue around the glans. That's good. Very sensitive there. Use your lips as well. It feels great. So smooth and warm and –'

She looked up at him. 'When I said I hadn't done this sort of thing before, I meant picking up a man in a gym. I do know what to do with him once I've got him, so shut the hell up and enjoy it.' She sucked him back in again, watching him boldly as she did so. His reply was gagged by a tightly restrained groan as she ran her lips up and down the whole length of his shaft, swirling and feathering her tongue over every rigid inch. His eyes closed with pleasure and her confidence soared. The smooth texture of that large glans against the inside of her mouth gave her an immediate rush of desire that was almost orgasmic. He slipped down the bench, thrusting up towards her. The power she held over him was now total.

His fingers twined in her hair as she took more of his length in her mouth, sucking, squeezing, using her inner muscles to build on his passion. His cock hardened even more, bringing him close to the edge as her mouth so eloquently translated what his cock was demanding. She pushed her bottom out, picturing her sex dripping and open, waiting for his attention. Suddenly she felt near to coming, imagining him pulsing inside her. Her towel fell away and her breasts brushed against the hot, fragrant wood, stiffening the nipples into rigid points. She concentrated on his testicles, lifting each one in turn with her tongue then sucking it into her mouth, pulling gently at it with her lips, watching his cock jump against the flat of his stomach. He moaned his approval, total rapture on his face as he gripped the wooden slats with white-knuckled hands. The intense heat in the room was making her heart race dangerously fast, the steam catching in the back of her throat. She moved up and loitered around his glans again, roaming her tongue up and down his shaft. He was too weak to thrust any more, so he had to take what she was giving, or choosing not to give.

'You're killing me,' he muttered. It could be true. Rachel's heart felt as if it would burst any minute, so she could imagine what the heat and the decadent pleasure she was giving him were doing to his bloodstream. She felt him tense, his balls lifting to empty their load. With exquisite timing she drew him all the way in, squeezing every inch of him. His hips bucked, and with a long, drawn-out groan he let go. Hot salty liquid hit the back of her throat and she sucked him dry. He slumped against the wall, gasping for breath.

'Oh, yes,' he murmured, as he floated back down. The heat was so intense, the steam so thick that his voice had faded. 'That was totally wonderful,' he said finally.

'Thank you,' she replied, 'but if you want more, first you have to feed me.'

'I thought I just had.' Her severe look made him smile. 'I was joking,' he added.

* * *

45

His name was David Fielding. He sourced fine gems for wealthy clients, and mostly dealt in diamonds. He was forty, not married and not living with his mother. His job meant that relationships were hard to sustain. She took that as meaning he was commitment-shy. It didn't bother her. She had too much on her plate at the moment to think about her private life on anything other than a physical level.

She went home to change, and arrived back at the hotel an hour later, wearing her favourite wraparound dress. Underneath she wore a cream voile bra with matching sheer panties, and a matching suspender belt holding up sheer stockings. The dress was also cream, contrasting nicely with her glossy conker-brown hair, the skirt tulip-cut just above the knee to reveal the length of her legs. It was held together with a single large, square, ivory button at her hip. The neckline plunged deep, but managed to remain discreet unless she chose to move in a certain way, giving her the choice of seduction. In the car her legs trembled as she remembered the man waiting for her at the luxurious hotel. She could be a whore, and if he thought of her as such she did not care. Her body craved sex. Having tasted the appetiser, she was greedy for the main course.

The hotel was actually an old manor house. The doorways were tall, the windows draped with thick brocade curtains. The lounge bar ceiling was high and coved and painted an antique dusky red. Cigar smoke mingling with the heavy scent of waxy, white lilies gave the place an atmosphere of expensive respectability. He was waiting for her by the wide doorway that led out to the veranda, watching a sudden rainstorm from a deep chintz chair. He was wearing dark, casual trousers and a cream silk shirt. No jacket or tie, but he still managed to exude quiet class. By his side was a tumbler of whisky. The waiter took her order of a gin and tonic and melted away. On the coffee table was a bowl of glistening pitted Spanish olives. She took one, sat down in one of the accompanying large armchairs and inhaled the sensual scent of rainwashed grass drifting in through the doorway.

'I hope those are stockings.'

'Of course.'

'Show me.'

Her heart thumped at the command in his voice. She let the skirt fall apart, showing off one long silky leg, and the elaborate lace webbing over her pale skin. At that moment the waiter appeared from behind with her drink. His young face was scarlet as he handed over her glass. Daringly, she winked at him. Since being in the steam room the devil had moved in. He allowed himself another look before fleeing. David was watching her with a steely look.

'You can flirt with other men but don't do it while you're with me. Understand?'

Casually she flipped her skirt back over her leg. 'That's a bit presumptuous, isn't it? How do you know I'll want to see you again after tonight?'

'You will, for the same reason that I'll want to see you.'

'And what reason is that, exactly?'

'I'll tell you after I've tasted you.'

A middle-aged couple were walking past at that moment. The woman flushed furiously while her husband looked embarrassed. Rachel thought how close she and Jerry had come to being just like them. Jerry always referred to sex as 'fiddling around'.

'Go to the ladies' room and put this on. I want you to wear it while we have dinner.'

David's voice pulled her back. He was slipping something small and heavy inside her bag. She looked at him, but his face was impassive.

While he was being shown the table she slipped away to the ladies' toilet. She pulled out the bag he had given her. She was expecting underwear but what she got was a six-inch black dildo. Thick and veined, fashioned from warm latex, the bottom end was winged so it would not get lost. The bulbous glans was bouncy yet solid, as though something was inside, but she could not see or feel anything when she shook it. The rubber was smooth and unseamed, an expensive toy. Although she was moist and receptive her muscles still protested against its impersonal hugeness. When she stood up and adjusted her panties over it she felt thoroughly stuffed, but somehow lewd and excited at the same time. Her muscles squeezed against the alien intrusion while her sex reacted by lubricating and opening even wider. Her panties were tight, preventing escape. A little unsteadily, she walked out to her seat, gasping involuntarily as she sat down, pushing the dildo up against her womb. David was watching her steadily.

'Do you have it in?'

'No,' she lied.

'I can find out.'

'Oh? How?'

'You'll see,' he said mysteriously.

They ate smoked salmon and duck in cherry *confit*. He talked about his job, but did it without affectation, not trying to impress her. How refreshing was that, she mused, thinking how unusual he was (that was already obvious, having presented her with a dildo less than four hours after their first meeting). At the same time, he steered clear of any exchange of personal information. He asked about her job, but in a perfunctory fashion, as if he just wanted her to confirm what he already knew. It didn't bother her unduly. Despite what he said before she presumed that he had no plans to see her again after that night.

Every time she shifted on her seat the thick dildo reminded her of its presence, flooding her panties with moisture. As she was halfway through dessert she felt the first soft pulsing deep inside her. Then the cock was moving up and down, fucking her from deep within. For a moment she closed her eyes, confused and overcome with the sensations the swelling cock was sending through her lower body.

'So you do have it in,' David said softly. The pressure increased.

'Stop it!' she hissed. Involuntarily she opened her legs under the table, mercifully hidden by the long, linen tablecloth, and tried not to give in to the mounting pleasure. He watched her fighting it, all interest in her meal gone. With the remote control he increased the pressure, watching her jolt and bite her lower lip.

'Please,' she pleaded. 'Not here.'

'Play with your nipples.'

'No,' she managed to moan. She clutched the table, trying to breathe. The tool inside her was swelling and squirming, making her body a slave. She wanted to spread herself out and let it fuck her to the limit but just as she was reaching the peak of her endurance he switched it off, plummeting her back down to earth.

'Play with your nipples, Rachel. Make them hard for me. I'll keep you screaming for mercy until you do.'

Suddenly desperate for the deep pulses to begin again, she did as he bid, using both hands this time to pinch and squeeze her nipples until they were tight buds. He watched them, running his tongue over his lips. Surreptitiously she pulled her dress to one side so he could see her cream bra, and the pink tip pushing against the mesh. He applied more pressure again. Her already stimulated body jolted into overdrive. Under the table her legs spread wide, letting the tool fuck her hard and deep. She slipped off her shoe and pressed her toes against his groin. To her utter amazement she felt his naked cock, upright and very hard, and his hand, palming it as he watched her.

He guided her foot to his cock and pressed them together. His other hand was on the table, concealing a small black box which held the controls to the vibrator. She could see his chest heaving slightly under the silk shirt but his face was not giving anything away. With her foot she braced herself against his cock as he shifted the vibrator to maximum speed and watched her eyes close and her mouth fall open as she tried and failed to overcome the dizzying heights of her orgasm. She muttered a series of tiny 'oh' sounds as she came, clutching her chair, hoping and praying that no one was watching her.

'You fuck,' she gasped, as soon as she could speak. 'You bastard fuck.' The words fell from her lips and she was shocked. She had never spoken to anyone like that before. Not even Jerry when he was being a prick.

'Glad you liked it,' he said, smiling coolly. 'Now you may go and remove it. We'll have coffee up in my room.'

She struggled to make herself decent again. 'How do you know I'll come back?'

'Because you want my tongue in your slit. Now go.' He was not amused any more. His voice held the same command as before, but roughened by anticipation.

In the ladies she gently removed the dildo. Where it had been she felt tender, her sex lips stretched wide and gaping. Tentatively she touched herself. He was right. She did want more.

As he reached for her in the privacy of his bedroom, she stopped his kiss with a hand on his chest.

'I was with the same man for twenty years. Despite what I said earlier, I'm still an amateur.'

David didn't smile because, as she was beginning to realise, it was something he just didn't do that often. She wondered why, but just at that moment it wasn't appropriate to dwell on such mysteries.

'There are no amateurs in this game, Rachel. You just

have to give in to what your body wants and not be afraid to express it.' He kissed her gently on the lips. 'Don't be afraid to tell me what you want. That is all I ask of you.'

She ran her fingers along his smooth jawline to his lips just as they covered hers again. As he drew her close to him she could sense his tensile strength, and almost imagined that it was strongly reined in so as not to scare her, fighting as he was against his own physical need. When the kiss ended, it was as if he had to force himself to stop, for fear of overwhelming her. His passion was disturbing for someone she hardly knew, with an intensity of meaning she could only guess at behind the relentless grind of his hips against hers. It was the way his fingers stroked the undersides of her buttocks, the way he murmured hot, unintelligible words into her neck and inhaled the fragrance of her hair. So caught up in these wonders was she that he had carried her to the bed without her even noticing. He drew one of her arms up above her head and held it firmly there, while with his other hand he dealt with the large button at her hip and flipped her dress open.

She held her breath as his fingers played over her body as if seeing it for the first time, not just a few hours earlier, entirely naked. The wonder on his face was endearing, like watching a young bridegroom on his wedding night, but then he dealt with the front clip on her bra with ruthless efficiency, gathering a breast in his hand and swooping down to suck at her nipple, as hard as a pebble. The sweet pulling sensation made her gasp. Her fingers found their way to his springy dark hair and held on as she rode the pleasurable wave, not stopping her hips from undulating in sheer delight.

He was in no hurry to undress either her or himself. She loosened his tie and unbuttoned his shirt, but there was no frantic shedding of clothes, as one might have expected. He removed her panties but left her dress and stockings and suspenders on, and it was somehow far more erotic when their naked flesh rubbed together accidentally and when they were least expecting it. Rachel instantly forgot her initial nervousness and remembered how she had seemed to Matt, like a goddess, someone he still yearned for. Unknowingly he had given her a confidence she had not possessed in her teens. She thanked him silently and spread herself before David like a sumptuous banquet. She clutched the pillow and sobbed her joy as his tongue fluttered mercilessly around her sex, strumming with pianissimo delicacy against her clitoris until that turgid organ submitted and she was soaring.

After that he took her every way, with seemingly boundless energy. On her side, with his fingers dug deep into the flesh of her hip, his cock felt huge and tightly packed into her weltering pussy. On her back he forced her to look into his eyes, challenging her to shy away from his potent masculinity. And on all fours she was his slave, spreading out her knees and arching her back in a way she had never done for Jerry, her hair tossing around all over the place, while David pounded her with such force that the breath was knocked out of her as she yowled like a farmyard cat.

Afterwards she fell into an exhausted sleep, his body spooned tightly around hers. Just before she drifted away she smiled to herself. Oh, yes, her buttons were easily pressed by suits in expensive cars. Everyone had to have one vice, didn't they?

5

She had left him while he was still asleep, leaving her business card with a note on the back, thanking him for their evening. It was worth a shot, even if she did not expect to see him again. He had given her the distinct impression that he was not to be relied upon, and she didn't want to be seen as an unwelcome presence in his bed the next morning.

Still, it would have been nice if he had called. By Wednesday night she had convinced herself that he would not, so it was time to forget about him. She went through this on Thursday, Friday and Saturday as well, before giving up once and for all. Almost. It was strange how this part of the mating game was no more fun now than it had been over 25 years before.

It was a pity Reginald Tagger wasn't giving her the same treatment, though. She had begun to suspect he was having her followed. On Monday night, as she put her milk bottles out on the doorstep, she saw a figure sink back into the shadow of a doorway on the opposite side of the street. Then on Thursday, at a hotel in Milton Keynes, a nondescript man had caught her eye briefly before turning away. He didn't appear to be doing anything except merging into the background. Once he knew she had clocked him, he disappeared.

On Sunday night she prepared the car for the week ahead. It was a labour of love. She liked nestling her bottom into the fleshy leather seats and running the duster around the little knobs on the dashboard, making the car shine on the inside as well as out. It always

53

smelled of clean leather and beeswax polish, and her smoking ban kept it that way. In the foot well of the front passenger seat she had her emergency box – surgical gloves, first-aid kit, buffing cloth and fire extinguisher – and in the glove compartment her list of useful numbers, including restaurants and hotels, should she be asked for recommendations. She checked that everything was present and correct before driving the car back into the garage and locking it up. As she was pulling the door down she saw two men standing at the end of the driveway, watching her. She locked the garage and faced them.

'Yes?'

The light was fading fast, but despite that they both wore dark glasses and black casual clothes. Beyond them, the quiet cul-de-sac was devoid of people. Even the kids forever riding around on their bikes had disappeared.

'Our boss wants to make sure you've got the message,' one said.

'It's a rough business for a lady,' said the other. 'I mean, what if your brakes fail one day?'

'Bad for business,' said the first.

'And there's battery acid. Nasty stuff if it gets in your face.'

'You've made your point. Get the hell out of here,' she said coldly.

'He wants to be nice to you, Mrs Wright.'

'Very nice,' the second one added, with a horrible wink.

'Fine. Now piss off.' She spat the words as venomously as she could.

They sauntered slowly away. As they disappeared around the corner another shadow caught her eye. Someone had been watching. Someone who didn't want to be seen. She stared at the place where they had been for a long time, but there was no further movement.

That night she went around checking all her doors and

windows before going to bed, feeling more uneasy about what she hadn't seen than what she had.

Friday afternoon at Heathrow. It was becoming a regular thing. Three weeks had gone by with no call from David Fielding. Why was he still bugging her so much? Because she had had great sex with someone who was prepared to put some soul into it, that's why. She decided that he must be incredibly ruthless to be able to do that and then cut her off so brutally. Which made him a bad person to know, and it was just as well she had forgotten about him. Really.

Rachel could hear Robyn Grodin long before she saw her. It was that shrill French voice and the click-clicking of her tiny kitten heels on the linoleum that gave her away. She was the first through the door, followed by Adrian, who wore the same seraphic smile he always had when he saw Rachel. Robyn swept through the airport like an international film star, draped in diamonds and linen this time, as the weather was warm. Every week she had different baubles draped around her neck and wrists, her tiny hands almost weighed down with rocks. Rachel thought it odd that they seemed to be for day wear only. At night she wore hardly any jewellery at all. From the droplets of conversation Rachel had heard it was clear she thought she did not need to impress their equally loaded friends with glitter, while the lower classes looked on in jealous awe. Rachel liked her less and less, but the image of her squealing like a piglet while impaled on Adrian's cock made her grin privately every time Robyn treated her to one of her haughty stares.

The pattern varied little. She would meet their flight from Paris and drive them to the Savoy. That evening she drove them to various large country houses, usually in Buckinghamshire. They seemed to have an endless supply of wealthy friends, some of whom Rachel had seen in

Sharma's copies of *Harpers & Queen*. There they would devour excellent food, drink copious quantities of wine and come out in the early hours, Adrian looking slightly dishevelled and Robyn looking as immaculate as if she had been put in a crystal display case and left there for the night. Rachel had no idea who else attended these parties, except for one occasion when she recognised a famous author who appeared each time with a different, and ever more beautiful, girl on his arm, sometimes two. She wondered how interested they really were in the clever conversation bouncing around the table, or whether they were content to be merely arm candy, with nothing more expected of them.

Then on Saturday morning, she would drive them back to Heathrow. Adrian was a very clever flirt, making Rachel aware of him even under the birdlike eyes of his wife. He made it clear that they shared something very intimate, and it would be only a matter of time before he attempted to take their knowledge to another level.

That afternoon she took them to the Knightsbridge hotel, but it was earlier in the day because Robyn wanted to explore Harrods and Harvey Nichols. Adrian declined to go with her, saying that he had to catch up with some unfinished business. Only Rachel had seen the gleam in his eye as he had said it.

She had been summoned to the bar lounge almost as soon as Robyn had gone. As always, he looked suave and handsome in cream cashmere slacks and a silk shirt; more cream cashmere was draped around his shoulders. The key to his room was on the table, glowing with radioactive temptation.

'Sit, sit,' he said, in his divine French accent, as thick as whipped cream.

Rachel sat. Adrian was holding a small parcel, exquisitely wrapped in gold paper. All Rachel's mental alarm bells started ringing.

'Would you care for some tea? Please do not be concerned. My wife will be away for at least two hours.'

As he said it, the tea came. It was beautifully presented with a silver teapot and two dainty bone-china cups, together with a carefully constructed cone of cucumber sandwiches, crusts removed of course. It seemed that refusal had not been anticipated. Rachel sat on one of the carved tapestry chairs opposite him. She noticed that the number to his room was 306.

'You're very kind, Mr Grodin. Thank you.'

'Thank you. And please, call me Adrian when my wife is not here. I insist. This is Lapsang Souchong. I hope it is to your taste.' He went through the ritual of pouring and serving. 'You do a wonderful job for us, Rachel. This is a small token of our appreciation.'

He held out the box. Rachel had her hands full with the cup and saucer but she put it carefully back on the table.

'Mr Grodin, I mean, Adrian –'

'Please.' He proffered the box. She took it and slowly unwrapped it. The velvet box was embossed with the word 'Asprey'. She opened it. Nestled in dark-blue velvet were a pair of diamond earrings, just the right size to be noticeably expensive. They twinkled at her in the light from the crystal chandelier above, as if mocking it. Diamond dealer, now diamonds. She felt stupidly near to tears. Jerry had never given her diamonds. Even their engagement ring had been cubic zirconia, all those years before. Now she seemed surrounded by them. Then she had an awful thought. Maybe she could sell them and –

'If you don't like them –'

'They're beautiful, but I can't accept them,' she said firmly, despising herself for her desperation. So much for being strong.

'But that is ridiculous! You deserve them. Take them and enjoy them, for me.'

She looked up at him then. 'For you? Or for you and Mrs Grodin?'

He grinned craftily. 'This is why I like you, Rachel. You're a smart woman.'

'Thank you, Adrian, but I can't accept them. You're my client . . .'

'OK, I see your problem. There is one solution.' He moved closer to her, so close she could breathe his expensive aftershave, redolent of high-class Parisian hotels and luscious afternoons in bed. 'If I cannot give them to you as your client, I will have to give them to you as your lover.' He pressed his lips to hers before she had a chance to move away. She was going to, but the sexiness in his golden eyes and the fact that she had never experienced someone who knew absolutely what they were doing kept her where she was. It was bad. He was her client and he was married. But she wasn't, she thought naughtily, as Sharma's words inveigled their way into her head just as his tongue slid between her lips. She let her tongue curl around his for a moment before drawing reluctantly away.

'So, you are not as English as I thought,' Adrian said softly.

'Adrian . . .' She had run out of words. She wanted to pick up that key and drag him up to his hotel room, but in doing so and accepting his gift it would make her a whore, wouldn't it?

'This isn't about love, Rachel. It's about passion and opportunity. Those are my commodities. Use them and enjoy your life.' He leaned over to kiss her again. Passion and opportunity, she thought, letting her tongue flicker against his. How delightfully European and wicked, like those deliciously intriguing hairless balls. It was time to cast away the inhibitions of the last twenty years, not to mention lingering memories of intense English diamond dealers, and grab herself a little fun.

'You are a very bad man, Adrian Grodin,' she said disapprovingly when the kiss ended.

'What can I say? I was born that way,' he replied.

Rachel picked up the room key and let it dangle from her fingertips.

'And I've been made that way. Lead on.'

It was like that advert on the television, the one about getting the flirting over with before getting home. Only she could not remember ever flirting with him. She could not even remember any fantasies she had had about him, but it was everything great extramarital sex should be: heated, frantic, slightly sordid. As soon as the door was closed he pushed her against it, his body hard up against hers and his tongue deep in her mouth. With shaking fingers he undid her shirt buttons, pulling the shirt apart and gathering her breasts up in his hands, burying his face in them with a deep groan.

'*Magnifique*,' he murmured, over and over, kissing them, pushing his nose into them, before freeing them from their cups of lace and sucking each nipple until it was tingling. She played on his desire, holding his hair firmly in her fingers and making him chase each nipple before he caught it and enveloped it with his tongue. She yanked his shirt free from his trousers, fumbling for the buttons as he pushed her skirt up around her waist and stuck a finger crudely into her panties. So much for appreciating the aesthetic beauty of the female form, she thought sneakily as he finger-fucked her with the lasciviousness of a randy businessman at an office party. He wasn't an artist: he was an opportunist. He had admitted that much himself, but right now it really didn't matter. His devotion to hedonistic pleasure was enough to keep her fired up and hungry for him. He was stepping out of his trousers and briefs and she was visually feasting on his hairless scrotum. It looked heavy and full, pink and silky. He sighed as her tongue slid against that smooth sac, and trembled as she felt compelled to suck one sphere into her mouth. It felt and tasted wonderful, rolling around in her mouth like a warm marble. His knees started to buckle slightly as she gave the other globe equal attention. His fingers were in her hair, holding her gently but firmly against him. As he sagged back against the door his hips were moving back and forth. His eyes were sleepy but his cock was wide awake, jumping every time her tongue reached new, untouched flesh.

'I like the way you suck me, *cherie*. You like them, yes?'

In reply Rachel drew his balls into her mouth again. Above them, the tip of his cock was glistening with pre-seminal fluid.

'*Cherie*, you make me want to come too soon,' he breathed, gently pulling her to her feet. He pushed her up against the door, held her knickers to one side and entered her with a positive thrust. She could see his reflection in the mirror behind him, his taut golden buttocks bunching as he filled her up completely. He paused, pinning her to the door, and smiled wickedly. Then she felt his cock shifting inside her. He was using his muscles to move his cock up and down against her pelvic wall. The sensation was mind-blowing. She wrapped her arms around his neck and leaned back against the door, letting his cock do all the work.

'You like, *cherie*?' he asked, but it was a rhetorical question. He was still doing it, seeking out that elusive G-spot, the only part of his body moving as they leaned against the door. She answered him with a squeeze of her toned inner muscles. As they tightened around him he groaned deeply into her neck.

'Rachel, Rachel, you are *fantastique*,' he purred, fucking her with long, slow strokes up against the door. Because she was tall he did not have to hold her, so they could both enjoy fully the pure carnal joy of raw screwing,

Rachel intoxicating herself on his spicy Etienne Aigner fragrance and the sight of his perfect butt muscles rippling under his golden skin.

'What if Robyn comes back early?' she whispered.

'She won't. Shopping is like sex to her.'

'I prefer the real thing,' Rachel said as he fluttered his tongue against her fat, rosy nipple. The sensation washed downwards, adding to the wetness already drenching his cock. He slavered at her other breast, leaving it singing and glistening with his saliva.

'It seems a pity to waste the bed,' she said, when she had had enough of the hard door against her back. He eased himself away from her and led her to the edge of the bed. He pushed her skirt up and examined her sodden cotton panties.

'I can tell you don't have a lover already,' he said sadly. 'But it pleases me that I am your first for some time. Am I right?'

She decided it was best not to be honest. 'That's right,' she said lightly.

'So you are aching for a little attention, no?'

She didn't like the way he made her sound so desperate.

'I'm pretty good at DIY,' she said. He looked puzzled, but she decided not to enlighten him. He hooked his thumbs into the panties.

'Next time you see me, you must wear silk,' he said, pulling them down and away. 'I like silk. It makes a woman smell good when she's aroused.' Without warning he pushed his face into her cleft. She gasped, holding only his shoulders for support as the warmth of his breath heated her private places to boiling point. When she felt the moist flicker of his tongue between her sex lips she almost collapsed. He guided her back on to the bed and kneeled between her legs, cupping her buttocks in his hands. She stretched out, resolved to relax and enjoy, and wondered why she didn't feel more nervous. It was probably because he was preparing to take his time, taking the pressure off her to explode with pleasure within seconds.

In the end, the skilled lapping of his tongue and his exquisite sense of timing brought her off faster than she could have believed. Her groans were guttural, urgent and obscene as he drew her body to its peak. Her legs spread as wide as they could, her buttocks lifting as high as possible as he licked and sucked and was sucked in by her insatiable pussy. And as she slowly fell back down to earth he caught her with his cock, pushing hard into her again and again, until she was back up there with the bad angels, savouring every lascivious peak. His smoothly handsome face had changed, had become reddened with lust, like some juvenile Bacchus determined to lose himself in hedonistic indulgence. His back bowed above her, letting her feel the full strength of his cock as it pulsated inside her. Then he opened his eyes and smiled slowly at her, holding his position, giving her every last drop of semen.

'Rachel, you are a vixen,' he said, and pulled out of her. He disappeared into the bathroom and came back with a warm wet towel, with which he washed her carefully. His cock was still hard, swaying heavily in front of him like a menacing cobra. He pulled on his small briefs, tucking his cock to one side. She had not noticed before how snug they were or how pronounced the bulge at his crotch was, but she would in future. The sight of that hefty package was almost as exciting as feeling him deep inside her. He saw her hungry look and moved to stand in front of her, taking her hand and placing it over the hot, shifting lump. His briefs were so sheer that his cock was plainly visible. She hefted his balls and stroked his shaft with her thumb.

'I must go,' she said, but she didn't want to. She

wanted to take that great piece of meat in her mouth and taste it again. Instead she instantly became businesslike and swiftly got dressed.

'Yes, you must,' he said, moving away and putting on his trousers. 'Why destroy something beautiful before it has even begun to grow?'

She was confused for a moment, thinking he was referring to his penis, but realised that, unlike David Fielding, he was intent on continuing their liaison.

'You will be driving us to Beaconsfield tonight,' he said.

'Of course,' she replied, formal now that her clothes were on.

'And on the way I shall think of you spread across that bed, and your pussy all sticky with my seed. What will you be thinking of?'

She smiled and gave his crotch one final, healthy squeeze, before slipping out of the door. She was learning very quickly that some questions just didn't need answering.

6

Maybe there was a sign above her with a big arrow saying, 'I've just been royally screwed by my handsome French lover,' or maybe it was because of the renewed sparkle in her eye, but she was aware of plenty of male attention as she walked back through the hotel to the car. And for the first time she found herself meeting their eyes and smiling. Without even realising it she had become a flirt, in a way she had not been before her marriage, and certainly not since.

'I don't know what's wrong with me!' she wailed to Sharma two nights later. They were sitting in Sharma's kitchen, eating a light supper of roasted salmon and new potatoes, garnished with radicchio salad. Rachel had bought a young New Zealand Shiraz to accompany the meal. Afterwards, they planned to take in a movie at the huge multiplex in Reading.

'Every man I meet I'm looking at him thinking, What is he like in bed? If he made a move, would I accept? And the answer is yes, mostly. Why am I like this? Is it the menopause or what?'

Sharma laughed comfortingly. 'It's stress, coupled with being with the same man for twenty years who wasn't that great in the bedroom department. You're just catching up, honey. You're exploring your sexuality and that's great! Lots of women never get that chance or are too afraid to.'

'What about you? Did you play around a lot before you met Colin?'

'Not much. Until I met him it wasn't that interesting. I

was lucky. We fit from the first moment. But that's me. You can't judge yourself by others. Go and enjoy it: be careful and be bad. Oh yes, I saved this for you. It's from last week's *Hello!*'

The picture was of Robyn and Adrian Grodin at a party thrown by some movie producer in Paris. It had been an opportunistic snapshot and the chance for some mischief by a member of the paparazzi, as it showed Robyn looking one way and her husband looking the other, eyeing up the barely covered backside of an unnamed blonde model. The narrative warned that he had started taking an artistic interest in his subject matter again, just when it seemed that marriage had safely quelled his ambition to unleash more of his lurid paintings on the outside world. It seemed that Sharma wasn't the only one who didn't rate him highly as an artist.

Rachel grinned. 'Maybe he should stick to giving head. He's pretty good at that.' She grimaced guiltily. 'Do you think I'm a bitch, doing that to Robyn?'

Sharma shrugged. 'He's a bit of a special case, hairless balls and all. And it isn't as if you don't need lots of sex right now. Just don't ask him to paint you.'

'I won't. And right now I seem to need lots of sex every day,' Rachel sighed.

Matt came sloping down the stairs, attracted by the sound of Rachel's voice. They changed the subject and talked about him going up to Oxford that autumn instead. Rachel insisted on clearing away the meal, and Matt insisted on watching her every move.

'I'll go and change,' Sharma said eventually, and swept out of the kitchen, leaving Matt to look at Rachel like a hungry dog.

'You look great,' he said, admiring her short linen skirt and light-brown legs. He looked as if he wanted to fall on her, but did not dare to. The silence and the longing stretched between them. His hand came up to touch, hesitated, then reached tentatively for her breast. She could see his Adam's apple bobbing as he swallowed hard, his fingertips lightly playing over her nipple.

'We can't do this, Matt,' she whispered.

He shook his head, jerkily, as if it were on a demented string. His breath was short and hot, his dark eyes suddenly feverish.

'Once more,' he whispered back. 'I've been listening to you saying how much you need to be fucked. I need it too. Help me.'

It wasn't a pitiful cry, but the husky plea of a man on the edge of his reason. She was hypnotised by it. He groaned and almost folded in two as he felt the light touch of her fingers slipping into the waistband of his jeans to pull him closer. He buried his face in her neck as she fondled the hard ridge in his pants. She could hear him whispering, 'I want you,' over and over, but her concentration was on the sounds upstairs, telling her where Sharma was. He was pushing urgently against her hand, fumbling with his zip and thrusting her hand inside the moist warmth of his trunks. She could smell his heat, his need, his clean, soapy skin as she wrapped her fingers around that delicate spear of flesh and began a slow, sliding movement, letting his stretched foreskin ride over the bulging top of his cock before pulling it back again, over and over, as he bit his lips and grunted and thrust against her.

'I want to be inside you,' he whispered hoarsely.

'This is all you're getting right now,' she whispered back. Sharma was clumping about in the bedroom. She had shoes on, which meant she would not be long now. But Matt wasn't going to take long either. She felt him tensing as she dipped her head and squeezed his cock between her lips. Almost immediately he coated her tongue with thick, creamy semen, thrusting so hard that his lubricated cock slid all the way in. She gagged a little, but kept swallowing the evidence until he was dry. She stood up again as Sharma's footfall sounded at the top of the stairs. Matt tucked his still-hard penis back into his jeans and zipped up. He looked flushed with arrogant success. Rather than making too-obvious, loud conversation, Rachel handed him her wine glass.

'New Zealand Shiraz,' she said, in a normal speaking voice. 'Tell me what you think.'

Sharma saw them discussing the wine, Matt with that sappy, half-cut look that he always wore when Rachel was in the room. Rachel smiled easily at her friend, feeling only slightly guilty at what she had done. It seemed as if Matt had recovered from his lust/love confusion and was going for all-out lust while he could still get away with it. And she was prepared to let him get away with it for a little while longer. She left the house with a clear conscience.

At least something was going right, she thought as she drove towards Heathrow to pick up the Grodins again that Friday. She had spent the last two days swathed in breathless, adolescent excitement. David had called out of the blue, saying he had been abroad but that he was picking her up on Saturday night for a proper date this time, as he called it. They would be going up to London, dining out, doing the stuff that people usually did before they ripped each other's clothes off. He had not actually given her the option of refusing. Not that she would, as all rules of being hard to get when faced with a worthy opponent had flown out of the window at the first sound of his voice.

Meanwhile, she dared not look Robyn in the eye the next time she picked them up from Terminal 2. It may have been her imagination, but Robyn's vivid blue eyes seemed to pierce right through her conscience as she climbed into the car. She was beautifully dressed, as always, in a cream wraparound cashmere coat as the weather had turned cool, and pearly round-toed Gucci shoes, her Vuitton hand luggage in tow. Around her neck she wore a platinum and diamond choker that would not have looked out of place at the Oscars. Again, it seemed a tad gaudy for the middle of the day. Rachel thought somewhat bitchily that money didn't necessarily mean taste or good judgement, as history showed time and time again. Adrian was by his wife's side, ever the adoring, attentive husband, but when Robyn wasn't looking he gave Rachel's backside a sneaky squeeze.

That night they were in Wiltshire. Robyn seemed to have friends in every county, ensconced in the kind of sprawling mansions that graced *Country Life*. On the way she was talking to her good friend Tim on her slim silver Nokia, and then a very famous designer called as they were arriving at the house. Sharma would have a field day, Rachel thought, knowing that the partition had been left open deliberately so that she could listen to the A-list conversations going on in the back. The message had been clear. You might be fucking my new husband, but I will always be far more influential and wealthy than you.

Fair enough, Rachel thought. At least I'll never marry someone suspecting they always had their eyes on younger, prettier women. She could see why Robyn had done it, though. Adrian was charming, skilled between the sheets and notably attentive towards her in public. As arm candy went, she could do a lot worse.

She was waiting in the dark for the party to end when Adrian found her. She was leaning over the car, gazing towards the house, lost in her own thoughts when she felt his warm hands slip under her jacket and the weight of his body press hers against the cool window. As his thumbs stroked against her nipples she was thinking of David. Forget him for now. Remember passion and opportunity instead. Adrian had told her to use him and, as he was a nonstarter in the meaningful relationship stakes, she was damned well going to for as long as she could. She had weighed up the probable loss of income after their affair ended against the short-term benefits he was offering, and had decided to go for the short-term option, because her physical needs were just as important to her as her financial ones. After she thought all this out, she was shocked at how calculating she had been in making the decision. But that was life, that was business and that was love, twenty-first-century style.

'Isn't this a bit risky?' she whispered, arching against his large, warm hands.

'Very risky, but I wanted to touch you. To smell you,' he murmured, rubbing himself up against her backside.

'Where's Robyn?' She kept her voice low, even though there was no one else around. The other cars were parked some way off, their drivers in a small huddle by the servants' quarters.

'Inside, being fucked by two women. She is occupied for now.'

His casual tone made her turn around. 'How do you know that?'

'Because this is what we do,' he said simply.

She tried to get her head around it, knowing she was being dense but not actually believing the truth.

'You mean swinging?'

He chuckled softly. 'Is that what you English call it? We come for good food, good wine, stimulating conversation. Then, after coffee, we explore our sensuality. Some times we share, or swap, or just watch. This time Robyn was ready to extend her experience so I came out here to extend mine. Is that so wrong?'

Put like that, she supposed it wasn't. 'Was the food ... good?'

'Excellent. I ate lightly poached asparagus spears,

sucked straight from our hostess's lusciously salty pussy, and fresh raspberries eaten off her divine breasts.'

'You're teasing me!'

'Non, cherie, I do not tease, but I am being very indiscreet. I want to concentrate on us. We don't have much time.'

'I don't believe in mixing business and pleasure,' Rachel said sternly.

Adrian was too busy working his hand up under her skirt to reply. She drew a sharp breath as he stroked her silk-clad cleft and worked his finger into the side of her panties.

'Are they really all having sex in there?' she whispered.

'Not all. Some are watching. I see this intrigues you, cherie.' He thrust his finger directly up her pussy, making her gasp. The unexpectedness of it and the thought of all those upper-class dinner guests feasting off each other like wild dogs had suddenly made her very moist. As his finger moved wickedly in and out she found herself caving in, moving sensuously against his hand, widening her legs so that he could fondle her more effectively.

'So, did you have cream with your raspberries?' she asked, as he deftly stripped her panties away. He was pushing her skirt up to her waist, unseen in the dark, hidden by the bulk of the big car they were leaning against.

'Yes. It was in a tiny silver jug. We poured it down her stomach, drank it from her navel and dripped it into her pubic hair where it looked like pearls. Quite enchanting. Then we spread open her sex lips and poured it among her folds until she looked as if we had all come on her already that evening. I drank first. The combination of cream and woman musk is a taste made in heaven. In fact...' He pressed his lips on to Rachel's and thrust his tongue deeply down her throat. 'Can you taste that?'

She could not put a finger on what he had tasted like,

but it was very sexy, as though he had already made love that night. She smiled in the dark and kissed him back, this time using her tongue to delve deep into his mouth. He brought up the fingers that had been exploring her pussy and ran them over her lips, so she was kissing him and sucking her juices off his fingers at the same time. The pulling of her lips on his fingers made his cock throb heavily against her thighs. She felt for his zip and pulled it down. Inside his trousers, his cock was bursting out of very small briefs. Still kissing her, he manoeuvred them down to rest under his balls. She shuddered deliciously as he cupped her buttocks and lifted her slightly, positioning her on his cock. As she felt him fill her up and impale her against the Mercedes' impersonal bulk she bit back a whimper of need.

'Oh, Rachel,' he breathed, moving deliberately and very lasciviously against her, slow-screwing her to the side of the car. 'I want more than this. I want a night with you, tasting you, exploring you. I want to feel your mouth and your tits around my cock. I want –'

She stalled him with another kiss, aware that they were in the open air, and that what she was doing was unprofessional at best, even if it felt damned good. The car was moving under his thrusts, not too noticeably, she hoped.

'Fill me up, Adrian,' she murmured, biting gently on his earlobe. 'Fill me up with cream.' The picture of the unknown woman sprawled out on the dining table, covered with food that was slowly being eaten from her flesh, was so arousing that she felt herself begin to rise up with each thrust, into an orgasmic haze. She was panting and pushing against him, excited by the mental picture and the tawdriness of being fucked against a car by a man whose wife was inside the house, being banged by two other women. Her orgasm was intensified by the need to keep quiet, while his was muffled by her mouth, all energy concentrated on three desperate plunges that ricocheted throughout her whole lower body.

For a moment they were silent, breathing heavily. Then he gallantly kissed her hand and went back into the house.

'I don't think I'll ever look at asparagus the same way again,' Sharma sighed. 'And I'm not even going to say that thing about men being like buses, all turning up at once.'

'You just did,' Rachel pointed out.

'OK, details. Start with David. How tall, how big, how rich?'

'In that order?'

They laughed over their linguini. Until then, Rachel had not told Sharma about her first meeting with David. It had seemed too good to be true at the time, and was followed by a week of pathetic pining that embarrassed even herself. Now she had a date in the bag, she felt comfortable sharing him with her best friend.

'Start with the crotch and work up,' Sharma said, grinning.

'No complaints there,' Rachel said primly, then held up her hands an approximate width apart. Sharma arched one eyebrow.

'Are you sure that isn't the one that got away?'

'All right, measuring distances has never been my strong point. He's six foot or so, fit, dark haired, forty and . . .' She trailed off, leaving a dramatic pause.

'Yes?' Sharma drummed the table eagerly.

'He drives a Porsche and deals in diamonds.'

'Bullseye!' Sharma shrieked in delight. 'You clever little witch. Do you have his number?'

'Right here.' Rachel patted her Fendi clutch bag.

'So when are you seeing him again?' Sharma was obviously hugely enjoying Rachel's good fortune.

'Saturday.' Rachel laid her arm across the table towards Sharma. 'Pinch me, please. This isn't going to last.'

Sharma gave her a token nip with her sharp finger-nails. 'So what? Enjoy it while it does.'

Saturday evening came and, for David's black...
Sharon's 'Fuck my pink' outfit isn't going to win.
Sophia gave her a look with her dress down...
made to want Philip's sudden it does.

7

Saturday evening came and, with it, David in black Armani trousers, a white silk shirt and black leather jacket, diamond stud in one ear. She heard the dull roar of the Porsche's engine as he pulled up outside. She thought the diamond and the black leather made him look dangerous and a little seedy, which lit a deep fire of excitement in the pit of her stomach. Her own outfit unconsciously mirrored his own. Black leather trousers, a crisp white linen shirt and Ghost perfume, together with spiky black ankle boots and a token splash of quirky colour with a Miss Sixty clutch bag, hand-painted with a picture of Marilyn Monroe. And to complete the look, the diamond earrings from Adrian, which made her feel dressed and expensive.

When she opened the door to David they looked at each other and laughed.

'Wow,' David said.

'We obviously have the same good taste,' she said, laughing and accepting his warm kiss on the cheek. He followed her into the tiny kitchen. It was very neat, as always, with only one pair of panties that had strayed from her washing pile on the way to the washing machine. She scooped them up and stuffed them behind the wine rack. David was looking around. The kitchen was a galley affair, separated from the living room by a breakfast bar. She saw him reading the sign on her fridge saying, 'Desperation Makes You Strong', in big black letters, but thankfully he did not comment on it.

'Have you been here long?'

'To answer your real question, the house is rented, so I'm not allowed to touch the magnolia, or swing any cats. This isn't my choice of décor, believe me.' She poured two glasses of crisp Soave, thinking she had deftly avoided any questions about her private life, but he was more persistent.

'So let me guess. A marriage break-up? You don't look like the rented-accommodation type.'

She felt a little affronted. 'So what do I look like?'

'A rather attractive woman whose husband has never appreciated you. Did he have the affair or did you?'

She didn't like the penetrating look in his eyes. It needled her soul and pushed her dangerously close to pouring everything out, from Jerry's abandonment to Tagger's threats.

'You don't pull any punches, do you?' she said, a little unsteadily.

'Neither do you,' he said, and took her wineglass to put on the table. He pulled her into his arms and kissed her hard on the mouth. When she responded, his whole body seemed to melt against hers. Eventually, she ended it.

'For a diamond dealer, your social skills are rubbish,' she said mildly. 'But if you kiss me like that again, I might find a way of forgiving you.'

Almost three breathless minutes later, they parted.

'Where are we going?' she asked.

'I'll explain on the way there,' he said.

The Porsche's seats looked a long way down, compared to those of the Mercedes. He saw her looking at the car and grinned.

'You like?'

'Of course.' This probably wasn't the time to say she preferred big, fat-cat saloons to anything else, not while he was dangling the keys in front of her.

'You want to take us into town?'

Her mouth dropped open. This was something else to tell Sharma. What other man would willingly hand over the keys to his beloved sports car to a woman he hardly knew? And tell her to drive into the heart of the West End?

'But what if I dent it?' she spluttered.

'Then you pay for it to be fixed. I've seen you handling that battleship like a Mini Metro, so I hardly think you'll be intimidated by this.' He jangled the keys. She took them.

'It isn't the car I'm intimidated by. It's you.' But she climbed in the driver's seat anyway. Her arse felt as if it were on the tarmac.

'What do you mean?' David asked, as he climbed in beside her.

But she shook her head and stroked the outrageously phallic gear knob. It felt good in the palm of her hand as she gunned the engine, which leaped into life like a tiger prodded with a burning stick. They pootled carefully out of the cul-de-sac and on to the main road. They drove calmly through the town, keeping as low a profile as was possible in a red Porsche, although Rachel could feel the muscular engine urging her to go faster, transmitted through the fat leather steering wheel and the hard, buttock-cupping leather seats. All in good time, she thought, pulling up beside a group of youths in a Subaru at the lights. Knowing she shouldn't, she looked over at them. The driver did a double take and revved his engine. She thought, no, I won't take them on. Too obvious and too childish. She was above all that. She gave a little 'don't care' shrug and waited for the lights to turn green.

In the end it was academic. Her brain, reacting to the exhilaration of being in a beast made for speed, instructed her foot to floor the accelerator before she had time to think. With the town and the Subaru far behind them, and the sign for the M40 up ahead, she felt a freedom that she had not felt for a long time.

At 110, with no one else around her, she began to feel vulnerable. Speeding tickets were bad for business. She slowed down and cruised at an acceptable 85. Only then did she look at David.

'How do you treat guys you're not intimidated by?' he asked, subtly picking his fingernails out of the soft leather seat.

'Oh, I'm sorry. Did I scare you?' She wasn't going to tell him that, one Christmas, Jerry had paid for her to go on a rallying course at Silverstone. It had been a pretty cool present, considering what a shit he was. Also, there were the cars he had bought when business was lucrative, which he allowed her to drive on occasions. All rude, crude and superfast, with yawning exhaust pipes and throat-ripping V8 engines. They had given her a taste for the fast lane, and she had missed being able to open up the engine of a really sexy car and let rip.

But back to haring along the motorway in David's shiny red Porsche 911. For a little guy it packed a punch, but she still wasn't convinced. Yes, the engine was mighty, but the looks reminded her of stripy-shirted merchant bankers with knotted silk cuff links. It was the 80s, packed into a froglike body and used as a phallic substitute. But then, her tastes were always somewhat off kilter to most other people's, underneath that clear-eyed, conventional appearance. No, she preferred her beloved S Class, the sugar daddy of them all.

'So, what do you think?' David asked.

'It's a bit obvious. I like my Benz,' she said without thinking, then grimaced at him. 'Sorry.'

He shrugged. 'Don't be. I don't like it much either. What would you have me drive instead?'

She thought for a while. 'An Aston Martin,' she said decisively. 'A Vanquish, like James Bond.'

He laughed suddenly, as though she had said something funnier than she realised. 'Shit! Let's change the subject.'

It was a shame, but she humoured him. They listened to Coldplay and drove on into London, not talking much, but it was a contented silence.

The restaurant he chose was on Shaftesbury Avenue, more low-key than she had expected of him, with only ten tables and an excellent wine list. The ambience was intimate, and they were treated with a deference that suggested to Rachel that he might have been there before. The conversation flowed as easily as the wine, but when she asked him about his work he seemed to want to play it down. She understood that he did not want to name names, and she did not push him, preferring to enjoy instead her succulent seared cod. He seemed far more interested in her line of work and who she worked for, but when his questions became too intrusive she smiled and shook her head.

'Client confidentiality, David, it's the same for me as for you.'

He reached over and stroked her earlobe with his thumb. 'So you won't tell me who gave you these?' he asked, obviously referring to her earrings. 'A gift from someone special, perhaps?'

She decided not to give too much away. 'A perk of the job,' she said, shrugging lightly.

'Some perk. May I have a closer look?'

It seemed an odd question to ask, but as he was an expert in diamonds, she didn't suppose it was too out of the ordinary. She carefully removed one earring and handed it to him.

'Don't tell me they're fake. You'll ruin my evening,' she joked, half-dreading what he would say.

He was examining the gems carefully. From his pocket

he drew out a loupe and gave the earring even closer inspection.

'Do you carry that thing around with you all the time?' She laughed.

'Everywhere. It's always in my pocket.'

'And I thought you were pleased to see me,' she quipped.

He looked up then, and suddenly smiled. She had the oddest feeling that it was something he had to remember to do. But then he handed the earring back to her.

'An Asprey diamond,' he said, with frightening accuracy. 'Very respectable, but not the best. If it were, you wouldn't be sitting here with me.'

'Where would I be sitting?'

'Who knows? Anywhere with a millionaire and a yacht?'

She leaned towards him. 'Maybe millionaires with yachts aren't my type.'

He leaned towards her. 'I can't think of any woman who would reject a millionaire's love tokens with the words, "no thanks, you're not my type."'

'Then maybe you should start mixing with a different sort of woman.'

She realised he was no longer smiling. Some raw point had been reached, and he did not know how to back down. She picked the earring up again and decided to change the subject.

'So, how do you tell if a diamond is respectable or not?'

He let out a breath, patently relieved to be back on safe ground. His hands cupped hers around the jewel.

'The cut and the clarity of colour. The brighter the sparkle, the more expensive the gem. The skill of the cutter is paramount. The more he cuts, the more facets there are, the more it will catch the light. See?' He turned the earring in the light. It twinkled gaily in the soft candlelight. 'And there's weight to consider. The heavier the jewel, the more value it has.'

'That sounds like a euphemism,' Rachel commented wickedly.

David chuckled, his diamond ear stud flashing in agreement. 'Last week I had a client who wanted a diamond-studded clit ring for his girlfriend. The thing was, she didn't know where she was supposed to wear it.'

'You mean, like, to dinner?'

'No...' He suddenly realised she was grinning at him and they laughed together easily, as if they had known each other for years, not days. He picked up her hand and, with his fingertip, stroked from the tip of her middle finger down to her wrist. It was a delicate, sensual gesture that reminded her that they were already lovers.

'How do you feel about porn movies, Rachel?'

The question diverted her attention from the exquisite honeydew melon sorbet. 'I've never seen one,' she admitted, 'so I don't actually know.'

'Would you like to find out? I know a good place not far from here.'

Rachel didn't know quite how she was supposed to feel about porn. Righteously offended or sordidly excited? She decided to go for the latter.

'Go on, then,' she said. 'I don't think you'll be satisfied until you've totally corrupted me.'

David's eyes held a new gleam, like the gold on his Rolex. 'I believe in satisfaction at all costs.'

Rachel unzipped her boot and slipped it off. His eyes widened when he felt her bare toes pressed against his groin. She did not say anything, but let her toes stroke him into hardness. He swallowed visibly, holding her gaze over his coffee cup, while his legs parted further under the tablecloth to let her fondle him.

'I don't suppose you've brought anything for me to wear?'

'Yeah, I have.' His voice had gone shaky and an octave higher than before.

'So why don't you give it to me,' she whispered, putting as much innuendo into the sentence as she could muster.

He reached into his jacket. Whatever it was had to be very small. He handed over a filmy white package and she went to the ladies' room.

Inside the package there were two items of clothing. Again, expensive and well made. In the softest black latex, the panties were as small as eye patches and the bra was a balcony affair, designed to push up and out. For a moment Rachel was puzzled, for on one side of the material it was covered with hundreds of tiny nodules that grasped at her skin like little fingers, pulling on it but so softly it felt like a constant caress. Then she realised that when the garments were on, they were designed to constantly stimulate and play with her most sensitive regions as she moved about normally, the idea being to keep her in an aroused state until David could finish the job later on. Trembling, she undressed and put on the panties and bra. Already aroused by the knowledge that he had thought all this out beforehand, when the tiny soft fingers clutched around her nipples and clitoris she had to bite back a gasp of pleasure. She tucked her own underwear into her bag and adjusted her makeup, then unfastened one more button on her shirt so he could see glimpses of the black bra. When she sat back down at the table his eyes were bright and greedy.

'You are probably the baddest man I have ever met,' she said, breathlessly.

Whenever she moved, she could feel the subtle tug on her nipples and, under her snug trousers, more fingers were ever-so-gently pattering against every sexual place, even tickling her backside. And she knew she was going to have to put up with it for another three hours at least before David released her from this prison of desire.

The cinema was more like a private club, tucked well down a barely lit street. The screen wasn't that big, and there were only enough seats for fifty or so people. There were others in the dark rows of seats, studded here and there, but no other couples. They sat near the middle, although Rachel would have rather sat discreetly at the back. With the smell of stale cigarettes and the slightly greasy feel to the seats, it wasn't a place for the faint-hearted. As they took their seats she was aware of the eyes of other men in the audience. Apart from a hooker in a micro denim skirt sitting with a man in a three-piece suit, Rachel was the only other woman in the place.

'Can't we sit at the back?' she hissed at David.

'And not let the others see how lucky I am?' he said with a grin. She realised then that this was a game of nerves.

'What if they try it on?' she said nervously.

'Relax. I'll look after you.' He held open his jacket so that underneath she could see a black leather holster, holding a small handgun.

'Do you have a licence for that thing?' she whispered.

He put his finger to his lips. She saw his earring flash in the dark, along with his white smile. 'If you want to leave, that's OK. No problem.'

'Who said I wanted to leave?'

He slid his arm around her shoulders and planted a deep kiss on her mouth. Suddenly she felt as hot and horny as a sixteen-year-old again, making out in the cinema in the middle of the afternoon. As the kiss continued, she realised that all those distant fantasies could now be followed through. There would be no telling off, no guilt, no fear. They could kiss and grope each other for the next two hours and nobody would care. The latex bra and panties continued to do their work, adding to the steamy sexual turn the evening had taken.

The room darkened even more and some truly awful music started, accompanied by the jerky opening of the faded red curtains. David took Rachel's hand and put it on his cock. He was very hard. She rested her head comfortably on his shoulder and began to watch.

The film was called *Camera Shy*, but the girls in front of the camera could hardly be described as retiring. There was no plot, just a series of scenarios set around a luxurious mansion in the middle of the woods. Over-blown décor, four-poster beds, a well-equipped gym and swimming pool. A beautiful blonde in a white lace basque was obviously the star of the show. She moaned prettily and spread her legs for a variety of huge penises, usually belonging to hideous men with suspect facial hair. Rachel watched with curious detachment. Close up, the endless pumping organs left her feeling bored and ready for the next thing. Glancing over, she saw the businessman being fellated by his blonde partner. His stare was fixed on the screen and his hand was on the hooker's head, pushing it up and down. A muffled chok-ing sound made her turn around. A man was two rows behind her, his hand moving jerkily in his lap. As he made eye contact with Rachel it started to move furi-ously. She looked away again, her face burning.

Another man had appeared on the screen, blond as Adonis and with a strong, handsome face. In fact, he reminded her a little of Adrian Grodin. He wore a smart suit, and with him was a short, pretty brunette in a white wraparound dress redolent of old Bond movies. They were in a room furnished almost entirely in white, but that did not matter. Rachel was waiting for them to get started.

They did, almost immediately. The woman dropped to

her knees before her partner and, in close-up, undid his zip. As his half-erect member fell out into her mouth Rachel felt her own sex warm up. The woman's glossy red lips closed around the thick shaft and pulled on it gently. It swelled to full hardness almost immediately, while she traced each throbbing vein with her tongue, running the tip all around the purple glans before taking him fully, up to the root. His hands were on her shoulders, his legs locked to stay upright. A brief glimpse of his flushed face showed the cords in his neck protruding with pleasure, his lips half open and eyes closed. She ran her lips up and down, her tongue round and round, in a seamless motion that seemed quite natural to Rachel. Her own sex felt hot and a little damp as the woman tongued his balls and pulled on each tender sphere with her small white teeth.

'Go down on me,' David whispered, pressing her hand on his cock. She gasped in delighted shock. He had exposed himself, not caring about being in such a public place. She greedily sucked him in, overheated by the vicarious thrill of sucking him off in such a seedy, dirty place. Moans and grunts and slapping of flesh emanated from the speakers, almost but not quite drowning out David's own quiet moans of encouragement. Behind them, the man who had been masturbating let out a long, sibilant stream of obscenities. Rachel felt David's lower body tense so she drew away, pulling his trousers over his cock to conceal their wickedness. The man behind them was staggering out of the cinema, holding his coat tightly around him. She smiled at David and met his hot kiss, while a large part of her said that she couldn't believe she was actually doing this.

On the screen the man was naked, sitting on a white leather sofa, his legs aggressively spread. His cock nearly reached his navel, and pulsed with all the blood racing through it. The woman stood before him and slowly unwrapped her dress. A shot behind the sofa took in the white quarter-cup brassiere and matching sheer lace panties covering a tiny V of closely trimmed dark hair. A pretty ribbon bow held the bra together at the front and two more bows at her hips kept the panties in place. She wore white hold-up stockings with a lavish lace trim, and white stiletto heels. She spread her legs, while he massaged his cock and watched her saucy smile inviting him to touch her.

Rachel was transfixed. After sticking an exploratory finger into her hole, the man pulled the bows loose, letting the panties flutter to the floor. She spread her legs wider as he ran his tongue up the soft creases either side of her sex. Rachel's legs involuntarily opened as well, and David opportunistically slipped his hand between them and began to rub gently at her, putting pressure on the tiny latex fingers massaging her most sensitive regions. In close-up the man's tongue flickered over his companion's folds, buried itself deep, then teased her clitoris with tiny little licks that made Rachel's own clitoris beg to be touched. Spreading herself open even wider, Rachel abandoned herself to it, her eyes locked on the man's tongue. The tiny fingers inside her latex bra tugged at her nipple, and the cool touch of her hand made her gasp. Her nipple was huge and stiff and singingly sensitive. She pulled at it, desperate to wring every ounce of pleasure out of her body. She wanted a cock, hard and huge and ready, and at that moment she would have done anything to get it. David kissed her again, a moist, hard kiss full of need.

'Let's go home and do it for real,' he said.

Outside in the street David was looking ragged and hungry, while she was sparkling and flirtatious, adding to the fuel of his desire. It was the most exciting evening she had experienced for a long time, knowing he was reacting to every time she gasped silently through half-open lips, or pushed her breasts forward at him so he could see them cupped in the small, enclosing bra. The journey home was completed in smouldering silence.

Once inside the house again he grabbed her immediately, using a thick hank of her hair to pull her back into his arms. The sound of clothing being ripped off was lost under their wet, open kisses. They stumbled up the stairs, tripping over his trousers and jacket on the way. He tugged her trousers off as she scrambled up before him and captured her on the top stair. The weight of his body on hers and the stair digging into her back was hideously uncomfortable, but she dug her fingers into his hips and ground against him as he devoured her with his kiss.

'You are so wild,' he said, raggedly.

'And you're insatiable. That's a pretty good partnership, don't you think?'

He did not reply, but pulled her to her feet and led her on up the stairs. There was only one bedroom, which was almost completely dominated by her bed. They tumbled on to it immediately.

'How's your clit feeling?' he asked, insinuating his body downwards for a closer inspection.

'Like it needs to be licked,' she replied. She had been in such a wholly aroused state all evening that now it felt like an overblown rose. She spread herself out so that he could inspect the panties and the pool of stickiness inside them. He slid them off and gave a low whistle.

'You're as swollen as a peach and twice as juicy.' He took her hand and placed it over her sex lips. They were gaping and open, plumped up to twice their usual size, and her clitoris was as big as she had ever felt it, fat and tender and the size of a grape. She cried out softly at the first touch of his tongue, delicately fluttering over the sensitised organ.

'I don't think I'm going to do this. I'm going to fuck you instead,' he said casually, but she grabbed the back of his head and thrust his face back into her desperate pussy.

'Do me or die,' she snarled, quite unlike her usual ladylike self. She felt his tongue worm deep inside her pussy, thrusting in and out, then travelling up and down each crevice to her clitoris, so knowingly that her orgasm was building, sending tremors through her body, making her moan and wriggle. But even through her ecstasy she could prolong it, guiding him to the exact spot to string out her pleasure, using him to keep her peaking until she was exhausted and had to push him away.

'Now you can fuck me,' she said breathlessly, still shaking with joy. He looked momentarily angry at the way she was calling the shots, but he was too far gone to argue. Her pussy was too inflamed and moist for him to resist. She held on as he lunged into her, watching his face change with every desperate thrust. He looked feral and almost inhuman with lust, with every muscle pumped and the veins in his neck standing out like whipcord. Then his eyes opened and seared her with such angry desire that her body melted, unable to cope with his sustained assault. She gave in to the warm orgasmic spread across her lower body, far gentler than his, because to match it would have surely meant destruction. She rode that delicious wave, spurred on by his growing growls of release, watching him with a sultry smile guaranteed to take him to his peak. It came with a roar, his eyes closing again with the intensity of it, while she held him and kissed him and lifted her body to his so that he could relish every single draining thrust.

'You didn't come,' he said, when he could speak. They were still joined, he supporting his weight on his elbows and looking down at her.

'I was too busy enjoying myself, watching you,' she replied.

He didn't seem satisfied with that. 'But you should have done,' he said.

'Why? Sometimes it's more erotic to watch someone lose control than it is to do it yourself. You should know that. You've done it to me, remember?'

David shifted his weight off her and they lay facing each other. His cock fell out and lay half-tumescent, along his thigh. She walked her fingers along it and it shifted slightly.

'I don't think you'll take too long to recover,' she said soothingly. 'I feel very satisfied but, if you think you can do better, I'm not going to stop you trying.'

This time he left her in the middle of the night. She did not ask him to stay, although she wanted to. When she called his mobile the next day it was turned off, so she left a message, just saying how much she had enjoyed their evening. She didn't overplay it, and put the ball back in his court again by suggesting he call her when he had time.

This time she really did expect him to call her, but by the following weekend resigned herself that he probably wouldn't. It was a shame, as she thought they had shared something pretty special, something that went beyond a blow job in a seedy cinema and a common enjoyment of props. She obviously had a lot to learn.

On the work front, things were looking up, and her diary was pretty much full for the next three weeks. It was just as well, because the phone became her main focus whenever she was at home. She scowled at it every time she passed it in the hallway, and it seemed to glow tauntingly at her from her bedside table at night. She was angry at David for making her feel like this, but angrier with herself that she had let him do it. Meanwhile, she resolved to not feel guilty the next time Adrian gave her the opportunity for a little illicit passion.

Once, she could have sworn she had seen David watching her from a distance as she picked up her passengers from Heathrow. At least, she thought it was him. They only made eye contact for the briefest of moments and then he was gone, carving through the crowd in a black trench coat that flapped around his calves. She called to him, but he did not respond. It was almost as if he had not wanted to see her.

She decided it hadn't been him, but his doppelgänger. It was easily done in a place where there were so many business people. After a while they all looked alike. And it would explain why he didn't respond when she had called his name.

She was still thinking about it when he called her that night, out of the blue.

'I saw you at Heathrow today. Why didn't you say hello?'

'But I'm in Capetown, Rachel. What are you talking about?' He sounded irritated but she felt a rush of relief.

'It was so weird. The guy was even dressed like you.' She laughed when she had explained.

'I'm going to have to change my image,' he said.

'I like your image,' she replied. 'It suits you.'

'It does? I didn't realise we knew each other that well yet.' There was a slight edge to his voice that she had heard once before, when they had been talking about millionaires and yachts. He seemed uptight, and she wondered why he had bothered calling her. The call ended without them arranging to meet up. It left her feeling dissatisfied and confused.

There was also another man that she had seen on several occasions, merging into the crowd in a black overcoat. One of Tagger's men, she guessed. But nothing more had happened to the car, and some of her peers had actually exchanged pleasantries with her, probably because they thought her time was limited, but it still made life slightly easier. She was learning to use her womanly wiles to disarm them. She didn't appear too clever, even though she knew her way around a car engine as well as any of them. Little did they know it, but she was beginning to charm them, playing on the disadvantages of being a woman in a man's world.

'I don't care,' she said, when Sharma remarked that any self-respecting feminist would have her burned at the stake. 'Men are men, and they don't react well to overly aggressive women. In a way what I'm doing is worse, because I'm playing on their weaknesses to get what I want.'

'Prick-teasing, you mean,' Sharma said.

'No! Being so nice they think they have the advantage. That's the game.' She nodded approvingly. 'I like it, actually. It's getting to be quite fun.'

'I still think you're selling out,' Sharma said, scowling so that her thick brows formed one long line across her forehead.

'No, Sharma. It's that other word beginning with s.'

'Sex?'

'Survival. With respect, it isn't something you've ever had to do, is it?'

Rachel had won the argument and, because she had, she paid for the meal, even though she couldn't really afford it. Sharma let her, even though she knew it too, because it was important to Rachel that she contribute to their friendship.

'Bitch,' Sharma muttered.

'Cow,' Rachel retorted, scribbling her signature on the bill.

'Cunt.' She was hushed by Rachel's warning finger.

'Now, now, there are middle-aged men present.'

Laughing, they linked arms and walked back home.

8

So when had she shed the tight, somewhat staid skin of her former self and become this flighty, somewhat devious siren devoted to exploring every avenue of her newfound sensuality? She was pondering this point in room 104 at the Ritz, while submitting to Adrian's Gallic charm. He had called her the previous day, saying he was in town, and she had no inclination to turn him down. It wasn't time yet to put her life on hold for one man, even one with a Porsche and a career in diamonds. And especially if he chose not to call her unless he felt like it.

Adrian was wreathed in a cloud of aftershave, suspect French cigarettes and supercharged pheromones. She had not explained to him about her financial and business problems. It wasn't what he wanted from her, and all she wanted to do when she was with him was forget, for a while, her life outside the baroque, mahogany four-poster bed they currently occupied.

Her stomach full of lightly poached quail, vanilla terrine and champagne, she was happy to muse while he ravished her breasts. He seemed totally enchanted with them, presumably because they were so much bigger and softer than Robyn's little torpedoes, with responsive nipples that sprang to life under his tongue. He could push them together to make a tight channel for his cock to force its way through, appearing at the top of her cleavage with the bulging end all gaping and dewy-eyed. And he was content to spend as much time as she could bear on exploring all the delights her pussy had to offer, with his tongue, his nose and his fingers, making her swoon with orgasmic pleasure. Afterwards he held her, spooning his body around hers. He had a hard torso, but not as hard as Matt's, and definitely not as hard as David's. His cock was about the same size as Matt's, but David had the edge when it came to girth. But those smooth balls drove her wild. Never before had she been so willing to lavish so much attention on a man without her tongue getting sore.

They were discussing the role of sex in the cinema, notably the great scene at the beginning of *Belle du Jour*, with Catherine Deneuve tied to a tree, and the perversity of *Blue Velvet*. But when he mentioned *Last Tango in Paris* and started stroking her backside, she knew what was coming next.

'Forget it,' she said easily.

'But why, my love? It is very *erotique*. That first push, the anticipation of pain, followed by dangerous pleasure, knowing you must stop, but not wanting to.'

He pressed little imprints of persuasion along her shoulders and neck with his lips.

'You're not selling it to me. If you ever had a large blunt instrument shoved up your backside, you would know why,' she said, turning around to face him.

'But I have, and it's very delightful. How else would I know?'

'You've ... been with a man?' She felt very naive for asking it, but she had to, or the curiosity would kill her. Strangely, she could imagine him with an older, darker, more sophisticated man than he. The image sent tremors down her body.

'Of course,' he said. 'Everyone should be buggered at least once in their lives.'

'So how did it feel?' She snuggled closer into his warm body, feeling the warm throbbing of his cock push insistently against her buttocks. Maybe it wouldn't be so bad, if he took it slowly and agreed to stop as soon as she had had enough.

'It felt as if all that existed of me was my rear and his cock. Nothing else mattered. Just . . .' He was trying to find the words in English to explain. 'Invasion. I was wide open to him, wanting him to take me over completely.' His cock pulsed strongly as his voice trailed away. She could sense him losing his way among the hazy erotic memories of it. 'I was young and Paris was very different then. Some of the clubs there still exist, but the clientele are different.' He shuddered elegantly. 'Rougher, no manners.'

'Was this guy your boyfriend or just a pick-up?'

He kissed her shoulder. 'My mentor. He showed me how to dress, how to treat women, how to appreciate good food and wine. In return I gave him my body and let him use it as a vessel for his needs. It was a good arrangement.'

She turned in his arms and looked up into his gentle, handsome face. 'Do you still see him?'

'*Non.* He had several students beside myself. He lives with one of them in Israel. And you have craftily changed the subject, my Rachel.'

She smiled slowly. 'No. I was going to ask what your most erotic memory was from those days. Maybe it will convince me.'

He lay back on the bed and stared up at the ceiling. 'It is a long time ago. Robyn . . . she does not like to think about it.'

It seemed as if he was reluctant to tell her, but his erection was still firm. She picked it up and dropped it again, watching it bounce against his taut belly. There was no tan line around his crotch, just dusky red balls proudly displayed against the backdrop of his golden skin.

'We were at a party,' he said suddenly. 'I was high on coke. I haven't touched it since meeting Robyn. I cannot as part of our prenuptial agreement. It is a shame because it makes good sex.' His cock slapped against his belly in agreement. 'Sometimes he let me hang loose like that, but it was very controlled. Two lines were all he let me have in an evening. I don't know where it was, but the toilets had holes in the walls, you know? Glory holes, they're called.'

'I don't know,' Rachel said honestly. She could imagine ... no she couldn't imagine.

'You stick your dick through the hole, and someone sucks it,' he explained.

'Isn't that kind of dangerous? What if they want to chop it off!'

'As I said, those days there was etiquette, a code of honour. I wouldn't like to say what happens now.'

Rachel bit back a smile. She couldn't imagine any etiquette for glory holes appearing in *Debrett's*.

'We went into one of these cubicles, my mentor and I. It was very small. He sat down on the toilet and unzipped me, made me hard with his mouth, then told me to put my cock through the hole. There was never any thought of saying no. I did as I was told. It is very sensual, having a mouth you cannot see drawing you in. The feel of that tongue, running up and down my cock, is something I get hard thinking about even now. He, she, whoever, was very good. I was bang up against that wall, so close my balls were also sticking through the hole. All I could do was hold on to the wall and take it. And then ...'

'Yes?' Rachel felt breathless with anticipation. The imagery was so erotic that she could almost see Adrian trapped against the wall, held there by his own desire to be pleasured by that unseen person on the other side.

'I could feel my mentor rubbing against me. He was

very hard, very big. I knew what he wanted but how could I? His cock was sliding between my buttocks. I was sandwiched and helpless, knowing that his cock would hurt me but wanting it so badly. He was talking to the person on the other side, telling them how I was reacting. They moved away, leaving my cock cold and bereft, but he would not let me back through the hole. He wet me with his fingers and spread my buttocks apart, then eased his great cock into me, while I sobbed and pleaded for mercy.'

By now Rachel was rubbing him slowly, running her fingers over the delicate flesh, so pumped up now with the distant memory.

'He was fucking me, not hard, but insistent, boom, boom, against that wall. My cock had wilted with shock, but that tongue had come back...' He pushed his pelvis up in sympathy. 'I was hard, so hard, being so fucked that I had no control. I was completely at their mercy. That mouth, pulling on me, the perfect symmetry of our cocks, working with each other. I cannot remember coming. I was in rapture, enslaved by cock and tongue.' He looked desperately at her, seemingly unable to move. 'Rachel, get on me. Fuck me, suck me, I don't care. I need ... something!'

Instantly she drew him into her mouth. His legs sprawled, opening himself up to her. His rectal opening was puckered but slightly open, as if anticipating that distant, rock-hard cock. She wet her finger and pressed against the delicate skin, and immediately it was sucked in. She pushed the finger in as far as it would go, timing it with sucking his shaft into her mouth right up to the root. Adrian grunted and bucked, out of his head with bliss. It took less than a minute for him to spurt, letting out a drawn-out howl. She prolonged the pleasure as long as she could, then gently removed her finger and rested back on the pillow to watch him catch his breath.

'You know me,' he was murmuring, over and over again. 'Rachel, you little vixen.'

That weekend yawned emptily ahead. The phone was silent and in that silence she thought of Matt, also on his own in the house while his parents were in Scotland for a wedding. They were not due back until Sunday night. The weather was gorgeous, inviting alluring thoughts of cool pools and green English gardens and bronzed young men in small swimming trunks. Sharma had said to drop in on him and see he wasn't wrecking the place, even though they both knew he wouldn't be. Even so, it was totally selfish and potentially dangerous, toying with the emotions of a vulnerable boy for her own gratification.

Matt opened the door an hour later. He wore chino shorts and a damp towel draped around his bare shoulders. His black hair was slick, droplets of water sparkling on his brown skin. They stared at each other. Suddenly Rachel had no idea what to say.

'I was in the pool,' Matt said, quite unnecessarily.

'Sharma told me to check on you,' Rachel said lightly. She looked past his shoulder into the house. 'Well, you haven't burned it down and I can't smell any pot, so I'll be off.' She turned to go, irritated at her cowardice.

'No! Stay a while and have a drink.' Matt grabbed her hand and pulled her into the house. 'Can I get you a Pimms?'

'Oh . . .' She shouldn't. Really. 'Go on, then.'

He was already mixing a Pimms No. 1, heavy on the Pimms. He handed it to her and led her out to the pool side. The pool looked as delicious as she had hoped. He sprawled out on the sun lounger opposite hers and swigged at his beer. He looked lush and beautiful, with darkly tanned skin and deep chocolate-brown eyes, his black hair pushed straight back.

'Why don't you come in for a swim?' he suggested.

'Now Matt, you know I haven't got my bikini,' she said playfully.

'That doesn't matter. It's just me and you.'

She sucked at her Pimms and looked at the cool, blue water. The sun was hot enough to fry eggs on the York stone slabs, so hot that the birds had stopped singing. What else had she got to do that afternoon? The thought of a lazy afternoon in his company had its appeal. She took another few mouthfuls of Pimms, ingesting just enough alcohol to loosen her inhibitions.

'You're right. No one is going to see, are they?' She unzipped her dress and let it drop to the floor. Of course, her simple white gauze bra and panties would be rendered totally transparent by the merest hint of water. He circled her, then pressed up against her back, pushing his penis firmly into the crevice of her buttocks.

'I shouldn't be doing this,' she said slowly.

'But you are. And one way or another today, I am going to have you,' he said huskily. Again she was reminded of the way he would be when he was in his thirties. Confident, arrogant, intensely sexual, thanks to her. She picked up her Pimms and took a healthy mouthful. It slid seductively down her throat. She slipped into the water with barely a ripple and swam a couple of lengths with lazy, accomplished strokes. He watched her, following her up and down the pool. She turned on to her back so that he could see her fat nipples poking through the now transparent bra.

'Christ,' he said hoarsely. She turned and flipped away from him, propelling herself through the water like a mermaid. When she turned again he was in the water right next to her. He pulled her close again and tugged at her small thong. With one deft move he was inside her, effortlessly. He moved slowly, so the water wouldn't splash against them. He ran his thumbs over her erect nipples and then sucked each one greedily through the wet fabric. His mouth was scalding hot. She guessed it was the young, eager blood pumping around his veins and into his cock, spearing her hard against the tiled wall of the pool. She reached back and got her Pimms, drinking deeply and feeling the alcohol heat up her blood even more. She did not need it, but she liked the way it heightened those drowsy sexual feelings that were turning her lower body to liquid.

Matt had pulled away and was hauling out of the pool. He sat on the edge, legs dangling in the water, and drew her to him. His groin was directly in line with her face. He pulled her half-out of the water so that her elbows rested on his thighs. She liked how light her lower body felt, floating away into the middle of the pool as she sank her mouth down over his cock. He leaned back on his arms and lifted his face to the sun, a good-looking, vibrant young animal with the world in his lap. She was very content giving him pleasure, stroking his naked buttocks, drinking the chlorine scented water from his cock and feeling very decadent in that enclosed garden, smelling of nicotianas and roses. The drone of a lawnmower and the occasional rush of passing cars were the only indicators that there was reality outside their sweltering, sensual world.

She heard a breath, sounding like a soft laugh. He was smiling, but not at her. Looking up, she saw three young men on the balcony leading out of his bedroom, watching them. She knew she should have been angry, but the Pimms and the heat had dulled her senses, and anyway, they were all beautiful creatures, staring raptly at her as if she were some kind of water goddess.

'Just me and you, I thought you said,' she commented sternly, but Matt could see she wasn't really angry.

'I think they'd like to join in,' he said.

'They can't,' she said gently. 'I'm not a whore, Matt. The only person I'm interested in is you.' And she gave his balls a long, loving lick, using the whole of her tongue to emphasise her point. 'If you have a problem with that I'll leave now.'

'I don't have a problem with that,' he replied breathlessly, closing his eyes again to enjoy the delightful waves of pleasure washing over him. She could feel the sun beating down on her back, and thought that if she carried on lazily licking him his cock could get sunburn. She wondered how it felt, being a man with his cock worshipping the sun and a woman between his knees, worshipping him. It would be interesting to swap sexes for a time, she thought, aware also of the three young men still watching them from the balcony. They weren't talking, but watching in a kind of rapturous silence.

Matt moved away and took her hands, pulling her out of the pool. He led her to a sun lounger and indicated that she should lie back and enjoy the sun. She did, sipping at her Pimms. With every mouthful she was feeling ever more languorous and sexy. She let her legs fall apart, aware that her dark bush was clearly visible underneath the flimsy triangle of the thong. Matt removed it and tugged delicately at the cups of her sodden bra, trying to expose her nipples. She could hear his breathing, thick and fast, and the way he swallowed as each perfectly formed, pink nipple popped out. She nestled into the cushions and sighed happily.

'I'm all yours, Matt. You bad boy.' She was saying that a lot recently, she thought wickedly, as Matt's wet tongue slavered over her breasts. She opened her eyes a tad, just to make sure it was him, not one of his friends that had sneaked down to get in on the act. Matt was doing it all right, sending the right messages down in little darting sparks from her nipples to her clitoris, over and over. Up above, the boys on the balcony were still there. She could see them, openly touching themselves through their trunks, a trio of erections for her to feast her eyes upon as Matt strummed at her clitoris and delved deep into her sexual passage. She gathered up her breasts and stroked the nipples, watching the middle youth, who was using one hand to lean on the balcony and the other to fondle his penis. When he saw she was watching him exclusively he pulled the trunks down and let his cock hang, rubbing at it unashamedly now. Then her eyesight blurred and she was in the middle of a wonderful, heady, orgasmic fog, too drugged with sensation to do anything but whimper at her teenage lover to fuck her hard.

He pulled her to the other sun lounger, sitting down first so that she was on his lap. Sitting up, she could see right up to the balcony a few feet above, and three naked cocks being furiously wanked as Matt gave his all into fucking up into her smouldering pussy.

'Oh yes,' she whispered breathlessly, leaning back and letting him do the work. Sweat and pool water made the six-pack of muscles on his chest and abdomen glisten. She held on, letting her breasts bounce all over his face and keeping eye contact with the boys above. They spurted one after the other, the first one thrusting his cock through the railings to shoot sperm out into the open air. The middle one was next and more copious. She could feel it splashing on to her breasts and face. Then the last, so overheated by the sight of her firm, tilted breasts covered in sticky sperm that he added his load to the slick already sliding down between her breasts. Matt gathered her to him, pressing their bodies together to enjoy the hard, sticky points of her nipples sliding across his chest, and he came, hard and grunting, biting his bottom lip and pulsing so hard she nearly came again as well.

That evening she drank Chardonnay and tried to stop melancholy thoughts of David invading her mind. The doorbell rang at ten o'clock. Her heart sank. It had to be

Reginald Tagger. No one else would call on her at that time of night. She stole upstairs and looked out the bedroom window.

Matt looked up at her. His bike was propped against the wall.

'This isn't going to become a habit, I hope,' she said firmly as she opened the door. He smelled of his father's whisky.

'I had a choice. Get drunk thinking about you or come to you,' he said, lurching past her into the house.

She should have called him a taxi, as she had drunk too much to risk driving him home, but now he was on the sofa, sprawled, looking up at her with those depthless dark eyes.

'So you did both,' she said disapprovingly, but her heart wasn't in it. When she sat next to him he pulled her into his arms and placed her hand between his legs.

'I've been fucking huge all evening, thinking about you with jizz all over your tits this afternoon. I was going to have a wank but it's such a fucking waste.' He kissed her, sharing the intoxicating taste of Laphroiagh. 'What else could I do, Rachel? It's your fault. If you didn't want it you shouldn't have come to me this afternoon.' The alcohol had made him sound whingy, but his kiss was firm and irresistible, his body hard under a tight white T-shirt. He shed it and pressed her down into the sofa, stripping away her clothes, diving down to her bare breast with a soft sigh. She held on to his hair and rode the lovely sweet feeling of his lips tugging against her nipples. An erotic thriller had just started on Channel Five. It seemed appropriate wallpaper set against their lazy, inebriated lovemaking. He wriggled down and began to lick at her, while she whimpered and lost herself in the drowsy luxury of his tongue exploring every private place. She was back on that hot patio, with three men standing over her, visually feasting on her flesh and pulling on their cocks. One by one, their come landed on her breasts like warm raindrops and, as she massaged it into her breasts, Matt's tongue lashed her clitoris so rhythmically that she began to come with slow, pulsating waves, whispering his name.

After that he could not wait. When he penetrated her he was so hard it felt like physical assault. She dug her fingertips into his buttocks and pushed him deeper inside her as he pounded her wine-drenched, sex-soaked body. He let go with a guttural grunt, his eyes wide open and boring into hers, before collapsing on top of her.

He wasn't too heavy, so she let him stay there, still inside her. She stroked his hair and kissed him, and his eyes closed. For a while she dozed, until she realised he was asleep, still half-inside her. He mumbled as she wriggled out from underneath him, but did not wake up. She covered him with a spare blanket and crept upstairs to sleep in her own cool bed. Lovely as he was, she was not prepared to share her bed with him and find him there in the morning. That was a privilege only someone older and more experienced could enjoy. Someone like David, she thought wistfully.

In the morning she overslept, to be woken by the doorbell. As she was pulling on her robe she saw Matt, dressed in boxer shorts and the singlet he had arrived in the night before, opening the door.

'No, wait!' she called, suddenly terrified that it might be Reginald Tagger, but it was too late. As she was halfway down the stairs she saw David walking through the door, looking at Matt, then at her, and drawing several conclusions that she really didn't want to explain right then.

'This is Matthew,' she stuttered. 'He's the son of a friend of mine.'

'My parents are away,' Matt chipped in, alert to the competition from the newcomer, who was radiating hostility and wounded pride. 'I'm afraid of the dark. Rachel helped me overcome it.' He slapped Rachel's rump. The look on his face was so smug that for one horrible moment Rachel thought that David was going to hit him.

She was torn. Tossing Matt out on to the street was unfair without feeding him first, but there was no way David was going to stick around while she cooked bacon and eggs.

'Matt, go into the kitchen and put the kettle on,' she said firmly, giving him a look that told him he had slipped up, big time.

'It looks like I wasted my time coming here,' David said stonily.

'No. I'm really glad you did. The bad timing is his, not yours.' She didn't know what else to say. 'I'm sorry,' she said.

'So am I.' David turned to go. She stopped him.

'When you didn't call after last time, I thought –'

'That you would jump into bed with the son of your best friend. Good move.' He shook her off and walked out the door. Suddenly she was furious at him.

'Well, screw you!' she yelled from the doorstep. He kept on walking. Aware that she sounded and looked like a fishwife, she beat a hasty retreat indoors.

Matt was prodding teabags in mugs, looking unrepentant.

'Don't you ever do that again!' she said, shimmering with impotent fury.

'Do what? Fuck you? You'll soon be back for more.'

The insolent tone in his face was the last straw. She did what she had never, ever done to a man before, and slapped him hard across the face.

For a moment they just stared at each other, stunned. Matt's cheek was bright red where she had hit him, but a slow flush was creeping up his neck towards his other cheek. He threw the teaspoon in the sink and stormed out, ignoring her pleas and apologies.

It wasn't until later that it occurred to her to wonder how David knew that Matt was the son of her best friend.

9

But she had bigger things to wonder about than that. Things like the £20,000 still outstanding to Reginald Tagger, and just over a week left before he came knocking on her door. She had been hoping for a miracle, but that wasn't going to happen, so by Wednesday morning she had decided to go to Colin's bank and take up their offer of a loan. Then she would pay Tagger and wait for the next demand, whether it be for sex or cash. Either way, she was truly in the shit. Maybe by then the miracle would have happened, she thought, feeling ultradepressed as she drove back home. She had informed the police of Tagger's threats, but they had said that unless he actually touched her there was nothing they could do.

On her penultimate weekend of freedom, for that was how she saw it, there was to be a party at Sharma and Colin's house to celebrate Matt's eighteenth birthday. She had not seen him since he had walked out. It was probably just as well. He needed time to reflect on why she had been so angry. But when Sharma called the next day, Rachel couldn't help asking how he was.

'Silent, moody, but glad to see his mother. And the house wasn't trashed, although the drinks cabinet looked a bit thin,' Sharma replied jovially. There was nothing in her tone that rang any alarm bells, so Rachel swiftly changed the subject.

On Friday, the actual day of Matt's birthday, Sharma invited her for cocktails. She was calm and breezy, as a paid party organiser was doing all the work. All she had to do was cruise around, issuing instructions, which she did with painful attention to detail. The marquee was already up, and the kitchen had been taken over by the caterers.

When Matt saw her he leaped up from his chair and gave her a warm kiss on the cheek.

'Sorry I was ghastly the other day,' he whispered.

'I'm sorry I was,' she replied, squeezing his hand. With the other she handed over his present. Even though she was dead broke she was determined to get him something decent. He opened the card and read the contents with growing awe. His mother smiled indulgently. She had been prewarned that he would be spending a day driving Ferraris as soon as he had passed his driving test, which would be any time soon. He gave Rachel a great big bear hug.

'I wish I could kiss you properly,' he whispered.

'Later,' she promised, letting him go.

Soon Matt and his father were arguing over the merits of the Porsche 911 over the Ferrari Marinello. Matt favoured the looks of the Marinello and the engine of the 911, and suggested that a hybrid of both might be his present from his folks.

'Dream on, kid,' Colin drawled lazily. 'If and when you get your licence you'll be getting a zero horsepower Corsa like any other kid on the block.'

'Or a Yaris,' Sharma chipped in.

'No!' Matt and Rachel said together, with matching grimaces. They laughed, Matt watching her with an openly adoring expression, but without the anguish of previous weeks. She winked at him, then saw Colin watching her.

'Kas are also good,' she said, smiling innocently at him.

'And where would I put my golf clubs? Because if I buy one of those, you can be damned sure he won't be driving it. He'll run off to Oxford in the Beamer.'

'Oh please, can't we talk about something else? Matt, I need you to go into town for me.' Sharma dispatched him with a ten-pound note and an order for Marlboro Lights. He went off, muttering theatrically about knowing when he wasn't wanted.

When he had gone, Sharma and Colin turned to Rachel, looking curiously businesslike.

'We have a proposition for you, Rachel, and because time is short I'll get to the point. We'd like to invest some money in Interlude,' Colin said carefully.

Rachel stared at him. 'But you can't! You'll never see a return on it!'

'Perhaps we have more faith in you than you have,' Sharma said. 'I think we all know that Interlude isn't going to survive without it, even if you work twenty-four hours a day for the next decade. There's the payment to Tagger, and you can't expand even if the business is there, because you won't be able to raise the capital. This way you will.' She shrugged, as if that was all there was to it.

Rachel looked at Colin. He shrugged too. She felt over-whelmed, but it was confession time. She looked down at her freshly manicured hands, struggling for the words. When she looked up, Sharma and Colin still had matching expectant expressions on their faces.

'There's something you should know, and when I've told you you'll probably want to take that offer back,' she said regretfully.

'Ah, this is about you and Matthew still sleeping together.'

'Colin!' Sharma was shocked. Not at the news, but at the baldness of his statement.

Rachel opened her mouth, and shut it again. All her carefully constructed sentences had gone out the window.

'We never slept together,' she began carefully.

'Oh, come on, Rachel. Don't do a Clinton on me. It's patently obvious by the way he's behaving towards you!'

'I said we've never slept together, but we have ... been intimate on a few occasions. Believe me, Colin, it won't happen again. I'm sorry.'

Colin looked so grave she was suddenly frightened. All the support they had given her and were prepared to give in the future, and she had rewarded them by fucking their only son.

'I don't really know what to say,' she stammered, aware that her face was bright red and that her hands were shaking.

Colin suddenly grinned. 'Then I'll say something. Thank you. Thank you, because you've given him an experience that every boy dreams of and few experience. I know I didn't.'

'He might have been better if he had,' Sharma said dryly. 'Anyway, I think we all agree that the situation shouldn't continue after tonight. It would be a shame to deny him on his eighteenth birthday though, don't you think? If you felt so inclined, of course.'

Rachel was left hyperventilating with embarrassment and shock. 'So you knew as well?' she said accusingly. 'My God, I thought we'd been discreet!'

'You had, but Matt hadn't. He's written it all in his secret diary. If you ever get famous, it won't do your reputation any harm at all, Mrs Robinson.' Sharma slapped Rachel's thigh and laughed fruitily. Colin joined her, hugely enjoying Rachel's discomfiture. She let them, knowing it was part of the payment.

'Is that a yes to our business plan then?' Colin asked.

Rachel could have wept with relief. How much more would they do before compassion fatigue set in?

'That's a definite yes, and a grateful thank you, but

this is to be a formal business arrangement. I won't take it as anything else.'

'But –' he protested, but Sharma stopped him.

'That's fine,' she said, with a friend's understanding that sometimes friendship was not enough. She and Rachel exchanged smiles.

'Thank you,' Rachel said, and went inside to cry in the bathroom.

The next morning she had a pick-up from Heathrow, meeting a flight from Capetown. She didn't usually do Saturdays, but this client was a potential regular. His secretary had called the week before to arrange it. His name was Mr Davis, and he wanted her to wear the chauffeur's cap, the woman said, without a hint of humour.

So Rachel stood at the barricade, making light conversation with the others and feeling like a female member of the Village People. But one cabbie even made a joke with her about it, so it was obvious her charm offensive was working.

To her surprise, the first person to appear through the double doors was David Fielding. He was sweeping the crowd, looking for his ride. Then he spotted her and came over. She really wished the ground would open up and hide her and that ridiculous hat.

'That's a beautiful sight to welcome me home,' he said. His smile was uncertain, as if he wasn't sure of her reaction to seeing him again.

Rachel wasn't sure how she felt either. 'I'm waiting for a client,' she said, and really, really wished she wasn't. Even after a 5,000-mile flight he was clean-shaven and fresh-smelling, almost as if he had been meeting someone special at the other end.

'Mr Davis? That's me.' He took her arm and steered her

towards the exit. With an effort she put her professional mask on.

'Do you have luggage?'

'No,' David replied. He was carrying a heavy flight bag and a laptop case. 'I like to travel light.'

They walked out into the car park. Rachel felt confused by his appearance, especially after their last encounter. She asked him about his trip, and learned that he went down lots of deep holes and drank lots of wine from the Capetown vineyards. So far, so good, so polite. The car was intact, with no obscene messages sprawled across the bonnet, and no sign of tampering. He waited at the ticket machine while she paid and fetched the car. She did the usual, opening the door for him, putting his bags in the boot. He let her do it, watching her at work with a faintly amused look.

When she slid behind the wheel and slammed the door he reached through the partition and grabbed her, tilting her head back to accept his kiss, his hand instantly inside her blouse to knead her breast. She caught it and moved it away.

'Isn't there something you need to say to me first?'

'Do I really need to?'

Oh hell, she thought. She didn't want to get into a deep, meaningful conversation right now. She placed his hand back on her breast and let him fondle it, turning her face back towards his for another kiss. Deep, meaningful conversations weren't on his agenda either, from the heat of his breath and the urgency of his tongue, working as far as it could into her mouth to drink her in.

'Take me to your place,' he said huskily. He put the hat back on her head and sat back to let her drive.

Later they were entwined in her large bed, amid sheets damp with their vigorous loving. David lifted her hand

and kissed each finger, then sucked each one into his mouth. The feel of his tongue swarming all over her middle finger and the pull of his mouth was so erotic that she could imagine how a man felt to be sucked off, and suddenly that was just what she wanted to do to him. But as she went to move down the bed he stopped her.

'Did you sleep with anyone else while I was away?'

This was a minefield. Previous partners, current partners; she had no idea about David and wasn't sure she wanted to know. But he did want to know, and something in his face told her to tell the truth, even though he might not like to hear it.

'That's a dangerous question,' she said, buying some time.

'I like living dangerously. Did you?'

'I didn't even know you were away until you called me. I didn't think I'd be seeing you again.' She moved away slightly, so she would feel less vulnerable if he grew angry. 'I did have a lover. He is married, so it isn't – wasn't serious. It was . . .' She smiled slightly, remembering Adrian's words. 'Passion and opportunity. Very pleasant, but that is all. What about you?'

David looked down at his hands. 'I haven't been with anyone since I met you,' he said quietly.

'I'm honoured,' she said, surprised. 'I hope it wasn't too much of a sacrifice.'

'For me it wasn't, but it obviously was too much for you.' He moved off the bed and began pulling on his clothes. His face was set and pale.

'David. I've just come out of a long marriage that ultimately meant nothing to the man I was with. I'm spreading my wings, that's all. When we first met you made it clear that commitment wasn't on your agenda. What was I supposed to do?'

The doorbell rang before he could answer. She thought she had better answer it to give him time to digest his answer.

With her silk robe wrapped firmly around her body she opened the door, expecting the postman. What she got was Reginald Tagger.

'Oh, no.' She tried to slam the door, but it was held open by his size-twelve black patent-clad foot.

'Any more thoughts on our little business arrangement?' he asked.

'You'll get the money a week on Monday. That's the deal, isn't it?' She hoped he would go before David appeared.

'Yeah, but I don't like how ungrateful you're being. The least you can do is show a bit of appreciation.' He shoved at the door, flinging it open. 'Why not right now? You're undressed for the part.' He plucked at her flimsy gown. Then his attention was drawn towards the stairs.

David looked tall and authoritative, and right then his bunched fists looked as hard as chunks of flint.

'I'm busy right now, Mr Tagger,' Rachel said firmly. 'I'll see you a week on Monday.'

'Yeah, with my money. Then we'll discuss the other thing.'

'No negotiation on that, Mr Tagger,' Rachel said quietly.

'We'll see.' Tagger continued to stare at David, then silently he backed off, slamming the door behind him. Rachel let out the breath she did not know she had been holding.

'And before you ask, that wasn't him,' she said lightly.

David's lips compressed. 'Are you all right?'

'It's nothing I can't handle,' she said, putting a dismissive tone back in her voice.

'Are you in some kind of trouble?'

She laughed easily. 'Up to my neck, and especially with you. Do you want some coffee?'

'No.' He sounded as if he were about to leave her, but with the speed of a hawk swooping down on its prey he caught her long hair and pulled her to him. His kiss was brutal, bruising her mouth, but the fierce longing behind it was so intense that she was spellbound, too over-whelmed by his tongue in her mouth to respond. Eventually he tore his lips away from hers and stared down at her, breathing heavily.

'Christ,' he muttered, as if he could not believe she had bewitched him. Then he was kissing her again, pressing hot imprints of passion all over her face, her neck, her breasts. Her fingers tangled in his hair and held him close. 'I'm sorry,' he muttered. 'I'm a stupid, possessive dickhead and I don't deserve you.'

They breathlessly broke apart. 'It's OK, I forgive you. This time,' she said. 'Coffee or bed?'

'I can't stay all day,' he said, pushing his nose into her hair. 'I wish I could, but I've got work to do.'

'You're being presumptuous again. I haven't forgiven you that much, anyway,' she said, tugging his velvety earlobe with her teeth. He clasped her buttocks and hoisted her up so she could wrap her legs around his waist, then took her back upstairs.

The taxi he had called to take him back to London was outside the front door, and they were just inside, kissing goodbye.

'I'll come back later,' he said suddenly. 'We'll get Chinese and a DVD and screw all night. How about that?'

It sounded wonderful, for any other night of the year. That night it raised a slight problem.

'I'm actually going out tonight. It's Matt's eighteenth birthday party,' she said hesitantly. 'Why don't you come with me?'

The words were out before she could stop them. Then she thought, why shouldn't he come? It would show Matt once and for all that she wasn't available any more, and Sharma had promised that there would be plenty of attractive teenaged girls to occupy him. So maybe inviting David wasn't such a great idea after all. Having just got him back, she didn't fancy fending off any competition just yet. Her differing thoughts must have shown on her face, for he seemingly interpreted the invitation as one made out of obligation. His jaw tightened as it always did when he was tense.

'No, it's OK. I don't want to cramp your style. Or lover boy's. I'll call you.' He kissed her swiftly on the cheek and went out to where a dark-blue BMW was waiting. It looked a bit smart for an ordinary taxi, she thought, with tinted windows and no sign of a licence plate. To hell with that, though. Why was he being so difficult? She slammed the door on the BMW's retreating rear end and went to find solace in more coffee and four chocolate digestives.

Matt's party was a typical Sharma affair. Buckets of Möet, miniature meaty nibbles spiked with cumin and coriander, together with tiny kebabs with lethal dip; a blues band in a marquee in the garden. It all sounded a bit staid to Rachel for a boy's eighteenth, but Matt had been enthusiastic and had helped with organising the music and the menu. There were fifty people milling around, all immaculately dressed, some related, some not. Sharma's own family were notably absent, because even after 25 years they had not forgiven her for marrying a white man.

Rachel chose a white sheath dress with a draped neckline and sleeves that hovered just below her shoulders. Her underwear was minimal as the weather was so hot, and her sandals sparkled with pink diamanté studs, buckled with a slender strap around her ankles. The dress had been from Debenhams in the Reading sales the afternoon before, but it looked lovely next to her lightly tanned skin. Sharma whistled approvingly as she walked into the garden, and greeted her with a kiss.

'My son will have an erection all evening,' she said with mock disapproval. 'You can't look that gorgeous and be single. Every woman here is going to hate you. You should have brought your man with you.'

'Not for the want of trying,' Rachel said resignedly. 'I don't think he liked the idea of having to fight for me.'

'Then he's a pussy and not worth your time,' Sharma said briskly. She caught the arm of a passing male in a dinner suit. He looked about thirty and startled at Sharma's claw shooting out to grab him. 'Rachel, Peter. Peter, Rachel. Peter's in finance.' And single, she mouthed, rubbing her forefinger and thumb together behind poor Peter's back to indicate he was loaded. 'Peter, take Rachel to get some champagne. She's a professional chauffeur, you know.' And she swept away, leaving the stammering, beetroot-red man to crumble at Rachel's feet.

Rachel shot Sharma a killing look and led Peter into the throng. She was kind to him for ten minutes (she timed it) then moved on, much to his relief as well as hers. After half an hour and two glasses of Möet she had relaxed into a serene happiness. Until then, with the excitement caused by David's unexpected appearance and getting ready for the party she had all but forgotten the McKenzies' capital investment, which meant she could put her all into Interlude and make it grow. Right now she didn't need to be distracted by complicated men with diamond ear studs or rapacious loan sharks. She could afford to hang loose and have a good time.

The party was already in full swing. Sharma had gone overboard with lights and the whole garden sparkled like a fairy kingdom. A young waitress in a tiny black skirt approached Rachel with a tray laden with full champagne glasses. She took another one and mingled, flirting effortlessly with some of the men. It was getting to be a habit and one she could get addicted to.

A light touch on her buttocks made her turn around. David? But no, it was Matt. He looked flushed with alcohol and attention, and stunning in white Calvin Klein jeans and a black silk shirt.

'You look fabulous!' she said, kissing him affectionately on the cheek.

'So do you.' He said it so meaningfully that it must have been obvious to the people they were with how he felt. He led her to the marquee and they danced until she was breathless.

'Now stop neglecting your other guests,' she said eventually. 'I'll see you later.' And she winked at him, letting go of his fingers at the very last second.

An hour later Sharma grabbed everyone's attention.

'I know all you want to do is party but first we have to get the Happy Birthday thing over and done with. It's the reason you're all here and he didn't want me to do it, but I'm his mother and I always get my own way.' She winked at Matt and revealed a large, mercifully simple, cake with eighteen candles. Matt squirmed as they sang to him, but he graciously made a short speech and thanked his mother, pecking her on the cheek to approving cheers.

As the party started up again Matt caught Rachel by the marquee and led her round the back, where it was dark and warm and no one would see them.

'Can I have my birthday kiss?'

'Of course.' She tilted her face up to his and slipped her arms around his waist, feeling him tremble against her.

'I want more than that,' he said when he broke away.

'So do I, but not under your mother and father's nose,' she said.

'I wish ... I mean, could we go back to your place? I want to end this night in bed with you.'

'That isn't going to happen. I have someone now,' she said, thinking wistfully that if only it were true.

'But I want you.' He kissed her again. 'You.' She felt him holding her hand against his groin and rubbing it up and down. He was hard. There had never been a time when he wasn't. 'Please, just one last time. You can't deny me tonight, Rachel. Please.'

He was right, of course. She could hardly deny him on his birthday. She led him to the deepest, darkest part of the garden and there he parted the folds of her dress and discovered how naked she was underneath. His fingers delicately probed and found her wet warmth, echoed by the warmth of her mouth against his. The evening was fragrant and very dark, the music seeming to be miles distant. She heard him unzip and smelled his musky fragrance. Then he was easing inside her, sighing gratefully as she caught her breath at his size. She stroked his hair as he plunged deeper, his breath scalding her neck.

'Matt,' she breathed as she surrendered herself to him, opening herself wider so he could fully enjoy her. 'Eat me,' she murmured, without even realising it. But he had heard, and pulled away with a soft squelch to drop to his knees. In the absolute dark she felt his breath on her inner thighs, and the tickle of his tongue against her distended clitoris.

'Oh, oh,' she sighed as his tongue traced around the circumference of her clitoris, before sucking it with infinite tenderness. She felt it pulse as his tongue batted against it. Frantically she pulled her dress apart and bared her breasts to the cool evening breeze, feeling her nipples draw up and spring erect. As she touched them his tongue hit the right spot and her orgasm flared upwards, so intensely it felt like white heat in front of her eyes. She squealed softly, biting her lips to stop the sound from travelling, her legs widening and sagging, snapping the delicate panties and leaving her bare and coming violently against Matt's relentlessly flicking tongue.

'Fuck me,' she muttered, out of her mind with pleasure. Her hands were under her breasts, lifting them up and offering them to him as he stood up. She was a blatantly sexual goddess, offering the whole of her sex to the priapic young god with his blazing eyes and sawing breath. She uttered a coarse, low growl as he lunged into her, holding her buttocks hard so he could give her as much as he had.

'I want your cock,' she hissed as he fucked away like a mechanical being, stifling his own grunts of pleasure. Her words sent him into hyperdrive, banging her into the wall like a man possessed. It was fucking at its most brutal and needy, she not caring about the love bites he was leaving on her neck, or the ruination of her underwear. It was Matt's birthday, and he deserved a decent present. She held on and almost swooned with pleasure as his pounding made her come again, heightened by the explosion in his loins seconds later. He nailed her to the wall, leaning against her with only his cock joining them together, his head back, prolonging gasps searing his throat.

'Rachel,' he whispered afterwards, covering her face with tender kisses. 'Thank you.'

'Happy birthday,' she said, smiling in the dark. He held her close, and she knew he understood that it was the last time. Just before they walked back up to the party she whispered, 'Goodbye.'

Unseen, she slipped back into the house to tidy herself and repair her make-up. He had left one small bite mark on her shoulder, and a sparkle in her eye, but they were the only evidence of their badness earlier. Her panties were somewhere in the undergrowth where hopefully the gardener would just discreetly dispose of them. She wasn't going to go and hunt for them that night.

Sharma was talking to a tall man by the poolside. She saw Rachel and beckoned frantically to her. The man turned and Rachel felt a leap of faith.

'David!' She checked herself from rushing towards him. Sharma pressed another two glasses of champagne into their hands and left them alone.

'She's pretty scary,' David commented, watching Sharma sweeping around the remaining guests. 'I got the distinct impression she was checking me out.'

'She's looking out for me, that's all.'

'Do you need someone to look out for you?'

'Now you're here I might.' Rachel grinned.

David looked around at the other guests, huddled in small groups. 'This isn't my kind of thing, to be honest. Can we walk in the garden?'

'Sure.' They walked slowly, towards the dark. 'Why did you come, if you don't like this kind of thing?'

'To see you in that dress.' He stopped and stared down at her. 'And to persuade you to take it off for me later.'

Glancing back, she saw Matt watching them. He was surrounded by the girls that Sharma had invited, hoping that one of them would tempt him away from Rachel. David followed her gaze.

'The birthday boy looks like he wants you for his present.' He placed his fingers under her chin and made her face him instead, then pressed a kiss very firmly on her lips. 'He can forget it. Tonight you are mine,' he said, leading her into the dark.

At the very end of the garden he continued to kiss her. No words were said, just the eloquence of their tongues communicating as words would never be able to do. They were pressed together, legs against legs, sharing the warmth of their skin. For a long time they just enjoyed the lazy pleasure of kissing, listening to the distant music from their dark canopy of lilac trees. She felt his stealthy hands gathering up her dress.

'Oh Christ, no knickers,' he breathed. 'And you're soaking wet, you hot little tart.' His kiss became deeper, more demanding. She could feel his erection insistent and demanding. It would have been easy to let him screw her there as Matt had done, but no, she wanted it to be different with him. She pushed him gently away.

'Why don't we go?' she said. 'I've done the rounds and Sharma won't mind.'

'I like the thought of fucking you at a party. Can we go into one of the bedrooms?'

'David!' But she was laughing as he kissed all around her mouth.

'Come on, live dangerously,' he whispered.

'We can't. Sharma's my best friend,' she argued. He was leading her by the hand up the garden again, keeping close to the edge so that the shadows would conceal them. There was an air of adventurous naughtiness about him as he stole around the side of the house. They ducked out of the way as two guests walked down the narrow walkway between the house and the garage.

'Come on,' David whispered. They slipped into the house via the back door that led into the utility room. 'What's down there?' he asked, pointing to a stairway leading under the house.

'Games room,' Rachel whispered back. 'But we can't...'

He guided her down the black staircase, into the darkened room, and closed the door. There was a pool table in the middle, and a large settee and sixty-inch-screen home cinema to one side. She knew this already, which was just as well. It was too damned dark to see anything.

'Don't turn on the light,' he said. As her eyes adjusted to the dark, she could see him as a black shadow picked out by the indistinct light coming from the garden through high, narrow windows. The smell of his aftershave told her he was very close. In the velvet darkness he pulled her close and kissed her again, before guiding her back against the pool table and gathering up her dress. She could smell his excitement at the danger of being found out. He was a risk-taker who thrived on hazardous situations, she thought, as he ground against her. That was why he wanted her in the steam room, and at the hotel, and the cinema. That's why he liked his fast cars. Something in him wanted to be very bad and, when she was with him, she wanted to be bad as well. She took control of the zip on his trousers and pulled it down. He wasn't expecting that. He groaned deep in his throat as she found his cock and guided him into her oozing pussy. It found its way in the inky blackness, just as nature intended. She lay back on the pool table and let him fuck her, putting all his weight behind each thrust. She felt dirty and lusty, like a barmaid being fucked by a whole bar full of bikers. She could imagine them all standing around the table, jerking off, waiting their turn. David's fingers dug painfully into her buttocks, holding her firm.

'Oh God, David,' she moaned softly as he screwed her with every ounce of his being, his thumb against her clitoris, giving her double the pleasure. 'Stop. Stop!'

He pulled her to a sitting position again and pulled out of her. He was breathing heavily.

'What's wrong? Did I hurt you?'

'No.' She reached for him and drew him close, stroking his face. 'I've got a little toy for us at home,' she whispered temptingly. She had gone shopping after their last date, hoping to use it on him when she saw him again.

'What kind of toy?' His breath was hot and feathery on her neck.

'I'm not saying, but it won't work unless you're desperate and rock hard.' She squeezed his erection. 'Just like you are now, in fact. You're ripe for it.'

She began to lead him back up the stairs, one hand in the waistband of his trousers, the other on his crotch. He pulled her to him once more and kissed her roughly.

'You've sold me,' he said.

As they reached the door they heard muffled noises coming from the room they had just left. It was the sound of kissing and laughing. In the blackness she could just make out two bodies pressed together. One of them was Matt's. She could tell because of his white trousers. His leg was draped over the naked thigh of the girl on the couch with him. They were getting down and dirty, fired up by what they had witnessed.

'Twice in one night,' Rachel murmured. 'Lucky for some.'

Back at the house she did not let David undress her. In the living room she pushed him on to the couch where he sat looking up at her. She kicked his legs apart until they were spread as wide as they could go. He went to undo his fly but she stopped him and told him to put his hands on the couch. He did as he was told.

'Is it hurting yet?' she asked, standing in front of him, swaying slowly to the soft music she had put on. He watched her sinuously moving body in the slinky white dress and did not answer. She ran her hands all over her body, cupping her breasts, pushing them together, slipping her sleeves down further so that her shoulders were completely bare. She leaned down, showing off the deepened valley between her breasts, then stood back up and inched the silky fabric up, past her thighs, peeling the dress away like an unwanted skin. She stood in small silk thong and bra, her legs endless in the high, strappy sandals. He swallowed, watching her intently. She slipped her hand inside the fresh pair of panties she'd put on and pulled out something he had not seen before, because until ten minutes previously it had not been there. It was a silver ring attached to a soft strap of black leather. It kept coming like magic scarves out of a magician's hat, and then his eyes widened as the end of a vibrator appeared. It was slim, long and black – a very evil-looking thing. His breathing had suddenly become very shallow.

'I'll ask you again. Is it hurting yet?' Her voice was sultry.

'Yes,' he said hoarsely, pushing his pelvis up in an involuntary attempt to get more comfortable. She reached down and unzipped his fly. In silk boxers his cock leaped out at once. She peeled them down and let it straighten up, leaning over him to do it, her breasts tumbling out of their small balcony.

'Don't even think about it,' she growled as his hand came up. It fell away again. She removed his trousers and boxers, and made him lie on the couch, hooking one leg over the top so he was totally exposed. Critically, she inspected his bright-red cock, straining with unfulfilled passion.

'I'm going to take things down a little before you lose it completely.' She slid her hands under his buttocks and opened him up, exposing his pink rectal opening. Above, his cock beat an insistent tattoo on his belly. She had remembered what Adrian had said, that every man needed buggering once in his life. She blew on the tiny hole and watched it pucker up, then licked around his balls and blew on them as well. David moaned, writhing slowly with every lick. She was thinking how different he felt from Adrian, yet his hair was soft and silky, not coarse and crunchy like Jerry's. She sucked one ball into her mouth and palpated it gently. Then the other, using her tongue to encircle and pleasure it. Her fingertip pressed gently against his arse, but her fingernail was too scratchy for her to slip it inside. She remembered the pair of surgical gloves she had in the first-aid box in the kitchen.

'Wait here,' she said, and gave his cock a long, loving suck to keep him ready.

She came back into the living room with the glove

already on and lubricated, just in case he thought to protest. Another suck, another swirling lick around his scrotum to keep him heady with anticipation and lust, then she pressed her latex-clad finger against his arse and pushed gently. David grunted but did not protest, even when her finger met with some resistance before easing in up to the edge of her fingernail.

'Rachel,' he moaned, tightening his buttocks around her fingers. She pushed further, lashing his balls gently with her tongue. It was obvious he had experienced this before, by the way he was sighing and moaning and telling her to fuck him more. She moved her finger in and out, pressing deeper each time, while she washed his scrotum and tickled his balls with her tongue. His hand was on his cock, rubbing it.

'Sit on my face, baby,' he groaned, and she did, giving his mouth a long, lascivious pussy kiss, wet with excitement at watching him masturbate himself while she concentrated on his balls and arse. For a long while they stayed like that, the pleasure mutual and deep and understanding, until his hips began to jerk and he moved her away so he could speak. His eyes were drugged with satisfaction.

'I want to come every which way with you,' he said in a voice thick with desire.

She reached over for the toy she had magically produced earlier. It was a silver cock ring, attached by a strap to a slim vibrator, designed to slip into the rectum. She lubricated the vibe and inserted it carefully into his backside.

'Oh God, that's good,' he moaned. 'Now can I get inside you?'

'Not yet,' she said firmly. She attached the strap around the base of his cock, running it under his balls and tightening it as far as she dared. He stared down at his tethered genitalia.

'I'm going to explode,' he said, as if it were a given fact. She turned the vibrator on. His pelvis jerked forward and he gritted his teeth. With the remaining length of strap she led him up to the bedroom. He stumbled after her, almost too aroused to walk.

'Now you can fuck me,' she said, lying back on the bed. His eyes were wide as the vibe pulsed in his backside. The strap around his cock was maintaining his awesome erection but restraining the need to shoot. He fell upon her and began to fuck her, violently, angrily, while she tormented him with her luscious breasts, running her tongue over her nipples, taunting him with them, not letting him suck them in.

'Free me,' he said tightly, when the need was close to becoming too much to bear. 'Free me, you bitch.'

'Free yourself,' she challenged him. He picked desperately at the strap, releasing his bulging balls and plunging into her again at the same moment with a triumphant war cry. The relentlessly throbbing tool and the build-up of need was too much and he let go with a tidal flood, unleashing an ululating cry of relief. The moment she felt that first huge pulse it carried her away, screaming and clawing at him, pushing up against him with frantic fury. The pulsing vibe prolonged his orgasm almost as long as hers.

'Shit!' he said, as she gently removed the vibrator from his backside. He flopped on to the bed and lay staring at her for a long time. Eventually his eyes closed. She pulled the duvet up over them both and fell into a heavy, satisfied sleep.

10

And he was still there in the morning. And he still looked good, facial shadow and all. He was asleep, sprawled on his front all over the bed. She watched him for a moment, thinking how pleasant it felt to have a man in her bed again. Don't get too used to it, she thought, going downstairs to put the kettle on.

She made Earl Grey tea, and took it back upstairs, intending to wake him up with a kiss. When she walked into the room, he was very awake and kneeling on the floor. The bottom drawer, the one that held all her lingerie and vibrators, was open and he was riffling through it, very delicately so as not to disturb anything.

'What the hell are you doing?'

Her voice made him jump guiltily. 'Just looking for some more toys,' he said, grinning winsomely.

She didn't believe him. What made her angrier – the fact that he had just lied to her or the intrusion into her privacy? She put the tea down, tempted to throw it at him, but realising that she would be the one who would be clearing up the mess. A horrible thought hit her. Maybe he was a panty collector, with a special place at home for all the knickers he had stolen from his women.

Then she noticed that her jewellery box was also open. Suddenly she didn't want him in her house for one second longer.

'Get out,' she said.

'Rachel, please –'

'I don't want to hear it. Just leave right now.'

'It isn't what you think.' But at least he was pulling his clothes on.

'It's obvious you don't care what I think. I should call the police and let them deal with you.'

'No, please don't do that.' A look of fear passed over his face. 'This is crazy, a big mistake. Will you at least allow me to explain?'

'No.' She waited for him to go down the stairs and followed him, fighting the urge to help him down with her foot. She flung open the front door. 'If you don't leave right now, I'm going to start screaming.'

'Rachel . . .'

'I mean it, David. Goodbye and go to hell.' She slammed the door violently on his heels and sank down to the carpet, her face in her hands. There were no tears. Been there, done that, she thought bitterly. One step forward, two steps back. What was it with men? In her next life she was going to come back as a cat.

It was the next Friday night, somewhere outside Gerrards Cross. Rachel waited for Adrian and Robyn Grodin. It would take a long time to dispose of her feelings for David. Even after a long talk with Sharma and a bottle of Chianti, she still felt bruised inside. He had not tried to call her. She wasn't sure what she should say to him if he did. Not that it was relevant, because it just wasn't going to happen.

The night was dark with no stars, and very little light coming from the tall windows of the large house. She could hear music, Beethoven, but it was difficult to tell whether it was live or on a sound system. There was a lone man standing in the light of the door, framed between the two pillars. He wore a dinner jacket, but his build and aggressive demeanour, legs planted firmly apart and arms around his body, put him strictly in the security field. The guests she had seen before were all stick thin, elegant, as fragile as hothouse flowers in their fine silk and cashmere.

And by now they would be humping merrily away, happy as pigs in shit. Threesomes, foursomes, who knew? She would have loved to have walked in and among all the rooms, seeing what was happening in them. How was Adrian doing it? She was very curious. Did he have his face buried in the breasts of some obscure member of the aristocracy? Or was he being buggered senseless by the host of the house in the wine cellar?

Her phone rang, stalling her musings. It was Sharma.

'Have you listened to the news this evening?'

'No. Why?'

'Reginald Tagger is dead. He was found stuffed in the boot of his car this afternoon.'

'You're kidding!' Rachel couldn't believe it. Did this mean that the debt was void? 'Do they know who did it?'

'You know the police, they don't like to give anything away. There was the suggestion that it was a professional job, though. Pretty handy, huh?'

'I should say. But what if he has brothers, sons, people to carry on the business?'

'Oh Rachel, don't be such a worrier. The newscaster said he had no family, so just relax. Hopefully the cops won't waste too many man hours on him. The man was scum.'

'Yes, he was,' Rachel said faintly. Past tense. It felt weird, this slow elation that was beginning to seep into her bones. 'Thank God,' she said.

'And whoever put a bullet in his head. I have to go, honey. Call me tomorrow.'

'I will.' Rachel hung up. She felt like dancing. No more baseball bats, no more threats, no more visions of being forced to have sex with the bullfrog.

'You look pleased about something,' a voice said

behind her, making her heart jump so far it made her feel sick.

'Oh God, Adrian, don't do that!' She landed in his arms. He held her close, pressing his lower body firmly against hers. She rubbed against him, relief making her respond more enthusiastically than she would otherwise have done. One of his steaming kisses added fuel to her elation and she found herself feeling horny for the first time all week. He worked his hand up under her skirt and inveigled his fingers into her panties.

'*Cherie*, you are very wet. Have you been having bad thoughts?'

'Not until you came along.' She laughed. 'What have you been doing this evening?'

'Nothing too outrageous, my darling. I've been talking to a gentleman who likes my paintings.'

'And you haven't wanted to fuck him?'

Adrian laughed lightly. 'No, but I'd like him to fuck me. He is the master of the house.' He nodded to the bridge over the small river. A svelte figure leaned across it, smoking a cigarette. She could just see his dinner jacket and black bow tie, but she could tell he was stunning.

'Very nice,' she said approvingly.

'I'm glad you approve, because I thought we could seduce him together. Robyn has been lured by these *femmes fatales* into the master bedroom. I have instructed them not to let her out for another hour. Do you think that is enough time?'

The man was sauntering towards them. As he drew nearer she could see that he was somewhat inebriated and probably high on some kind of illegal substance, but he was very good-looking, with short, brown, straight hair and high cheekbones over flawless white skin. With a shudder she realised that he reminded her strongly of David. He looked at Rachel as if she were a particularly fine breed of thoroughbred mare.

'I say, she is lovely,' he said, slurring his words slightly. 'I'm Justin.' He took her hand and kissed it gallantly. 'My wife is somewhere, being rogered senseless, so we're in the clear. Shall we go into the servants' quarters?' His accent was Oxbridge, very well bred. Rachel felt herself weakening, even though she should have protested at not having any say in the matter. Justin had his hands on Adrian's waist. She could see Adrian's erection pressing against his trousers, and feel the warmth of his breath, quick and excited.

'Come with us, *cherie*,' he said softly. 'He can fuck me and I can fuck you.'

It sounded very tempting, considering she had no one to answer to but herself at the moment. Well, why not, she thought. She locked the car and went with them over the short courtyard to a small door into the servants' part of the house. Upstairs there was a bedroom, from where she could see the cluster of cars, including her own. The room was very softly lit, and just big enough to hold a vast bed. Adrian reclined upon it like an indulged Roman emperor and removed his trousers. He had tight-fitting briefs on, silk and as translucent as onion skin. His cock glowed visibly through them, hard and bulging. Rachel pattered her fingertips against it.

Justin sat on the other side of Adrian's legs, also admiring the restrained Gallic member. Then he cupped Rachel's head in his hand and pulled her close for a deep, tonguing kiss. He tasted of cigarettes and single malt, belying his clean-cut appearance, but it didn't repulse her. His fingers were toying with Rachel's buttons, exposing her breasts in white lace, his tongue tracing patterns around her lips as his trembling fingers did the same around her nipples. Underneath them, Adrian was running his hands all over his body, enjoying watching them making out. The briefs were still doing their job, holding him back but bulging more than ever. He drew Rachel down into his arms and began to caress her, removing the remainder of her clothes apart from her stockings. Justin lay on the other side, rubbing up against Adrian with his own erection, straining against black trunks.

For a while they all enjoyed this sensual feeling of skin against skin, not speaking, happy to let their hands do the talking. Then Adrian motioned to Rachel to remove his briefs. She and Justin peeled them down, setting him loose. While Justin concentrated on his cock, Rachel lavished attention on his balls, alternating each lick with a flicker against Justin's tongue. They smiled at each other as they pleasured the Frenchman. Justin removed his pants, revealing an erection maintained by a silver cock ring that encircled the base of his shaft. He manoeuvred on top of Adrian and gave him his cock to suck. His eyes became sleepy with lust as Adrian pulled on him, making his cock swell to almost twice the size. Rachel did not feel left out. She was too turned on by the sight of these two beautiful men ravishing each other to wonder what was going to happen next.

Adrian rolled over and buried his face in her breasts. At the same time, Justin spread her legs and began to lick all the way down the inside of her thighs. He licked all the way around her quivering opening, not touching that devastatingly sensitive point, and washed out her navel with a long, delving tongue.

'You smell of lilies,' he said, sniffing all around her sex like a dog and sending her skin shimmering with anticipation. She could feel his fingers, long and exploring, stretching the inner walls of her pussy and feeling around. 'As tight as a silk glove,' he proclaimed. While his fingers were still inside her, crooked slightly so that she was doubly aware of them, he thrust his tongue deep up inside her pussy. With Adrian concentrating on her nipples, his balls in her face so that she could suck contentedly on them, she was in seventh heaven.

Then she felt two tongues down there. Adrian had shifted, sending his cock deep into her throat as he joined Justin in his ongoing exploration of her folds. She spread her legs as wide as she could and relaxed back, almost gagging on Adrian's cock, but the joy of having him fuck her mouth while he shared her pussy with another man's tongue was too erotic to be spoiled by minor discomforts. With his weight on her body he could feel the full effect of her first jolting orgasm, almost too intense to bear. Her cries were stifled by cock, the restricted airflow taking her to heights she had never known before. She felt dangerously close to passing out as her lower body became a law unto itself.

'Oh Christ, she's ejaculating,' she heard Justin murmur in the distance, before his tongue mercifully brought her to another peak. She clawed at Adrian's back and undulated wildly, no longer in control of her own body. In her head she could hear nothing but fireworks, feel nothing but wave upon wave of pleasure, and see nothing but velvet darkness above Adrian's pale backside. She slapped it hard, making him grunt into her overheated sex.

'Do it again,' he rasped. She hit him again, and his cock jolted inside her mouth. Again, and she tasted his salt. Again and again, raising a rosy blush on his skin until he seemed to pause, then flooded her mouth with hot, creamy semen just at the moment that she could no longer concentrate, too intent on her own secondary climax. Or was it the third? She had given up counting.

Afterwards they lay replete, their limbs tangled. Justin lay back on Rachel's lap and swigged whisky straight from the bottle, his hips rotating slowly as Adrian sucked him. Adrian's cock was semitumescent after his recent orgasm, but still looked good enough to eat.

'I could do this all night,' Justin drawled, nuzzling further into Rachel's breasts. 'It's a pity the old witch is back tomorrow night.'

Rachel wondered what old witch he was referring to. Obviously not his wife, as she was elsewhere in the building, succumbing to a spot of decadent indulgence herself.

After a while Adrian crawled to his knees. His cock hung heavily downwards, but sprang up again as he backed on to Justin's tongue. His moan was loud as Justin doused his arse with saliva and guided his cock in. Rachel moved around and sucked on Adrian as Justin impaled him to the hilt. Adrian's eyes were bulging and his mouth was opening and closing like an oxygen-starved fish.

'*Mon Dieu*! I have not done this for so long,' he moaned as he lay, still fully kebabed, along Justin's prone body. The two men spread their legs to alleviate some of the pressure. Adrian's cock drummed against his belly.

'Ride us, little chauffeur,' Justin said.

Rachel thought that first she would give both pairs of balls lavish attention. Both men keened with pleasure as her warm tongue lashed them again and again.

'Get on before we come,' Justin managed to say. His hands were on Adrian's hips. Rachel straddled the men and sank down on Adrian's cock.

'Oh, sweet Mary,' Justin moaned, thrusting weakly up into Adrian. Rachel put on the chauffeur's cap and winked at Adrian, running her tongue lewdly around her lips and thoroughly enjoying the spectacle they made. Justin grinned savagely back and began to pump, hard and strong into Adrian's tightly clenched backside. Adrian's legs were braced to give him more thrust, while Rachel bore down on Adrian's cock with all her strength. In the middle, Adrian was being fucked to death, his eyes closed with bliss, the tip of his tongue just visible between his lips.

'Someone give me some coke,' Justin moaned. He motioned to an exquisite Japanese bowl by the bedside, filled to the brim with white powder. She couldn't believe the amount of cocaine she was actually looking at. It had to be worth thousands.

'How much?' she whispered.

'I don't care. Just give it to me before I shoot!' Justin had shed his aristocratic shield and was now a wild, fuck-crazy animal. She scooped up a little coke on her finger and held it to his nostril. He inhaled deeply.

'More. Other side.'

She did it again, waiting for a reaction.

'Me too,' Adrian said urgently.

'But Robyn —'

'Do it!' He sounded different, dangerous and desperate. She gave him the coke. Then the reaction hit both men. It was a huge burst of energy, roaring from Justin's cock to Adrian's and up into Rachel's soaking pussy. Adrian began to howl, his eyes white, a sheen of sweat beading his brow as Justin began to fuck him brutally, his teeth gritted in a primeval grimace. Together they held Rachel down so that she could not escape this tidal wave of lust. Adrian's hands were on her breasts, grasping them wildly.

Then he pushed her away. 'Not you. I need cock,' he urged thickly. He continued to massage himself, hips churning, riding the cocaine-fuelled high. Justin man-oeuvred out from underneath Adrian and kissed his ear.

'I'll get you some,' he whispered, and staggered off the bed. 'You can go now,' he said diffidently to Rachel, who was kneeling on the bed feeling stunned and helpless. He left the room, leaving her to stare after him. Their selfishness suddenly repulsed her. She had given head in a sex joint in London's seamy backstreets, but even that didn't seem as tacky as what she had just done.

'You had better go if you don't want to get bum-fucked,' Adrian said in a slurred voice.

'Robyn's going to be so mad at you for using coke. You could lose everything,' she said coldly.

He laughed hollowly. 'Fuck her and fuck you. You are not my mother.' He groped for the bowl of coke. 'Run away now, Rachel. We won't be needing you any more tonight.' He chopped out a couple of lines and hoovered them.

Rachel grabbed her clothes and ran from the room before he became too animated. In a deep doorway opposite, she pulled on her clothes. As she was about to step out into the corridor, footsteps made her freeze. It was Justin, but he had two other men with him. One wore evening dress and a truly frightening black rubber mask over his face, with holes only for eyes and nose and a silver zip across the mouth. His trouser zip was undone and his cock stuck out like a crude beacon. The other wore substantially less. He too was masked, and there was a contraption of leather straps and silver rings around his waist, leaving his buttocks bare and his cock sheathed in a black leather sleeve. At the tip a chain was attached, and Justin was leading him with it. They were giggling, sounding high. She knew that if they caught her, she would have no chance. The door remained half open, so she could see the men, all snorting lines. Adrian's eyes were wild, his manner feckless.

'Which one of you brutes is going to have me first?' he drawled. Rachel felt compelled to see what would happen next. Justin retrieved some silk scarves from the bedside table and gagged Adrian while the man in the leather bondage held his hands apart. Then Justin produced a red leather box, resembling a large jewellery box. He opened it up and pulled out a handful of sparkling gold chains and diamond necklaces. He giggled with childish glee.

'I've raided the safe,' he crowed mischievously. 'Now you can fuck the family jewels while I fuck you!'

Rachel had no way of knowing whether the jewels were fake or real, but Adrian moaned through his gag and lifted his hips as Justin wound gold chains and necklaces dripping with diamonds and other precious gems around his cock. When it was completely covered with jewels, Justin wrapped his hand around it and began moving it up and down. Adrian's eyes rolled and his hips moved with Justin's hand. Carefully, the other two men flipped him over. He was as compliant as a drowsy dog as they pushed pillows under his stomach, which lifted his backside up and exposed him totally, as well as keeping the jewels in place around his cock. Justin tied his hands to the bed head and his ankles to the railings at the bottom. It looked hideously uncomfortable, but Adrian was obviously enjoying it. The bowl of coke was handed around, and the man in the suit kneeled in front of Adrian, guiding his cock into his mouth. The one with the leather sheath began to lash Adrian's buttocks with the chain that Justin had lead him in with. Adrian's moans were muffled and loaded with pleasure. When Justin unzipped his trousers again and thrust his cock into the bowl of coke Rachel decided she had seen enough. She tiptoed out of her hiding place and ran down the stairs. No one followed her. She reached the car and locked herself inside it, shivering violently.

A few minutes later, a sharp rap on the window nearly made her throw up. It was Robyn Grodin. Only it didn't look like Robyn Grodin. It looked like a woman who had been hauled through hell and back, her black mascara smudged, her usually immaculately coiffed hair more reminiscent of Sid Vicious than Audrey Hepburn. Without waiting for Rachel to get out of the car she wrenched the back door open and climbed in.

'Take me back to London,' she rapped, though her machine-gun voice lacked its usual fire. Rachel didn't argue. She started the engine and turned the car around, expecting to see Adrian Grodin running after them, waving his fist.

It didn't happen. When they were out on the main

road Rachel glanced in the rear-view mirror. Robyn was huddled in her wrap, looking furious.

'Are you OK?' Rachel asked, expecting the query to be shot down in flames.

But instead of a rude response Robyn shook her head. She looked bitter. 'No, but I will survive.' She riffled in her clutch bag and found something that cheered her. 'No, take me to the Marriott at Heathrow.'

'Will do.' Rachel wanted to ask more but dared not. It wasn't her place. Besides, Robyn's face had settled into a more familiar look of self-satisfaction. When they arrived at the hotel Robyn left her without another word. Rachel wasn't bothered. She really didn't mind if she never saw her or Adrian Grodin again.

She pointed the Mercedes back towards Henley. It was way after midnight, and now she felt exhaustion creeping insidiously up on her from behind. With uneasy, half-formed thoughts drifting around her head she drove homewards, taking comfort in Mary J Blige singing 'No More Drama'. No more drama in her life either, she thought wryly.

Too soon, it seemed.

Blue flashing lights behind her made her check her speed. On the M40 she wasn't breaking any rules. She shifted into the slow lane to let the blue and white pass. It didn't. In the split second that she realised they were for her, she noticed another, moving out, around and in front of the car, forcing her to slow down. She felt sick. She was alone in the dead of night. Carjackers sometimes posed as policemen, didn't they? But they looked like the real McCoy, crouch-running towards her and hauling open the car door, screaming at her to get out of the car. Pulling open the rear doors.

'There's no one else,' she heard someone call, and then she was pressed against the side of the car, hands feeling her all over. Too stunned to speak, she had the presence to register the guns and the overbearing voice telling her she was under arrest for the murder of Reginald Tagger.

She was turned around, more roughly than was necessary. In front of her was a chunky man in plain clothes, smoking the remains of a cigarette. He looked unkempt in a cheap brown suit and with a supercilious look on his face. She held her breath, thinking, Don't antagonise him, don't swear, don't do *anything*. The detective nodded to the waiting police officers. One stepped forward and put cuffs on her. She kept silent until she saw a rangy young man climbing into the Mercedes.

'Be careful! That's my livelihood!' she yelled at him as he slammed the door. The detective lit another cigarette, holding it between his thumb and forefinger like a Cockney wide boy. Fine, except his accent was strictly outside the M25.

'Detective Inspector Bailey,' he said. 'You're going down, Mrs Wright,' he added, nodding his head sagely.

'Not on you I'm not,' she retorted. She was led to the first police car and helped into the back seat. She was grateful that at least they didn't plonk a hand on her head to shove her in. The young officer sitting next to her seemed almost embarrassed. She didn't want to embarrass him more by making eye contact.

The wait at the station was horrible. Druggies, hookers arguing with their pimps, shaven-headed Friday nighters all stared at her as the relevant paperwork was filled in. She was made to stand among them, still cuffed and incongruous in her smart black suit, silk blouse and immaculate patent heels.

'Thought a classy bitch like you would have known your john was a cop,' one frizzy-haired woman sneered. Rachel opened her mouth to retort that she wasn't a prostitute, but checked it just in time, as she was surrounded by them.

'Shut it, Sandra,' the man behind the desk said tersely. Systematically Rachel was stripped of all her belongings. Her clutch bag, her watch, all of her jewellery. Then she was made to take off her shoes, which she found particularly humiliating. Eventually she was summoned to a dingy interview room.

'Sit,' Bailey said.

'Woof,' she said, sarcastically, as she did so.

He leaned down and pushed his ruddy, piggy-eyed face into hers.

'If I were you, I'd watch your mouth. No one likes a smart cow in here.'

She smiled weakly. 'Thanks. I'll take that as a compliment.'

They held eye contact. She had noticed earlier the thick wedding band on his left hand. Who would want to marry someone that butt-ugly, she thought, as the game of eyeball chicken continued. Her eyes began to smart and she looked away so she could not see the satisfied smirk on his face. He sat opposite her. Another man hovered in the background. He switched an ancient tape machine on to Record.

'Tell us about your relationship with Reginald Tagger,' Bailey said.

Rachel stared at him. 'I've never had a relationship with him!'

'But you owed him money, didn't you?'

'My husband owed him money. He took out the loan in my name, then left me in the shit to go sunbathing in Brazil. Tagger came to me for the money.'

'And he threatened you when you said you couldn't pay?'

'Yes. But I didn't –'

'So you had the motive to take Tagger out, and the opportunity.'

'How? I couldn't do anything like that!'

'Like what, exactly?'

'You know damned well what!'

'But you could have paid someone to do it. It was a contract job, Mrs Wright. Very convenient for you.'

'Very, but even if I wanted to, I can't afford a contract killer! If you look at my finances that is plainly obvious.'

Bailey leered nastily at her. 'There are other forms of payment, Mrs Wright, as I'm sure you well know.'

It was a good job she was handcuffed. Otherwise she would have slapped him, and assaulting a police officer wasn't a charge she wanted on record, let alone murder.

'Fine,' she said coldly. 'I'm not saying one more word without a lawyer present.'

'That's your call, Mrs Wright. Interview terminated at one-fifteen.' Bailey ended the interview and told the officers to take her to a cell. They led her to a tiny room and pushed her inside. There was a narrow bed against the far wall. No windows, or anything else that could be used as an escape route, or weapon, or implement of suicide. The air smelled of stale body odour.

The door was slammed again with a loud, metallic crash, the loneliest sound that Rachel had ever heard. She buried her face in her hands and wept. More than anything she wanted her friends around her like a warm, comforting duvet, not to be shivering in a dark room, wondering if her life was about to go down the toilet for the second time.

She curled up on the scratchy grey blanket and closed her eyes, wishing herself far away. On and off throughout the endless night she dozed, woken frequently by the crashing of distant doors, the echoes of voices loud and aggressive, and by the lumpy mattress underneath her body. When she woke up again it was morning and she was desperate for the toilet. Distant cheerful whistling came closer and the small window in the door was opened.

'Morning, ma'am,' an older male voice said. Through the small square he looked so much like her own long-dead father, with the same kindly, seen-it-all-before eyes that she wanted to cry.

'Can I use the loo?' she asked tremulously. A woman police officer came and escorted her to the lavatory. She was ill humoured and not prone to small talk. Rachel did what she had to do and went out into the corridor again.

'Thanks for being polite,' she said to the kindly officer as he led her back to her cell. There she waited for a long time, so long that the clanking of keys woke her with a start.

She was taken down the corridor to another room, furnished only with a white Formica table and two plastic chairs. Bailey came in ten minutes later and switched on the tape recorder. He looked even uglier than he had the night before, and smug with it. To her shock, he announced to the tape that it was eleven a.m. She had obviously slept more deeply than she had realised.

'You're involved with some pretty interesting people, Mrs Wright. I understand you were at a party last night?'

'I was working last night. I took some clients to the party.'

'Who were they?'

She sighed heavily, knowing she had no choice. 'Monsieur Grodin and his wife. If you look in my diary in the car you will see all the details.'

'Already done. So you don't go into the house and join the guests?'

'No.' She took a reluctant breath. 'This time I did, briefly. But not the main house. I went into the servants' quarters.'

'Why?'

'Mr Grodin asked me to.'

'Why was that?'

'He . . . we . . . wanted to spend a little private time.'

'Doing what?'

'Oh, use your imagination!' she snapped at him. Bailey exchanged satisfied looks with his companion.

'Was anyone else there?'

'Yes. A younger man. His name was Justin.'

'Had you met him before?'

'No.'

'But you had sex with him.'

Rachel glared at him. 'What the hell has all this got to do with you?'

Bailey moved closer to her. 'Mrs Wright, the Lady of the Manor arrived home early this morning to find her house filled with drugged-up toffs all porking away like rabbits. Meanwhile, a million pounds' worth of her precious gems have gone missing, and there's Reginald Tagger, festering in the boot of his Mercedes. Finally, there's you, a cash-strapped chauffeur, linking all three cases. So if I were you, I'd stop asking questions, and start answering them.'

There was a tentative knock on the door. A man stuck his head around the door.

'Godzilla's coming this way.'

Bailey cursed under his breath. He terminated the interview and went out.

Rachel waited. In the distance she heard voices. Angry voices, echoing down the corridor and coming closer. She tried to make sense of them but couldn't understand who was saying what.

'Jesus Christ, why couldn't you idiots have waited for me?'

'We had enough to pick her up, so we brought her in.' It was Bailey, not sounding quite as cocky as he had the night before.

'Wonderful, and in doing so you let the real perps get away! This is my call and you knew that, Bailey! If you've blown this operation your arse is on the line forthwith!'

'Oh, come on! You could have brought her in days ago but you chose to get a couple of pokes in first! Now Tagger is dead and –'

A thud shook the wall, making Rachel jump. Then calming voices, telling the two protagonists to break it off, to cool down. Rachel sat up, curiosity replacing fear.

'You no longer have authority on this case, Bailey. The whole damned mess from Tagger up belongs to us now. Be grateful.'

The door crashed open. The man who entered the room was blazingly angry, and for a moment the mask was so fixed that she did not recognise the person behind it.

He turned and shut the door, and when he turned again he had just about controlled himself. They stared at each other for a long, silent moment. Rachel could not speak.

'I'm sorry,' he said at last.

No, she still couldn't speak. The words just weren't there.

'It was handled badly,' he said, clearly uncomfortable under her disbelieving stare.

At last she found her voice. 'So that's supposed to make me feel better, being arrested by the man I've been sleeping with for the last two months? Oh yes, and the one I caught with his hand in my knicker drawer and jewellery box? I should bloody well say it's been handled badly!'

'No, you shouldn't have been held like this.'

But Rachel was now mad as hell. 'Wouldn't it have been a great date? Hey, honey, why don't we skip the porn show and I'll show you what it's like being arrested by armed men in the middle of the night! What a blast! You'll experience first hand the beaten-up hookers and their pimps, the drunken skinheads, and come to know what it's like to receive verbal abuse six inches from your face! And the highlight of the evening is a spell in a real police cell, sweat, fleas and all, while you contemplate your future, which seems to be dictated by people who don't give a shit! You know something? That makes me feel really hot! You want to make out now? Maybe I'll give you some really juicy evidence!'

'Shut – up.' His voice was tightly measured, but he slammed his palms so hard down on the Formica table that it threatened to collapse. She flinched, but never lost eye contact.

'You must really love your job,' she said softly. Commitment-free sex, with the booty to close the case thrown in.'

'That wasn't why I made love to you,' he said, equally softly.

'Come on, David, you never made love to me. You fucked me, and it was a perk of the job. You think I'm stupid?'

He drew a packet of Dunhills from the top pocket of his Yves Saint Laurent suit. As he flicked the lighter she felt a tug in her chest. Unlike Detective Bailey, this man knew how to smoke and make it mean something. He leaned against the wall, watching her through heavy-lidded eyes.

'You're not stupid, Rachel. You've been dealt a bum hand.'

'Oh please, don't start pitying me! Just tell me why I'm here, then let me go.' She desperately wanted a cigarette as well, though she had never smoked in her life.

'I can't do that yet.' David opened the door and ordered the man outside to get tea and pastries. Rachel suddenly realised she hadn't eaten or drunk anything since early the night before. Her skin felt dehydrated and her clothes wrinkled and grubby. He grabbed the chair opposite hers and spun it around, straddling it and sitting comfortably. How sexy was that, she found herself thinking, then put the hideously inappropriate thought down to shock.

'OK, tell me about Adrian and Robyn Grodin,' he said.

'Shouldn't you be recording this?' She motioned to the tape recorder on the table by his elbow. He drew on the cigarette and waited patiently for her answer.

'As I told Mr Bailey, they are regular clients. They fly in from Paris and I take them to a hotel in London.'

'Where else do you take them?'

'After that I drive them to their friends. The addresses are in my log book in the car. I write down the address of each drop and pick-up. It's standard practice.'

'Have you ever met any of these people?'

She hadn't, as a rule. The place for drivers was in the driveway. The hosts had no interest in them. She had not been offered so much as a glass of water. Once she even had to pee in the rhododendrons after one hostess sent a security guard out to say they were not allowed in the house under any circumstances.

David watched her with that same cold, speculative expression as she spoke. He was unrecognisable from the dubious diamond dealer she had grown reluctantly to care for. It was a pity that the image of him rummaging in her panty drawer just wouldn't shift.

'What about Justin Longmere? Lord Justin Longmere, to be precise.'

This was going to be worse than embarrassing. She braced herself. 'I met him briefly last night, yes.'

'Outside the house?'

'Yes. Well, no, not exactly.'

'What did happen, exactly?' His question dripped acid.

She told him, watching a small tic on his temple move every time he clenched his jaw. After that the questions came thick and fast, with no let-up. Why did she have sex with him? What happened next? Did she have any idea who Justin was? Answer: no, she didn't realise he was the son of Lady Longmere, former Conservative MP and squeaky clean as Mickey Mouse. On and on it went until her head spun.

'You're not a normal cop, are you?' she said eventually. During the last hour he had not written anything she had said down, or recorded it in any way.

'Tell me more about Adrian Grodin,' he said. 'Did you learn anything while you were sleeping with him?' He sounded bitter. She didn't feel at all sorry for him.

'Only that he was a veritable Baryshnikov of cunnilingus.'

David's eyes narrowed. She could see his jaw moving as he fought back some evil retort. She could see the question in his eyes. What about me, he wanted to ask, so desperately she could almost hear it.

The slap of a brown envelope on the table made her jump. From inside he drew an official-looking typed document, which he pushed towards her, together with a fat Mont Blanc fountain pen.

She began to read, painstakingly, so as not to be caught out later by something she had not understood. There was a lot of jargon, but the upshot was that anything she heard in that room was not to be repeated outside. If she did, she would find herself on a fast track to the nearest court for whatever shit would stick, which at that moment seemed to be quite a lot. At the bottom there were two lines, one for David's signature, and one for hers. Resignedly she picked up the pen and signed her name. David did the same. His signature was jagged and angry, not unlike the man himself. He lit another cigarette and drew on it with quick, palsied movements, roaming around the room.

'I lead a specialised unit affiliated with MI5. We deal with drug smugglers, minor terrorists, international crime cartels. This isn't strictly under our jurisdiction, but for certain reasons we have been given the job of tidying it up. This has gone to a pretty high level. Politicians, celebs, people who don't want their names connected with wild orgies in the middle of the countryside. It was

Lady Longmere's house you went to last night. She came back early, as Detective Bailey explained to you, and found some items of jewellery missing. Very valuable items, in fact. That was a coincidence, but Bailey bringing you in wasn't. He wanted to look good for the Commissioner and shot his wad too early in the attempt. Consequently Grodin slipped the net before we could question him.'

She frowned, trying to assimilate this new information. 'Sorry, what do you mean, "slipped the net"?'

'Grodin's got form, years ago, for fraud. We've only just found this out but now we know he's been casing the houses of these people for weeks, taking notes, photos, whatever he can in order to get good-quality copies made of the jewels that take his eye. Then when party time comes around again, he swaps the real gems for the fakes...'

'And Robyn wears them through Customs,' Rachel finished for him. That was why Robyn seemed so lavishly adorned. It saved awkward questions about the contents of her hand luggage, but it raised another one. 'Is Robyn in on it? It seems crazy when she's heiress to a fortune anyway.'

'Come on, Rachel, everyone knows that millionaire heiresses *are* crazy. She was in it up to her neck, but she's just gone boohooing back to Daddy saying Grodin forced her into it. Now nobody believes that for one second, but it's a convenient way of making her look good and dropping Grodin deep in the brown stuff, without any proof to the contrary. And Valmez isn't going to question it when Grodin blackmailed Valmez into giving his blessing to the marriage in the first place.'

Rachel threw up her hands. 'Back up a minute. Didn't she want to marry him?'

'Yes. She was doing it out of spite to her father. But a couple of days ago she found out that Grodin was using coke and doing all the things that he had promised he wouldn't do once he was married to her and she went up like a rocket. Grodin had even signed an agreement saying he wouldn't. But I guess old habits die hard.' He gave her a pointed glare, which she met with a catty smile. Inside she was thinking, So that was why Robyn wanted to make a hasty getaway. She had probably discovered Adrian stoned out of his head with a male member of the British establishment implanted in his backside. It would be enough to make any wife go into orbit.

'So what did Grodin have over Valmez?' she asked.

'There's some nasty past history in the Valmez family that the old man wanted kept hidden. In the forties and fifties he was a Nazi sympathiser apparently, which isn't good publicity for any foreign diplomat. *Le Monde* is rumbling on about it as we speak, but quite frankly, that isn't my problem. Valmez and Lady Longmere have been friends for a long time, and I'm under pressure to solve this neatly, discreetly and with no press involvement. And right now I don't know how I'm going to do it.'

She examined his face. He looked stressed, as if the last few hours had been hell. It probably had been, with a high-ranking French diplomat giving him earache, and a titled British battleaxe breathing down his neck, threatening to end his career.

'You'd better give me my cue to start feeling sorry for you, because right now I'm not getting it,' she said coldly. 'And if you really are a spy your technique stinks.'

'That's MI6,' David said wearily.

'And what about Reginald Tagger? They're trying to pin his murder on me!'

'They are bloody idiots, blundering around in the dark. Their evidence is circumstantial and, besides, we already know who did it.'

Rachel looked up. 'You do?'

David gazed levelly at her. He sat back in his seat and casually let his jacket fall open. She remembered the handgun he had shown her in the cinema, and her eyes widened. She pointed silently at him but his expression remained immobile.

'As the media said, it was a professional job.'

Rachel let out a long, disbelieving breath. 'Does that mean I can go home?'

'We haven't finished with you yet.'

'You mean you still don't trust me.' Her tongue felt wooden.

'It's my job not to.' He stood up and headed for the door. 'You need to clear your diary for the next two weeks.'

'What! Why? What's going on?'

'Can't say at the minute. You'll just have to trust me.'

'Oh great, another challenge,' she retorted as he left the room.

While waiting for David yet again she ate the pastries and drank the tea, lukewarm but better than nothing. The kindly police officer gave her some magazines to read. They were back copies of *OK*, *Chat* and *Prima*, not her thing at all, but it was a sweet thought. Within half an hour she knew how to knit an Easter egg cosy, prepare a three-course meal in five minutes and Put The Spark Back In Her Marriage. After that, everything David had told her began to make sense.

If the Valmez and Longmere family were old friends, then that would explain the Grodins' ability to gain access to the houses of people they hardly knew. Fine.

Robyn was a stubborn, spoiled woman, and Adrian's dubious past and taste for the finer things in life were probably irresistible, especially as she took pleasure in needling her long-suffering father. Not that Rachel had much sympathy with him, if what David had said was true. And if it was, surely Lady Longmere would want to distance herself from such a man, being the staunch supporter of the Conservative party that she was?

Eventually David came back and, at last, took her out of that horrid room. The gloomy corridor smelled as fresh as a mountainside in comparison, and the sunlight streaming though the high windows never seemed so bright. Then they were out in broad daylight that hurt her eyes. But not for long. She was escorted to a big black Mercedes with darkened windows, the vehicle of choice for small-time gangsters, shadowy government organisations, and her. Maybe it was time to change her mode of transport, she thought wryly.

One of the men drove. The other sat with her in the back, sandwiching her between him and David. She was very aware of David's dark-suited leg pressing against hers. It did not need to, not in a car that big, but even from him she was glad of some warm, bodily contact.

'So what were you really looking for in my lingerie drawer?' she asked.

The other man stared steadfastly out of the window.

'Evidence,' David replied shortly.

'Of what? That I wear knickers?'

The other man was still staring out of the window, but she could see his mouth twitching.

'I was looking to see if Grodin had given you any jewellery that might in fact belong to someone else,' he said patiently. 'Just remember that you're not out of the woods yet. Save any more talk for when we get to the office.'

They were in the car for another long, silent half-hour. Over London Bridge they drove, to the south side of the Thames, and into the underground car park of a faceless office building.

They led her to David's office and motioned to a chair. She looked around, concluding that he was probably quite senior, as the room was totally private and furnished in a spare luxury not afforded outside his door. The two other men sat down, their faces bland and immobile. It felt like an inquisition. Once again, she knew this was not normal practice. David sat down in the creaky leather chair behind his desk and leaned his elbows on the table.

'Rachel, these gentlemen are from Special Branch. They have been seconded to work with me on this problem. Our methods are our own, and Lady Longmere has stressed that we should use any means to close this matter soonest. She would prefer to avoid those "Smooth Frog Rips Off Toffs At Sex Party" headlines. I think you see our problem.'

Quiet sniggers around the table. David silenced them with a look and scratched his ear, smiling wryly.

'Sometimes I think these rich buggers get what they deserve, being taken in by paste diamonds and a French accent.'

'I was taken in, too. What does that make me?'

'Right now, I don't have an answer to that.'

'Guilty until proven innocent, right?'

'That's not how it works.'

'Bullshit.' She put every ounce of feeling into the word.

'Your personal feelings have been made clear, but I'd appreciate it if you would put them aside and help us.'

'And what if I don't want to?'

'You'll be charged with obstruction. Put the blunt way, this isn't a favour I'm asking you, Rachel. This is me saving your arse.'

'Oh, not you wanting to avoid directing traffic for the rest of your working life?'

His mouth set in a grim line. The other men looked at the ceiling.

'Mrs Grodin has told us that Grodin supplies gems to a character in Jamaica called Jermaine. Have you heard that name mentioned before?'

Rachel shook her head. 'Never.'

'He's known in the rap world as the King of Bling. He deals in platinum and diamonds. Tupac was a customer. So is P Diddy, apparently. Grodin is one of several suppliers but we don't know yet whether this guy is clean or not. Anyway, Mrs Grodin suspects that her husband will go to Jamaica to score with the latest batch of stolen gems. If he succeeds then he'll take the money and go underground, leaving us jackshit to charge him with. But he is a man of habit, and he doesn't know that Mrs Grodin has turned on him, so with any luck he'll be chilling out at his hotel before doing the deal with Jermaine, who isn't even there at present. He'll be back later on tomorrow, but he won't be in the mood to talk business until after his wife's birthday party next Saturday. Apparently he isn't a man who likes to be hurried, but either way we have to act fast.'

'But if you have reasonable grounds to think he might be handling stolen goods surely you can do something,' Rachel said.

'If we had the support of the local authorities, maybe, but he's good for the economy. Owns a couple of bars and a swanky hotel, and sponsors drug rehabilitation programmes for young drug users. If he goes belly down, so does his cash. But back to Grodin. We believe he has in his possession a diamond and white gold necklace stolen from Lady Longmere. It's worth around a million, so she's pretty keen to get it back.'

'Right,' she said slowly. She remembered Justin's comment about raiding the family safe. Shit, he must have been lathered. And being the opportunist he was, even in his drugged state it would have been easy for Adrian to help himself in the ensuing confusion the following morning. Then it was a case of hopping on the next plane to wherever to contact Jermaine for a quick sale, before disappearing with enough money to live in coke-addled obscurity, being buggered to death.

OK, the last bit was a guess but, if Robyn had found him, he would have known that their marriage was history, and he was unlikely to risk going back to Europe for a very long time.

'I think that's a fairly reasonable judgement,' David conceded grudgingly when she put this to him. The other men nodded in agreement. He opened a flat, square box lined with plush, dark-blue velvet. 'This is the fake that Grodin left in Lady Longmere's jewellery box,' he said. The necklace twinkled saucily at her, as if letting her in on its secret.

'That's a fake?' She said it with awe, reaching out to touch the stones. The necklace was made up of several strands of diamonds approximately the size of her little toenail, forming a delta that would disguise the crêpeiest of necks. The longest strand was around six inches long, designed to sit neatly between the breasts.

'Worth around five hundred pounds,' David said dismissively. 'Actually, it isn't even that good.' He snapped the case shut, causing her to retract her fingers rapidly.

There was a slight pause.

'Well, it's been a fascinating afternoon,' she said briskly, 'but why exactly are you telling me all this?'

The second man leaned over to her and spoke for the first time. 'What we need is a ground operative, someone to distract Grodin while the necklaces are swapped.'

'A woman would be ideal,' the third one added.

They all looked at her. She was aware that her lower jaw was scraping the floor. She pulled it back up.

'No way,' she said. 'No way in hell.'

11

The deal sounded simple enough. To fly to Jamaica, in some sort of disguise of course, fuck Adrian stupid while the necklaces were swapped and move to a discreet distance to witness the showdown between Adrian and Jermaine when the latter found out that the rocks were, well, just rocks. Then David and his men would move in for the kill.

So they didn't say it quite like that, but Rachel had been round the block enough times to read between the lines. Under the steely supervision of David and his men she cleared her diary for the next two weeks, as instructed. A couple of clients had not taken it well, but there was nothing Rachel could do about that when she was threatened with an odious police cell. Two days before, she had allowed herself to hang loose a little and enjoy life. What a mistake that had been.

When she asked to call Sharma he refused.

'I'm damned sure this isn't standard procedure,' she retorted.

'You're right, it isn't. As I said, we're a special unit.'

'In other words, you make up your own rules. You're worse than Tagger, using the handy cover of law and order to get your kicks,' she said sourly. 'Just tell me why you want me to do your dirty work?'

'I'll tell you when it's appropriate. Right now I need to know that you're up to the job.'

She thought before replying. The gun wasn't there, pointing at her temple, but it may as well have been. Even so, she wanted to prove to him that she damned well could do it. Even more, she wanted to prove it to herself.

'Yes,' she said decisively.

'Good. We'll be with you every step of the way. I realise this could be dangerous, Rachel, and I don't want to see you getting hurt.'

'Too late for that,' she muttered.

Late that afternoon David drove her in near silence to visit Lady Longmere. She was still in shock and very upset, he said, both by the duplicity of her long-time friend and the stupidity of her son and daughter-in-law, who were actually supposed to be looking after the house while she was away. Rachel could sympathise with her, imagining how it must have felt to walk into her beautiful house to find it full of drugged-out strangers, then to discover she had been robbed and, on top of that, a dear friend was just about to be exposed as a closet Nazi by the French media. Not a good day by anyone's standards.

Lady Longmere was still a beautiful woman, with perfectly coiffed white hair and willow thin in pearls and grey cashmere, but her mouth was tight with anger and her piercing blue eyes cold as chips of Arctic ice. Rachel felt as if she were being assessed like a potential scullery maid. She was glad she had worn her Roland Cartier court shoes and black Talbots suit. Her long dark hair was held back in a sleek chignon.

They were sitting in the drawing room. The house looked different during the day, with the mid-afternoon sun glaring off the yellow Cotswold stone. Rachel had not appreciated in the dark how huge the house was, nor how extensive the grounds, with striped verdant lawns and colourful borders full of herbaceous flowers. And in the distance, the Thames sparkled like a silver ribbon, studded with even tinier white pleasure boats.

There was no sign of Justin. He had conveniently gone

to Tuscany with his wife, Felicity. Rachel suspected that they had been despatched while the whole thing was sorted out. She was relieved. Facing Justin again while David was with her wasn't something she really relished doing.

'I hope you understand your position, Mrs Wright,' she said, still clearly distressed. 'I am ... inconvenienced by the events of last weekend. Therefore, I am going by Mr Fielding's advice. You will not mention this to anyone. If you do, you will be held in contempt. Is that understood?'

'Clearly,' Rachel said, thinking that she had not felt this small since being in the headmistress's office at high school.

'Others who have found themselves in a similar position have accepted that they will never see their valuables again, but they do want this man caught and punished, and you are going to assist us.'

'Yes. In any way I can.'

Lady Longmere fixed her with a steely look. 'Indeed, but I need your assurance that you will not be treating this trip as a free holiday. Is that clear?'

Rachel's mouth dropped open. She looked at David for support. None seemed to be forthcoming.

'And I hope it's been made clear to you that I have not been asked, but told to risk my business and my reputation in order to save yours, through no fault of my own!'

Lady Longmere pursed her thin lips in disapproval. 'I see. I knew it would come to this. Would fifty thousand pounds ensure that you carry out the mission to our satisfaction and keep quiet about it afterwards?'

Rachel was highly offended. 'This isn't about money! I don't know what I'm doing! All I want is this stupid charge taken away and the chance to get on with my life! I do not want your money, Lady Longmere.' She needed some air. Forgetting about the protocol David had briefed her about on the journey to the house she escaped into the garden and let the July sun warm her face. A swathe of pastel-pink stocks wafted their peppery scent past her nose, but she couldn't appreciate them. She guessed she had blown it with the old bag, but she wouldn't be bought, not by anyone.

'Hey,' David said softly behind her. 'Nice work. She thinks you're pretty cool.'

Rachel laughed shortly. 'Cool? Was that her expression?'

'Well, no. She said you seemed like "a decent gel".'

His attempt at an aristocratic dowager's accent made her laugh despite herself. They stood together in that peaceful, fragrant garden, and Rachel thought how nice it would be if he put his arm around her right then. You're a sap, she scolded herself. He's lied to you from the first but you'd still jump into bed with him. Not that she would let him know just yet. A few more days of not knowing wouldn't do him any harm.

The next morning she looked at the suitcase full of alien clothes, plus the silky blonde wig lying like a Persian cat on her bed, and she laughed.

'You are joking!'

'He cannot recognise you, Rachel. You have to become this woman, convincingly, or the whole thing is blown.'

Just before lunch he had arrived, together with a woman in a white uniform, carrying what looked like a large tool box. She was there to administer the St Tropez tan and the false nails and tell Rachel how to fit the wig.

Four hours later she was plucked, bronzed and blonde, blowing lightly over her new porcelain nails, painted with pearly white varnish. She had also shaved off her pubic hair, just as an extra precaution. It felt very strange and slightly prickly, and looked weird, even with fake tan plonked on it. She walked out of the room, wrapped in a safe towelling robe and glared at David from under the frothy blonde fringe.

'You think this is funny, don't you?' She went to the suitcase and picked up the first item her fingers touched. It was a very small T-shirt in thin silky jersey, so low cut she was sure her navel would show. Other items included a faded denim skirt the same width as one of Sharma's pelmets, and breakneck white stilettos adorned with little red bows. She picked up one of them by the heel as if it were a dead rat. 'Did I irritate you in a former life or what?'

'Just try to remember just how much is riding on this.' David sounded unsympathetic.

'Yes, my business. Just spare me the patronising pep talk, please. I'd like your assurance that there aren't ten men in the background having the five-knuckle shuffle at my expense, but if you say I can trust you one more time, I swear to God I'll swing for you.'

David motioned for the woman to leave them alone. When she left he slipped his arms around Rachel's waist. She was too busy levering herself into her five-inch heels to fend him off. Losing her balance, she had to cling to him to stop herself from falling over.

'You'll be fine. Act as thick as shit and no one will notice you. You know the type I mean,' he murmured.

'Yes. The type my husband left me for,' she replied tersely, attempting to struggle free of his arms. 'How much of a slapper are you expecting me to be?'

He held her tighter. 'That's up to you.'

'I didn't think I had any choice in the matter.'

He nuzzled into her neck. 'You're a wild animal, Rachel. I don't believe anyone can really make you do something you don't want.'

She felt his hand drift lower, under the short skirt to

stroke the inside of her leg. She grasped his fingers and moved them away, stepping lightly out of his embrace.

'So you'd better tell me my name for the week,' she said. 'Let me guess. Tracey? Sharon?'

'Kim Clarke,' he said curtly, visibly annoyed at her rejection. He snapped the locks on his briefcase and pulled out an envelope. Inside was a passport and plane tickets. The photograph inside the passport was her, but not. She stared at herself in the mirror, then at the passport. It looked suitably foul, computer trickery at its most finely honed.

Looking at David's tense face, it occurred to her that she actually needed him on her side when they were three thousand miles away from home.

'Um, when this is over, will I see you again?'

He glared at her. 'That depends, doesn't it?'

'On what?'

'On whether you screw up. If you do, you'll see me in court.' He slammed the briefcase shut with telling force. 'Time to go,' he said, and did not wait for her to follow him.

It was surreal, catching her reflection in the glass outside the terminal building and seeing a tousled blonde bob instead of her usual sleek dark hair. Even though she had refused to have her real hair cut off, it didn't feel as uncomfortable as she had dreaded, and the wig was easier to put on than she had anticipated. But although the hairstyle was acceptable, the clothes were going to take a whole lot more time to get used to. She had chosen a relatively modest jersey dress, before realising that it rose six inches up her thighs every time she sat down. Her feet were already aching in strappy Faith sandals. They clicked loudly on the linoleum as she walked through the airport with her case trailing behind her.

Act blonde, she thought. She ran the gauntlet of the cabbies and chauffeurs, most of whom she recognised. God, what if they recognised her? She could kiss goodbye to any credibility for the next millennium. And what the hell were they staring at?

She glanced down, and saw that the Wonderbra was doing its job a little too effectively. She discreetly pulled the neckline of the dress back up over her burgeoning cleavage and cursed David to hell. She felt like Lily Savage.

The first-class seats were suitably spacious, which was just as well because David bought a *Daily Telegraph* and proceeded to read it from cover to cover, encroaching on her personal space every time he turned the page.

Food came, and coffee, together with those little cartons of cream. She pulled the tab on one and aimed it at David's lap.

'I'm so sorry,' she gasped innocently as the cream spurted on to his expensive suit.

'Don't be. It's the air pressure that does it,' he said, baring his teeth at her.

'And I thought it was my light touch.' She winked at him and enjoyed the discomfort on his face. Something about him in that damned suit had sent all her hormones haywire again. How come her sexual morals had left her so easily? She could look at this deceiving son-of-a-bitch and still easily imagine leading him by the cock into the toilets at the earliest opportunity. She blinked, trying to erase the image, but it would not go.

The time passed. She read the tourist bumph warning about the hustlers and the no-go areas, and thought that maybe Jamaica wasn't going to be all about powder-white beaches and palm trees, as she had thought. It was bigger than she imagined, and bikinis were strictly for the beach or poolside, unless she wanted to be accosted by every male under the age of seventy. Suddenly she was glad that David would be with her every step of the way, even if he was being a prime arsehole.

Eventually she dozed off, and in her dream David was also asleep, his newspaper in his lap. Stealthily she slipped her hand underneath it and felt for his crotch. She fondled him into full hardness and watched his face change as he woke up. He looked shocked at first, then conspiratorial, unzipping his trousers and fumbling through his silk boxers. He stopped as the stewardess walked past, but then Rachel's hand was on naked flesh, hot and hard and demanding. His face was flushed, his breathing unsteady.

'Let's go to the toilets,' he whispered raggedly, moving her hand away again.

In her dream she agreed, as simple as that. He went first, then she did, slipping into the tiny room when no one was looking. He was already unzipped, his cock sticking straight out like a big blunt spear. She immediately sucked him into her mouth, closing her red-painted lips around him and leaving lipstick on his boxers. He was rocking back and forth, biting his lips to stop the grunts becoming too audible, but then he wanted her to stand up, so that he could peel down her dress and nuzzle into her tits. Further aroused by the sweet pulling sensations trickling down towards her clitoris, she pushed up against him, her fingers stroking his balls, all soft and heavy. Then her hand wrapped around his shaft and she was rubbing him as he rubbed against her, still sucking on her tits, his smart suit and neatly combed hair all untidy.

'I'm going to be hard all week because of you, you hot little slut,' he said hoarsely, and she didn't mind his crudeness, because she understood his need.

'Get that fat prick inside me,' she whispered into his ear. A little manoeuvring, and she was kneeling up on the toilet, her knees killing her, her stilettos jabbing into his legs. His hands were on her hips and he was easing in and out of her soaking pussy, holding her sodden panties to one side. His thrusts became quicker, harder, but no less deep, bringing them both to a shuddering climax that left her feeling weak and helpless.

'Oh, yes,' she murmured, and suddenly woke up, realising she had spoken out loud. Then she realised that her hand was actually in his lap. She withdrew it as if escaping a white-hot flame and turned bright red.

'Good dream?' he asked sardonically.

She brazened out her embarrassment and smiled sweetly. 'Wonderful, thank you.'

12

The hotel was opulent, looking over cocaine-white sand and endless blue ocean. Rachel's room was spacious, cool and expensively decorated, with large statues of Greek gods in cold white stone, so smooth it invited one to touch it. There were fresh flowers, reverential staff, a bed as big as a football stadium, and a large sunken bath and a balcony overlooking the sea. The thought that Adrian might well be here right now under the same roof made her shiver. This would be her home for the next five nights, unless it all went horribly wrong. Then she would be on the next flight home, probably in a box.

To distract her from such unpleasant thoughts she decided to venture out for a while. After dumping her bags down, David had disappeared, saying he would be back later and reminding her as a final shot to stay out of trouble. Despite that, the warm sunshine bathed her face and lifted her mood as it had never done in England, where there was always the threat that it wouldn't last. Here, she was sure, the sun was almost constant, and one could enjoy it without feeling as if it were a guilty snatched pleasure. She dressed in a simple white T-shirt and shorts that weren't too short, tied her blonde hair back with a bandanna and tried to look as uninteresting as she could to avoid the inevitable hustlers. Thus armed, she emerged from the hotel on to the vivid, bustling streets. For a while she walked, just enjoying the explosion of colours created by exotic flowers tumbling from the balconies of old, faded hotels, the smell of sizzling jerk chicken, the array of glistening tropical fruits and the jabber of richly inflected voices. Old men in rags puffed on fat stogies of ganja, watching her with yellow, bloodshot eyes. Young boys tap-danced on street corners with bottle tops hammered into their sneakers. She became an expert at the firm but polite rebuff when offered anything from slices of papaya fruit to a 'real good time'. It didn't happen as much as she had feared, but she was still exhausted by the time she got back to the hotel an hour later.

Relieved to be back in the cool quiet of her room, Rachel took the wig off and had a shower. The moist late-afternoon heat made her drowsy, so she lay on the bed, let the ceiling fan waft cool air over her naked body and closed her eyes.

When she woke up, a man was standing over the bed.

She opened her mouth to scream, but then realised it was David. He looked pretty acceptable in a navy polo shirt and cream cargo shorts, his calves as tight as rope knots and no socks to grace his slim feet, shoved in Tods sandals.

'It's show time,' he said, throwing a towel to her to cover her nakedness. He took her place on the bed and stretched out to wait for her.

'So what do I need to do?' she said as she reapplied her St Tropez moisturising crème to keep her tan looking convincing.

'Grodin isn't here yet, but he will be, the day after tomorrow. We managed to get Jermaine's chauffeur to talk.'

'How?' Rachel asked suspiciously. 'Did you break his ankles?'

David smiled coldly. 'A kilo of coke did the job. I'm not fussy how I get my information.'

'I know that already,' she retorted. The smile disappeared.

'We were right, though. Jermaine only arrived back

last night. He has a place a couple of miles up the mountain, a big pink hacienda called Santega Heights. That's his home and he keeps it private. Business is strictly dealt with down here on the level. But as I said, there's a big bash on Saturday night at one of his bars. Jermaine's wife will be forty.'

'Nice for her.'

'Indeed. We need to know if Grodin's going to be there. If he is, we'll have a chance to swap the necklaces.'

'We? So you're not expecting me to ensnare and bed him and do it myself?'

David laughed shortly. 'Of course not! We're can't let an amateur screw up an operation like this!'

Rachel whirled round and faced him. 'So why the hell am I here, dressed like Dolly Parton? Is this your idea of entertainment?' She felt her voice rising and cooled it. No one was going to accuse her of not being professional.

David treated her to a cool stare. 'I wanted you here,' he said simply.

'Why?'

'For my own amusement. Why else?'

She opened her mouth and closed it again. Something wasn't right. 'I don't buy it. You couldn't bankroll this on your own, and I can't see any secret government bodies letting you take a tart on business unless you were the Director General.'

'Quite. You could be useful to me and, as I have the right to withhold any further information from you while you are in my custody, I wouldn't bother questioning my motives if I were you,' he said casually, flicking his lighter. He sat comfortably back in the armchair, watching her. She was aware of his sizzling gaze as she started on her make-up.

'Glad to hear I'm not just part of the wallpaper,' she muttered, jamming the horrid blonde wig back on her head. She eschewed her normal Estée Lauder for silver

Bourgoise eye shadow on her lids and black eyeliner. Her lips she kept a natural colour but highly glossed. Finally she chose a white bikini, over which she draped a long silk sarong printed with blue and white tropical flowers, fastening it to one shoulder with a silk lily from Johnnie Loves Rosie. The underwire of one bra cup was actually a bug, with a range of a thousand metres and apparently waterproof. David had assured her that an operative would always be less than half that distance away. She had said tersely that she hoped he was a fast runner.

'Jermaine's place is a hundred yards down the road, the one with the white lattice and blue umbrellas. It's called Jays' Bar,' David said, when she was finally ready.

She had already seen it. Along Montego Bay's hip strip, it seemed like one of the classier establishments on offer.

'They operate a very strict dress code, especially for the women, but the ladies like it because they can go to the bar alone without being hit upon. Any man wanting to introduce himself has to do it through one of the bar staff. If she's interested, great, if not and he makes an issue, he's out, with no refund on his thirty-dollar entrance fee. The women don't have to pay,' he added, answering her next question.

'When you say a strict dress code?'

'I mean, fresh manicures, make-up, no denims or T-shirts.'

'What about this?' She motioned down at her dress.

'Fine,' he said dismissively.

'Thanks,' she said dryly. 'So what do I do now?'

'Go to the bar, hang out, see who's around. See if you can pick up anything about the guest list for Saturday night, but be careful. They don't like too many questions. You're on holiday for a week, if anyone asks. If they want more then keep it simple. That way you'll remember your story.'

'I'm not that bloody stupid!'

'Sorry.' He grimaced with his apology. 'But you're an amateur and it's my job to make sure you're safe.'

'You don't have to keep reminding me how amateurish I am. If I had my way I'd be back home being a professional chauffeur.' She grabbed her bag and marched past him towards the door.

'You look stunning, by the way.'

The unexpected compliment threw her. She looked away, resisting the urge to tuck her hair coyly behind her ear. Oh please, she thought to herself, don't go all girly now.

'Don't get used to it,' she said shortly.

'Just remember I'll be watching you at all times.' His tone implied that he didn't trust her to stay out of trouble. It was like a kick in the stomach.

Entering the lush entrance to Jay's Bar felt like approaching the Temple of Doom. A bouncer built like the Berlin Wall watched her impassively behind black Wayfarers, even though the sun had just about set by then. Then he smiled, revealing alternate white and gold teeth, scaring her even more.

'Good evening, my lady,' he said in a rich Jamaican accent, and stood away from the entrance in the white picket fence so that she could go through. 'The bar is to your left. Please enjoy your first drink on the house.'

'Thank you,' she said faintly, silently promising that she would enjoy her drink like a good girl. Promise.

The bartender oozed charm, flipping glasses as if born to it. He welcomed her with a dazzling smile, thankfully all white this time, and asked if she would like a cocktail.

'What would you recommend?' she asked. The reggae music, just loud enough to make one's body move but not to hinder conversation, was beginning to jiggle through her veins. There was no need to fear. Just relax and enjoy.

The bartender was spinning glasses, shaking, mixing. A dash of champagne, a splash of pink mush that seconds before had been whole strawberries and a flash of white rum, all prettily presented with a dark-blue Jay's Bar swizzle stick and a silver glittery straw, topped with a sliver of lime and a strawberry. He presented it to her with a flourish.

'For you, ma'am. A Silver Mercedes.'

Her stomach swooped. Had she been nobbled already? She took the long, tulip-shaped glass from him.

'Wow, how did you guess?' she said unsteadily.

'It's the King of Bling's speciality, ma'am. Named after his mama's vehicle of choice.' He laughed fruitily.

Coincidence, then. Her facial features relaxed. 'And mine,' she said gaily. She took a sip. Oh, she could get used to this. The cocktail was fruity, fizzy and wickedly alcoholic. She thanked him and he moved on to serve two more women who had come in after her.

She tried to look relaxed as she propped up the bar. Her blonde wig felt better than she thought it would.

Be the hair, she reminded herself, sipping her cocktail and checking surreptitiously around her. People occupied every table, beautiful people in designer shirts, skinny dresses, golden tans. Then her blood ran cold.

It couldn't be. Not here. Not in paradise. Her recent past could not so cruelly leap up and smack her in the face.

Abandoning her cocktail, she fled from the bar. She ran on to the beach and stumbled as her stilettos sank into the sand, still warm from the heat of the day. She kicked them off and continued to run until she was enveloped in darkness. Only then did she allow herself to cry, the great heaving sobs that had not come for six months. Not until now, seeing her lousy, good-for-nothing husband in all his banal reality, less than twenty feet away from her in Jay's Bar.

As she caught her breath, leaning against the prow of an old fishing boat, she heard someone call her name. Not her own name, but the one she had been given. Kim, as in Basinger. David jogged up to her. She could hardly see him in the darkness, and with only the light of the moon to guide her, her first slap was slightly off target.

'Why didn't you tell me?' Too breathless to scream it, her voice was a mere hoarse shriek.

'I couldn't risk you refusing to come.'

'You didn't give me any choice,' she snarled at him. 'This was you saving my arse, remember?'

'All right!' David ran his fingers through his hair, looking agitated. 'I thought you were involved, OK? I didn't expect you to react like this!'

'How the hell was I supposed to react? Give him a big kiss and say, "Hi darling, where's my alimony?" What the hell is he doing here?'

David looked relieved to be on slightly smoother waters. 'Jerry works for Jermaine as his bodyguard and driver. He has been for the last three months. Your relationship with Adrian Grodin and Jerry's connection with Jermaine just seemed too much of a coincidence.'

'Well, they do happen.' Her voice dripped acid.

'I know, but not often enough, in my experience.'

'I hope you're satisfied now,' she said bitterly.

'Rachel . . .' He reached for her but she thrust him away.

'I hate you,' she said vehemently. She began to walk back up the beach.

'Where are you going?' David called after her.

'To fix myself up. I'm hardly going to be allowed back in looking like this, am I?' She motioned to her ruined make-up and messed-up hair.

Fifteen minutes later she was back at the bar, hidden in the darkest corner so that she could discreetly observe her husband. And there was Jerry, looking obscenely tanned and cheerful, with a young, attractive woman adorning his arm. A great rolling wave of rage swept over her, threatening to snap the slender stem of her cocktail glass. How could he look so smug when he had left her floundering in so much shit back home? At least one thing cheered her considerably. He was dressed in a hazardous, technicoloured-yawn-print shirt, teamed with white nylon Bermuda shorts. He might consider himself a player, but would never be convincing unless he rethought his wardrobe and did something surgical with that paunch, which had grown considerably with the good living of the last few months.

She checked out the women next. There was a young Jamaican woman, glossy carmine lips widely parted in laughter, but her eyes were shrewd. She caught Rachel's eye and smiled slightly. No territory worries there. Was she just fucking Jerry to get closer to Jermaine? Anything was possible. And what had he done with Kelly the temp? Sent her back to Reading?

Sharp right, Rachel saw her, moving towards Jerry. Hips swaying under a short white sarong, baby-pink bikini top that just about covered her nipples. No regard for dress code, Rachel thought. Her appearance at Jerry's table confirmed the down-classing of that corner of the restaurant. They were getting shrivelling looks from other women, while quite a few men stared openly at Kelly's blatantly displayed, jiggling chest. Rachel looked back at Jerry. No doubt his connection with Jermaine had allowed him to wangle a table dressed as he was.

She lightly tapped her sparkly gold nails on the counter, wondering what to do next. She didn't particularly relish spending the evening watching her ex schmooze with the local wildlife. Nor did she want to go back to her room. The driving reggae music and laughter around her was making her hungry for company.

'Don't stare at them,' a man murmured beside her. Rachel spun round and concentrated on her cocktail.

David had appeared beside her, suave in a white dinner jacket. 'And watch how you walk. On your way back up here you looked like Margaret Thatcher.'

'I was trying to dodge the hustlers,' she hissed defiantly.

'Is this gentleman bothering you, my lady?' The bouncer from the entrance was standing over David, waiting for her nod. She smiled sweetly at David and gave it. The bouncer pointed one porky finger towards the entrance. There was no need for words. His dark glare said it all.

'I get the message,' David said coldly, and left before he was helped out by the scruff of his neck.

The sound of a mobile phone needled through her thoughts. It was Jerry's. He answered it so loudly that for a moment she was back in Henley, watching *Trigger Happy TV*. She grinned involuntarily, again catching the eye of the dark-skinned girl. Jerry kissed her and Kelly the temp roundly on their cheeks and said, 'Sorry, girls, the boss needs me,' in a voice ringing enough to let everyone know how important he was.

Kelly the temp pouted sulkily and huffed off. The other girl came up to the bar and sat next to Rachel. She ordered a strawberry daiquiri and offered to buy Rachel the same.

'Thanks,' Rachel said, thinking she would be pissed by the end of the night. David wouldn't approve, but after the way he had treated her he could go stuff his problems up his MI5 backside.

'No sweat. I'm Amelia. You are?'

Rachel gulped the wrong answer back down. 'Kim,' she said, sticking out her hand. Amelia took it and looked at her diamond-tipped nails.

'Hey, nice manicure. You're English, right?'

'That's right,' Rachel said. The girl was really quite beautiful, with tightly curled black hair cut in a very short crop, coffee skin and fine bone structure. With very small breasts and a lean, almost boyish figure, she didn't look Jerry's type at all.

'You around here long?' Amelia asked. Her accent was American, and her wide eyes were speculative. Rachel had the distinct impression she was being checked out.

'A week. I'm on holiday.' She wanted to be friendly, but needed to be careful, especially when sitting right in the bear pit owned by the King of Bling.

'On your own?' Amelia asked abruptly. 'That's no fun, is it?'

She knew that Rachel was hiding something. Time for the acting skills she hadn't used since high school to come into play.

'Since you're asking,' she said heavily, 'I'm recovering from a bad relationship actually. No . . .' She paused. 'Two bad relationships. At the same time.' She grinned to show she wasn't being heavy, but would she please stop interrogating her?

Amelia seemed satisfied with that. 'Fair enough. I won't ask any more. You can tell me more though, if you want.'

'Nah, I want to enjoy my holiday, thanks very much. What about you? Was that your boyfriend? He looked allright.' Just in time she remembered to drop her Home Counties voice and let Essex creep in.

Amelia laughed derisively. 'He isn't my boyfriend. He likes lots of girls.'

Rachel gave her an arch look. 'All at once?'

Amelia realised she was joking. She smiled secretively and moved closer to Rachel's shoulder.

'Sometimes. We call him Jo Blo because he really likes having his dick sucked. One of my girls sucked him off for over an hour once. And –' she leaned over and lowered her voice to a whisper '– if he's been away for a week with Jermaine, sometimes he gets so desperate, he needs a girl to give him a blow job once an hour for a whole day!'

'Blimey!' Rachel's eyes widened and this time she wasn't acting. The one thing, the only thing, she remembered liking about Jerry were his big, heavy balls. They were immense, like those of a bull. She could imagine him sustaining enough seed to last through a day, but actually getting off? That was some kind of record. He had never seemed that highly sexed when they were together. Maybe because Kelly the temp had been doing the business in the office. Poor girl. No wonder her bottom lip always looked like a milk jug.

'Oh! So you're a –' she dropped her voice to a whisper, '– a hooker?'

'I was. Now I manage some local girls. Don't tell me you're shocked. I came over because I thought you were one. The last thing my girls need is foreigners taking away their business.'

'Oh, I won't being doing that.' Believe me, I definitely won't, she thought. Not in a million years with Jo Blo. 'What about Kelly? Is she one?'

Amelia's slender brows drew together. 'Who?'

Rachel realised her mistake. 'Oh, I thought I heard her name ... the blonde one,' she stuttered. 'She looked really pissed off.'

'Oh, Sherry. She's a dumbass. He brought her with him. God knows why. She's as thick as shit. She turns tricks for some of the other guys in Jermaine's team but she doesn't get any cash for it.' Amelia looked at Rachel's tanned body. 'I'm surprised he hasn't noticed you yet. He likes his white meat, does our Jez.'

'Oh, I wouldn't dream of treading on your toes.'

'Honey, I wouldn't give him to you. He's trash. I'm just looking out for my girls. We don't ask for trouble but, if it comes our way, I sort it out.'

Rachel could see how. When she frowned, Amelia had all the aggression of Grace Jones.

'Do they get into bother then?' she asked, more

sincerely than she should have done, but she was genuinely interested.

'It happens. Some of the new guys, if they get out of their heads on cheap ganja, they can get heavy, you know? Think they can handle it and they can't so they take it out on the women. But not the King of Bling. He's a businessman, he don't hold with the trade and he has them all by the balls, I can tell you. Man, Jez thinks he's in a cushy position, but one whiff of wacky baccy on the job and he'll be out of Jamaica on a cargo plane. Jermaine don't take any prisoners when it comes to drugs.'

'He's pretty scary, huh?' Rachel suggested, hoping she would talk some more.

Amelia nodded. 'He's a good man, though. Good for business, takes care of the poor kids in MoBay and Kingston. Some of his business is right on the line but that's the ghetto, you know? It's a pity some of the guys around him are such pricks. They don't have the morals he does. He goes through guys like shit off a shovel. He needs them loyal and some of them just don't get that.' She looked momentarily angry and frustrated.

'Oh.' Rachel nodded, but she didn't pursue that line of questioning, for fear of appearing too interested. They talked about what there was to see on the island and Rachel could feel the jet lag creeping up on her like an inexorable tide. After she had yawned for the fifth time, in between talking about her fictional job as a marketing secretary, she apologised and excused herself. Amelia said she would be in the following night if she wanted to meet up for a drink. Rachel wondered why she was being friendly. Maybe she suspected something. She wished Sharma was there so that she could talk to her. Sharma would know how to play it. Rachel was floundering in the dark at this point, not knowing which way was up.

Back in her room, removing the wig was like shedding a horrid, itchy skin. She let her hair swing free and sighed with contentment, wandering naked to the balcony to look out over the sea. The moon sent a shimmering, ever-moving stream of light out to the horizon, accompanied by the small bobbing lights of night fishing boats further in to shore. The air was warm and fragrant, soothing away the shock of seeing Jerry again. And for the first time since he left her, she thought of revenge.

13

She slept long and deliciously, waking after nine o'clock the next morning. Down at the dining area, on the veranda overlooking the sea, she ordered coffee, pink grapefruit juice, and enjoyed a bowl of fresh papaya, melon and mango, slathered in Greek yoghurt. A *pain au chocolat* followed, with more coffee. As she was savouring the last mouthful, David joined her.

'Tell me now that you hate me,' he said.

She couldn't tell him anything, with her mouth full of crumbs. She leisurely drank the last of her coffee, dabbed the remnants from her lips with a stiff square of white linen and looked at him.

'I hate you,' she said.

He looked exasperated. 'How can you say that, when for the last half-hour you've looked like heaven has moved to earth?'

'Because your appearance at this table clearly indicates that it hasn't. Presenting me with Jerry like that was really cruel. Go away.'

'I'm going,' he said acidly. 'In a few moments you will be joined by two operatives. They will explain who they are and what their function is.'

And he left, slipping through the foliage like a ghost.

Rachel sighed and ordered more coffee. As she sat back to drink it a shadow fell over her table. She looked up. A young Latin American man was standing there. He swooped and kissed her heartily on the cheek, introducing himself as Carlos.

'Baby! I'm sorry I'm late. Will you forgive me?'

'Er ... yes?' she replied, presuming that was the right answer. He gave her a dazzling smile.

Carlos was a very interesting development, despite the white suit and black satin shirt, unbuttoned to his washboard stomach. When his twin brother, Pepe, arrived, she felt surrounded by an embarrassment of riches.

'David says we are to entertain you,' Pepe said, in an Italian accent as rich as tiramisu. 'He is in the office, doing paperwork.' He shrugged as if he could not understand why David would choose to do that over amusing her for the day.

They took her out of the bay on a sleek, blue, cigarette-shaped speedboat and took her for a high-speed tour of the south side of the island. For a while she completely forgot about Jerry and David and Adrian, and the inevitable collision course between them with her probably getting squashed in the middle. They kept her involved with light-hearted, superfluous small talk all morning, carrying on her deception when she started to flag with the air-headed disguise. Talking and acting dumb was harder than she could have imagined. She commented on this halfway through superlative lobster thermidor at lunch time, eaten at a bar on the beach, feet away from the sea gently licking at the sand.

'Just keep asking stupid questions and let them ramble on for ten minutes after each one. Nod as if you understand but look blank as if you plainly don't, and no witty comments,' Carlos reminded her.

'Sarcasm isn't good,' Pepe added, nodding wisely.

'And don't use words of more than three syllables.'

'That's a given,' Pepe said.

They were both enjoying themselves hugely, given licence to ogle her chest as much as they pleased and run their hands over her bottom. Hang on, how much of this was professional attention to detail, she thought. Not that she minded. To look the part she had to be as hands-on as they were and, as jobs went, she could think of worse things than flirting outrageously with two gorgeous strangers. How they managed to stay in such buffed-up shape was a mystery, as they had matching gargantuan appetites for rich food.

'Lots of sport,' Pepe said, wiping papaya juice from his chin.

'And sex,' Carlos reminded him.

'Lots and lots of sex,' Pepe corrected, with a lascivious grin.

After lunch they packed themselves into an old Golf GTI and headed up into the mountains. After a while she got used to Pepe driving at Italian speed down the dusty, cattle-strewn roads, while looking behind him to talk to her. Carlos shouted out directions and warnings.

'Hey, watch that cow, man!' Then, 'Shit, you just put that guy in the ditch!' Rachel looked behind to see an old man with an overturned cart of pineapples, shaking his fist. He wasn't hurt, but she was quite relieved when they parked in a luscious forest and quiet prevailed. Birds sang high up in blue mahoe trees, while all around the senses were assaulted with a vermilion burst of colour and the heavy scent of lush vegetation. Distantly there was the constant rush of water. Carlos carried a picnic hamper and Pepe led the way down a narrow, verdant path towards a clearing in the thick cluster of trees ahead. The rushing sound grew nearer. It was coming from a waterfall shooting two hundred feet above them from the mountain, into a diamond-clear pool surrounded by smooth, round rocks. As Rachel stood in awe she felt someone rush past her and saw Carlos's naked butt flash briefly before he dived into the water. Rachel settled down to sunbathe in the stream of dappled light filtering through the trees and dibble her toes in the cool water. Pepe appeared like a water sprite in front of her, droplets of water clinging to his long eyelashes.

'Come on,' he said.

She motioned to her blonde hair. 'I can't,' she said regretfully.

'OK,' he said, shrugging, and disappeared again. She settled down by their pile of clothes and closed her eyes. Swiftly she opened them again as she felt herself being rolled off her rock. Her shriek was cut off as her head disappeared under the water. She emerged coughing and swearing, to the riotous laughter of the two men. They were pointing at her bedraggled hair and gutshot expression, holding their stomachs as if in pain.

They played for a while before Pepe opened the hamper and produced cool tubes of Red Stripe beer, together with spiced beef patties enclosed in a thin, golden crust. Afterwards they snoozed, Pepe with his head on Rachel's lap and Carlos at her feet, idly playing with her toes. They made subtle moves on her but she wasn't in the mood. They were like playful, affectionate puppies but her insides still yearned for someone who didn't care, and she wasn't healed enough yet. They accepted her gentle refusal with good grace and took her back to the hotel.

'If you need us for anything, we will help you,' Carlos said, kissing her on the cheek.

'Anything at all,' Pepe added, with his own kiss, this time directly on the lips. She didn't mind that at all. She thanked them and went back to her room to get ready for that evening.

She waited until after eleven o'clock before going down to the bar. Hopefully, Jerry would have already gone or be too pissed to recognise her if he decied to try his luck. She dressed carefully, in a cropped halter top and white palazzo pants, so sheer that her tiny thong could clearly be seen underneath. When she sat at the bar, it would just peek out over the top, like those unfortunate celebrities snapped and disgraced in *Heat* magazine on a regular basis. Sharma would be appalled, she thought gleefully, suspecting that she had begun to enjoy her role far more than she possibly should. As it was ostensiblly her night off, she decided to leave the bug in her room. If she got lucky, she didn't want anybody listening in.

David appeared in her room as she was applying the last coat of Maybelline to her eyelashes and confirmed her suspicions.

'You're enjoying this, aren't you?' he said, looking her up and down.

'What girl wouldn't, given the opportunity to be someone totally out of character for a week?'

'Are you out of character?' He sounded cold.

'You want me to be professional, and I am being. Don't load me with your personal issues right now while I'm dealing with my own.'

David wandered out on to the balcony and stared gloomily out at the fiery sun, sinking down over the velvet ocean. She joined him and silently they watched the sun disappear. At the very last moment, a flash of the most vivid emerald green spread like lightning across the thin line between ocean and sky.

'What was that?' she gasped, awestruck by its beauty.

David looked bleak. 'An omen,' he said darkly. 'Christ, this could get messy.'

'Oh, only now you've figured that out? For some of us it already is,' Rachel retorted sharply, irritated by his apparent lack of ability to see beauty in anything. Even the diamonds he had purported to work with had been respectable, quality or high class. Joyful adjectives like beautiful, alluring and bewitching probably weren't in his vocabulary.

'Did you enjoy yourself today?' He barked out the question, as if he really didn't want to know the answer. He probably already knew that Carlos and Pepe were walking hard ons, and he definitely knew that she wasn't averse to fucking on the first date. She could see all his assumptions rising to the surface, and decided that right then he didn't deserve to be put out of his misery.

'The boys were very attentive. I was left feeling absolutely stuffed,' she replied innocently, referring of course to the food they had plied her with.

It was too much. He stalked out of the room and slammed the door.

So there she was again at the bar, in the velvet dark. Another night, another Silver Mercedes sliding easily down her throat. She thought of the sun-drenched, carefree sex Carlos and Pepe had offered her, and thought that sometimes she could be incredibly dense. How could she have turned them down because of some grumpy government official with an eye on his career and nothing else? For David was turning out to be just that, she thought resignedly. Where was the risk-taker with the diamond stud and the dodgy collection of sex toys? Had he really enjoyed being that person, or was he ruthless enough to make it convincing while despising her for falling for it?

Jerry suddenly appeared, cutting off her depressing thoughts in their prime. Rachel felt breathless as he approached the bar and ordered a Red Stripe. He had had a skinful already that evening, judging by his bleary expression. Rachel wondered what she had ever seen in him. He had always been chunky, built like a long-distance lorry driver, her mother had said, somewhat disparagingly. But now he looked more like a Yorkie bar, 75 per cent fat. Even now, it hurt to admit that her mother's reservations had been well founded.

She fluffed her hair around her face and sucked at her straw, hoping he would crawl back to his table, which was occupied by three giggling women. But Jerry obviously had his blonde radar switched on, and it was in full working order, despite the booze he had consumed that evening. There was no recognition in his eyes as they came face to face, just a dull, blatant interest, concentrated solely at her chest.

'Hello love, you on your hols?'

No, I'm a spy, working for a shadowy government organisation. That's what she was tempted to say, but Jerry didn't go for smart women.

'Yeah.' She giggled, fluttering her Miss Piggy eyelashes at him. 'You?'

'Nah. I work for the head honcho around here. I'm a chauffeur.'

'That's pretty cool. What do you drive?' Straight for the important stuff. He'd appreciate that.

'A red Bentley Continental. And a bulletproof S Class Mercedes,' he boasted.

'Ooh nice! I love a big fat Benz. Does he let you use them in private time?'

'The Benz he does. The Bentley is his pride and joy. More than even my life's worth to dent it.' He looked around the bar as if to check if there were any other women he could pick up if he had no success with this one. He still had not looked at her face.

'Have you met anyone famous?' she asked, shimmying her chest at him.

'All the time,' Jerry said, trying to hide a beer belch and not quite succeeding. 'Shaggy, J-Lo, Ashanti. You get to know 'em all after a while.'

'Wow, that's great!' What a prick! Had she really been married to him for almost twenty years?

'Nic Cage was here a few weeks back. He's a pretty regular bloke,' Jerry was saying. 'And Joaquim Phoenix.' He pronounced it 'Jo-quim'.

'OK, I'm suitably impressed! Do you ever see anyone obscure?'

He stared at her. She silently cursed her stupidity for letting her guard down.

'What?' she asked. Without the 't' at the end, Essex style.

'Oh, nothing. You looked and sounded like someone I used to know. Shit, that was scary.'

'Nah, not me, babe. I'm a pussycat.' She hid the fear in her voice with a fresh wad of Wrigleys spearmint. It had been Sharma's advice. If you want to sound common, chew gum while talking. And it worked, too. 'Your job must be wellpaid,' she said, her eyes bright with greed. 'I bet you get loads of women after you.'

Jerry grinned stupidly. 'I do pretty well out of it. It's a big buzz.'

'I bet.' Like leaving your wife to pick up your debts was a real challenge, she thought sourly. She lit a slim cigar with surprisingly steady fingers. She had decided that smoking something would stop her getting rat-arsed on cocktails and would give her a shield to hide behind, but she drew the line at cigarettes. It was fascinating, talking to her unwitting husband as a potential pick-up (as he obviously thought). She filled her diaphragm with air and let her chest swell and lift another two inches. Jerry's eyes were down there, ogling them shamelessly. His white chinos were very tight but, because of his beer belly, it was difficult to tell if he had a hard on. She sucked suggestively on her straw.

'A little bird told me there's a big party going on here tomorrow night. Is that anything to do with you?'

Jerry smiled indulgently. 'Jermaine's missus is hitting the big four-oh. She wants it all done right and, if anything goes wrong, it's my ass on the floor.' He said 'ass' like an extra from a spaghetti Western, and nodded as if confirming to himself his own key role in Jermaine's existence.

'Ooh! Anyone famous coming?' she gushed breathlessly, cringing at herself.

Jerry slurped his beer. Within five minutes she knew the guest list for the party the following night, but it didn't include Adrian Grodin. Jerry moved closer to her and breathed Red Stripe fumes all over her face. Rachel held her breath, praying that he wouldn't recognise the small mole on her temple. Her face was covered in a ton of make-up, but he was so close, she could see the whites of his eyes. They were an unhealthy sepia colour. He was obviously a fan of the ganja when Jermaine wasn't looking, and in quantities which meant his exalted position was sure to be for a limited time. But his attention was soon back on her inflated chest. He had just been checking to see that she wasn't a complete dog. He had his standards, after all.

'Fancy a dance?' he asked her breasts.

'Yeah, all right,' she replied.

They had never danced together in twenty years of marriage. He had never wanted to, but in six months it seemed that he had caught terminal Saturday Night Fever. It was painful to watch. She moved her body naturally to the pulsating beat, while he hip-thrust and jiggled inappropriately like a drunken father at his son's wedding. Just as she wondered how much more of this she had to put up with, a tall man in a white linen shirt and cream chinos approached her, cutting in with ruthless efficiency. He took one of her hands and put his other hand on her waist, and started to guide her around the room in a slow Tango. Very intimate, very sexy, and it had taken less than two seconds. She was getting good at this.

'Shouldn't you have asked first?' she said playfully.

'He is . . . asshole. Why should I?' he replied in broken English.

'I meant, ask me,' she said pointedly. He moved with the sinuous grace of an eel, inveigling his leg between hers and dipping her like a professional. It was easy to forgive his cheek, as over her shoulder she could see Jerry glaring at them. But he was soon appeased by his harem of patient beauties, leaving her to enjoy the attentions of her white knight, or rather, her bronzed hero, with his slicked-back black hair and skin the colour of clear honey. He had a slim moustache, very neatly trimmed. It looked soft and glossy, and if he didn't have it he would look just like . . .

Hang on a minute. Her expression didn't change. She let him guide her around the dance floor, happy to continue the pretence if it meant that David would continue to dance with her.

'I'm Kim. Who are you?' she asked playfully.

'Marco.' He dipped her again, and their bodies were for a brief moment joined from toe to shoulder.

'You dance very well,' she said, 'but my mother told me never to trust a man whose name ended in o.'

'Your mother is a wise woman.'

She wasn't sure whether David knew she had clocked him. Maybe he did, but he was happy to continue the pretence. He certainly seemed to be enjoying himself. As his hard body moulded against hers she felt her loins fizzing for release. The tension of the last few days had taken its toll, and despite the sex-bomb disguise, she had felt as sexy as a spayed bitch. Not any more.

'Can we get out of here?' she asked as the music ended. 'I'd like to walk.'

'But what about your mother?' Still in that seductive Spanish accent.

'She didn't say anything about trusting men whose

name ended in d,' Rachel whispered, taking his hand and leading him out of the bar.

They walked up the strip until it became quieter, with less neon and thumping music. Although it was nearly midnight they stumbled across a small place on the beach where they watched fat, juicy Tiger Bay prawns being barbecued and served up with spicy salsa sauce.

'How did you know it was me?' he said as they ate their midnight feast with long, rum-based cocktails filled with fruit and crushed ice. He had removed the moustache, on her request. Facial hair wasn't really her thing.

'Did you really think I wouldn't? When you've been connected to someone physically and emotionally, you will always know them.'

He stared at her for a moment, but declined to comment. 'So do you think Jerry realised it was you?'

Rachel sighed. 'I was married to him. Sadly, that's not always the same thing, even after twenty years.'

She didn't want to dwell on that unsavoury part of her life, not now, not here, with the exotic scent of hibiscus and spices hanging in the warm air. She wanted to know more about David, and this would probably be the only chance she would get. He wasn't a man prone to giving a lot of information about himself, but with the alcohol and the heady tropical surroundings, maybe he would be more open with her.

She ordered more drinks and gently began to probe him. At first he was unwilling, grudgingly admitting that he had been born to a family with high expectations. Even though he had exceeded them, it was not in the way they had intended, so he was still considered a maverick. A black sheep, as he put it. He faltered, but suddenly Rachel had the unnerving feeling of a floodgate being opened. He didn't know what he wanted. Sometimes he wished he was poor and had to struggle to get where he was. His life had been too easy, so he tended to make it as difficult as possible to compensate. He didn't know who he was, or who he wanted to be. Disguising himself was a dirty pleasure that he despised himself for. She was seduced by his sensitivity, his admission of his vulnerability. As she watched him, lit by a single candle and the light of the moon, she wondered how privileged circumstances could produce a man such as this. Don't dive in, she warned herself. He may not be all he seems.

After their meal they walked further on, down into the darkness, where other couples had retreated for their own, private parties. Finally he drew her into his arms.

'I wish I was Marco. Then I would be able to make love to you.'

'Who says you can't?'

'The old dilemma of business and pleasure –' His words were cut off by her lips. She could feel his reticence, but she wasn't going to let him go without a fight. Life was too short, Sharma would have said. Her arms curled around his neck as she held him in place. She could feel his body resisting, then giving in. The sound of the surf rushed through her head as the kiss heated up. His mouth tasted of tequila as his tongue found hers. Lost in the sudden passion of it, she did not notice being borne down on to the sand until she felt its sugary warmth against her back. David was kissing her throat, her neck, leaving behind hot, wet imprints of passion.

'Talk to me in Spanish,' she breathed as he ran his tongue down towards her breasts and between them, leaving a cool, silvery trail of wetness behind. Her nipples sprang up in response, only to be scalded by his lapping tongue.

'*Me vuelves loco, senorita. Te quiero,*' he murmured, unzipping her pants and manoeuvring her out of them. If anyone had been walking along the beach, they would have tripped over them, rolling together in the sand. It

187

was getting in her hair and everywhere else, but she didn't care. She had seen *From Here to Eternity*, and this was her Deborah Kerr moment. All thoughts of chaste 50s romances went out of the window as soon as she felt his fingers opening her up like a flower of paradise and his tongue delve into her pussy like a humming bird drinking nectar. She gripped his hair and rode his tongue, biting her lips so her moans weren't too audible. As if sensing her need for release he concentrated on her clitoris, playing it until she was keening with joy. Her fingers played over her nipples, measuring their pleasure against the spikes of sensation coming from below. Her orgasm was prolonged and glorious, stoked by the location, the man and the situation, oozing sexual opportunity.

He came up to kiss her, sharing her copious juices. At the same time he thrust into her, filling her up so completely she felt totally at peace. She moved against him as the sneaky waves lapped against their legs, soaking the remainder of their clothes. He rolled her over and over, kissing her, murmuring Spanish endearments into her ear. Another wave pushed further up the beach, soaking them up to the middle but still they fucked, moving so naturally together it was as if they were meant to be joined forever. As the next wave hit he rolled her so that he would take the brunt of it. She sat up on his lap and began to slow-fuck him, so deeply she could feel herself losing control. His shirt was sodden and transparent, clinging to a body solid with muscle and strong enough to lift himself out of the waves with her still on top of him. His hair was no longer slicked back but tousled, strands flicking over his lean face, angry with lust. He picked her up, her legs around his waist, and carried her up the beach to the warm, soft sand under the palm trees, where he proceeded to screw her violently and silently. Rising up and up, towards fucking overload, she felt that swooping dive of release as he let go, groaning her name.

'Rachel, my love.'

There were a few heady moments of absolute peace while they regained their breath. David staggered to his feet, brushing sand from his soaked clothes. Suddenly Rachel sensed an awkwardness in him, as if he had said something he shouldn't.

'Well, that wasn't my best career move.'

He tried to sound light-hearted, but it was as if he had thrown her head first into icy water. He looked up and noticed her stunned expression.

'No, I meant ... What I mean is ...' He floundered, no doubt realising he was unable to dig himself out of the yawning chasm he had just fallen into.

'You shouldn't have done it? It's a bit late for an attack of professionalism now, isn't it?' She took deep breaths to calm down.

'You came on to me, remember?'

Unbelievably, he was going for the defensive, men-can't-help-it approach. Words couldn't adequately describe how grubby she felt right then.

'I didn't hold your dick upright and force you to fuck me,' she snarled. 'You managed that all by yourself.'

He said nothing, adjusting his clothes as if he had just had a sleazy encounter with a cheap prostitute.

'Why?' she said finally, shaking with disappointment and anger.

David finally looked at her. 'All I said back there, about my family, everything, it's all true. I've just never had the opportunity to open up to you before. But the sex was a mistake. You should know that.'

'Open up to me? You've used me as an emotional punchbag, fucked me, then cast me aside like a piece of trash!'

'Sorry,' he said, and he started to walk back down the beach.

'That's all right then, isn't it!' she shouted after him, dashing away hot, angry tears. 'When all this is over, seek help!'

14

After recovering her composure she tidied herself enough to get back to the hotel room. She hoped her wig was on straight. It was all ratty at the ends from the sea. She felt grubby and weary and cheapened by David's cruelty. In her mentally weakened state she even thought that Jerry might have been a better proposition for that evening.

Talking of whom, she turned a corner and saw him, leaning against the Benz, chatting to Amelia and two other women. Rachel ducked out of the way and took a circuitous route back to the hotel. It was a dark street, probably not the wisest of moves after midnight.

Within one hundred yards of the hotel she was proved right. She felt an arm around her neck and another snatch her purse. Then she was dragged into an alleyway, kicking and squeaking underneath the hard hand covering her mouth.

'Shut up, bitch.' A woman's voice. Rachel nodded when she saw the small round muzzle of a handgun. The hand was taken away. In the dim light she saw Amelia's fierce face. She was with three other women, all looking at Rachel as if she had crawled out of the sewer.

'Who the fuck are you, really?' Amelia spoke for all of them. 'I called your name back there and you didn't even turn around.'

'I didn't hear you.'

'Uh-uh. Your name isn't Kim. You called the other white bitch a different name as if you knew her the other night. I thought there was something funny about you. Why are you snooping around?'

'Look, you have to trust me. I'm not –'

'We have to do shit for you. What gives?'

Rachel looked at their angry, suspicious faces. They had no intention of letting her go until she gave them what she wanted. She sighed and raised her hands.

'Careful,' Amelia said, holding the gun dead level to her heart.

Rachel peeled away the blonde wig. 'My name is Rachel Wright. I'm Jerry's wife.'

This they weren't expecting. One even laughed.

'No shit!'

Amelia wasn't convinced. 'So why the get-up?'

'Because six months ago he dumped me after twenty years of marriage, leaving me to deal with his failing business, his debts, the whole shooting match. I don't care about Jerry, but I do care about what he did to me. I've built up my own business from scratch, only to see it threatened by what he's playing around at here. So I've come out to kick his arse.'

'How were you going to do it?'

Good question. 'I don't know,' Rachel said honestly. 'I'm winging it hour by hour. Believe me, I'm not out to cause you trouble. There's other stuff going down too. If you'll help me, I'll help you stay out of it.'

Amelia stared at her for a long, breathtaking moment. She turned to her three companions. 'It's OK. Go home,' she said to them. They melted away. Amelia still had the gun pointed in Rachel's direction. She walked her down the quiet street, into a blind alley, and checked all around her to make sure they were alone.

'What kind of stuff?' she demanded.

Rachel knew she was in too deep, but now there was no way out of it. She was too much of an amateur to bluff.

'Just remember you're on your own here. You need us to keep your ass covered,' Amelia was saying.

'I appreciate that. Have you heard of Adrian Grodin?'

'Oh, shit. What about him?' Amelia muttered. She looked so anxious that Rachel was immediately concerned for her.

'What's wrong?'

Amelia shook her head as if the question was too dangerous to acknowledge. 'What of him?'

'He's coming tomorrow. He's doing a deal with Jermaine but he's been trading stolen goods. There are plans afoot to end it.'

'He's been dealing hot ice to Jermaine? Is he insane?'

'Who knows? What do you know about him?'

Amelia looked reluctant to tell, but she lit a cigarette and blew the smoke out on a long sigh.

'I supply coke to the guys. Jerry, some of the others, they don't know shit from sugar. I could give them baby powder and they'd think it was angel dust. Grodin isn't so easy to fool. One of my girls gave him the low-grade stuff by mistake and he figured what we were doing. He threatened to tell all if we didn't do as he wanted.'

'Which is?'

Amelia looked sick. 'Pervy stuff. Up the ass, doubling up, all sorts. We're straight, you know what I mean? We do it to earn a living but we won't go in for all that.'

'Fair enough, but why were you supplying duff coke when you knew how dangerous it was? And you're calling Grodin insane!'

Amelia smiled pityingly. 'Grodin is greedy, but we need the money. We have to pay for protection from the law and some of us have kids. If the police found out what we were doing, our kids would be taken away and our landlords would throw us out.'

'But doesn't Jermaine look after you?'

'Jermaine is respected, a businessman. He looks after the poor kids but he draws the line at hookers. We provide a service for his men; we keep them happy in their spare time, but it's out of sight, out of mind, no involvement on his part.'

Rachel tried to think through this minefield of information. 'So if he isn't running the protection racket, who is?'

Amelia sucked on the cheroot and glared at her. 'Take a wild guess.'

'Oh no!' Rachel ran her hand over her mouth. Like a snake devouring its own tail, the circle was never ending, and it always came back to Jerry. The two women stood in silence for a very long time, moving closer into the shadows every time they heard footsteps passing in the street. Two cats started having a scrap, with hisses and staccato yowls of rage. It was time to go.

'Amelia, what pisses Jermaine off above anything else?' Rachel said hurriedly before they parted company.

'What do you think? Disloyalty, lack of respect, being unprofessional, take your pick.'

I will, Rachel thought. 'If I need your help, can I count on you?'

Amelia laughed shortly. 'You know where to find me.' She slipped away, out of the alley, out of view in a few short steps.

Back in the hotel room Rachel locked the door, stripped and took a long shower. Lying on her bed and waiting for sleep to come, her mind was whirring. Disloyalty, lack of respect, being unprofessional. Sounded like someone else she knew, she thought bitterly.

Also haunting her were those three tender words David had whispered so sincerely, and the potential meaning behind them, contradicting the treacherous man he was turning out to be.

She woke the next morning, unrefreshed and uneasy. Another shower and a long time replenishing her tan and adjusting her disguise didn't help, but the sumptuous breakfast did, up to a point. If only she could be herself and not this other woman, getting alternate salacious looks from men and irritated ones from their women.

'Can I sit here?' A fat man with a dubious tan and a camera was ready to plant his bottom on the chair opposite Rachel's. She decided to be polite at least.

'You could, but my man is coming in a minute and he won't like it.' She smiled to show she meant no offence.

'Tell you what, let me give you this.' He gave her a card with the name 'Darren Hawes', and giving his profession as a journalist, which was doubtful, as his employer was a British tabloid rag. 'You've got a nice look about you, miss. If you want some work, I think I can get it for you.'

'What kind of work?' Rachel asked curiously.

'You know, glamour shots, in the newspapers.'

'You mean, like, Page 3?' She had to choke back a derisive laugh.

'Yeah, if you want to aim that high.' He gave her a lecherous wink. 'Call me.'

'Thank you, Mr Hawes,' she said as he ambled away. When he had gone she started laughing. Her, a Page three model? Just wait until Sharma heard about that!

She was still laughing when David joined her at the table and ordered coffee.

'What's so funny?'

'I've just been asked if I'd like to be a Page 3 girl,' she said, then remembered in a rush, that she was supposed to be angry with him for his appalling behaviour the night before. 'I would so like to hit you right now,' she added coldly.

'I know.' David caught her hand before it was whisked swiftly away. 'The pigeon has landed. He will be in the hotel in half an hour or so. Do not approach him straight away. He usually sleeps for a few hours before going to the pool bar. Take it from there.'

Rachel felt a cold creeping sensation in her lower regions. 'OK. What if I let something slip?' Like last night, she was thinking. And she thought she had been so careful.

'Just try to relax. This is a contingency, just in case you strike lucky and he offers to take you to the party.' He dropped what looked like a sugar sachet into her lap, unseen by anyone else. She grasped it and tucked it into her bra. 'A Mickey Finn, to be used in emergencies, say . . .'

'If he wants to have wild sex with me instead of going to the party, you mean.'

David's lips compressed. 'It takes effect within ten minutes, bear that in mind. And one swallow will keep him under for an hour. But as I said . . .'

'Emergencies only. Thank you.'

'It isn't going to happen. Don't worry.'

She would try, but in the grand tradition of simple plans, something was bound to go wrong. Her bottom felt cold again, and all at once she needed the bathroom. She excused herself and left.

She passed the morning with shopping. The small craft shops and fashion stores amused her for a while, as did a coffee by the sea in a cappuccino bar surrounded by fringed parasols. The coffee came served with three tiny blienets, round doughnuts sprinkled with cinnamon sugar, which went some way to quelling her jittery stomach. She bought a silk throw for Sharma in vividly dyed batik, and mused over silk boxer shorts for Matt, before deciding that they were best left on the hanger. Their liaison had been closed very neatly, and such a gift would only give him other ideas.

After a light lunch of okra soup and home-made corn bread, she wandered back to the hotel, steeling herself on the way for duty. She dressed carefully. A shimmering gold thong bikini, straps on the top and the bottoms of which could be gathered to show as much or as little as she liked, rather like pulling at curtains. She fiddled with it for quite a while. The minimal covered only her nipples and her pudenda. The maximum covered barely more than that. She covered her bare buttocks with a gauzy matching sarong and slipped her feet into kitten-heeled bronze mules. With her hair moussed and golden body paint applied to whatever area of skin she thought would catch the light, she thought that, if Adrian didn't notice her, he was as blind as Jerry.

It seemed that the less she wore, the more high-maintenance her look became, she mused on her way down to the poolside. Once there she chose a sun lounger close to the bar and settled down to while away the afternoon with her book.

An hour passed, then two. She spit-roasted her backside, then her front, and remembered all the reasons why she hated holidays by the sea with nothing else to do. Meanwhile, a group of teenage boys horsed around in the pool, diving, belly-flopping and generally providing some amusement with their shows of testosterone-charged bravado.

Then, out of the corner of her eye, she could see him, the man she had been waiting for. He floated in wearing a long white shirt over exceedingly small cream swimming trunks and white leather Gucci mules. He looked deeply tanned and smug, casting his eyes over the females around the pool as if choosing one from his very own, personal harem. They all reacted in some sort of odd Mexican wave, sucking in stomachs, pushing out breasts, flipping hair, except for Rachel, watching him discreetly from behind her copy of Pat Booth's latest bonkbuster. Although the shirt came to his mid-thigh it was open, and one couldn't help noticing how nicely filled the small bikini briefs were. Hers were not the only pair of eyes zeroing in on his lower regions as the shirt slipped from his body. He let it float down to a waiting chair before walking to the diving board. The boys made way for him, laughing quietly and nudging each other as he poised on the very edge on tiptoe. They were waiting for him to make a prat of himself.

After ensuring he had everyone's attention, he executed a graceful swallow dive and sliced through the water like a gannet, with very little splash. He came up again on the other side of the pool, flipping his golden hair, letting the droplets fly like diamonds across the legs of the women fawning over him from their chairs. There was even light applause, which he acknowledged with a stiff little bow as he climbed out of the water. The small swimming briefs had turned almost translucent, even verging on the obscene, Rachel thought. But irresistible all the same. Interestingly, no one approached the diving board after that, not even the hot-blooded youths that had been showing off earlier.

When Adrian had done thirty lengths he hauled out of the pool, padded to the bar and ordered a Manhattan, perching on a stool less than ten feet away from Rachel's sun lounger.

The bartender did his trickery with the cocktail shaker and the bourbon, topping it with a juicy green olive. He pushed it over towards Grodin's immaculately manicured fingers.

'Good to see you back, sir,' he said.

'Thank you, Philippe. It's good to be back.'

That exotic French accent still did the business for her heart, which began to race even more as his gaze alighted on her and stayed there. He took a cigarette out of a packet of Gitanes and lit it, still watching her. Through her purple graduated Gucci shades she gave him an answering smile before turning her attention back to her book, thinking that she really did need the bathroom again.

She went before he could talk to her, but left her book

so that he knew she was coming back. She smiled slightly as she walked past, her hips rolling in a slow rumba under the transparent sarong skirt, but as she reached the toilets she realised that her nerves were more to do with excitement than with fear. After replenishing the make-up that had melted in the eighty-plus-degree heat, and spritzing with Tendre Poison, she went out to face him.

Walking through the foyer, she heard a familiar voice. Robyn Grodin, of all people, was standing at the reception desk, giving hell to the unflappable receptionist on the other side. Rachel loitered by the array of magazines and American newspapers and listened.

The room Robyn Grodin had just been given was smaller than the one she had last time, and the Jacuzzi wasn't as bubbly as it should have been and, from all accounts, she had just checked in. On her own. Rachel strained to hear. The receptionist called her Mrs Dufont.

'It is Madame!' Robyn Grodin actually stamped her foot. 'And tell your staff not to alert my husband of my presence. I want it to be a surprise for him.'

'Of course, Madame. A wonderful surprise,' the receptionist said smoothly, without a hint of sarcasm.

Rachel melted up the stairs to her room as a young porter almost broke his back lifting Mme Grodin's pan-technicon-sized suitcase.

She grabbed the phone and dialled David's number. He answered straight away.

'We've got a problem,' she said breathlessly.

'How big?'

'About five-two.' She told him what she had heard.

'Shit.' He paused. 'Wait there.'

Fifteen minutes later he knocked softly on her door. Carlos and Pepe were with him.

'I've made some enquiries. Robyn Grodin had another row with her father and now she's saying she made up

199

everything to get back at Adrian for having an affair. Until just now her father had no idea where she was. She's a loose cannon and she must be taken out of the picture. The problem is how we're going to do it.'

Rachel looked at the testosterone-charged Italian stallions standing beside him, and it was blindingly obvious.

'It's perfectly simple,' she said. David folded his arms and waited, ready with his imaginary air gun to shoot down whatever she had to say. She looked at Carlos. 'You and Pepe, use your imagination to distract Mrs Grodin. It'll be a piece of piss because she's sex mad and she really, really loves her food.'

'Yeah?' Carlos looked hopeful.

'Definitely. And I think I'm onto a winner with Adrian, which means you can swap the necklaces. When he gets randy later on I'll slip him the Mickey Finn and get out of there, leaving him a note, thanking him for being such a tiger in bed.'

The men looked at each other. Pepe shrugged. 'Sounds good to me, boss.'

'You think you can keep Mrs Grodin for as long as it takes?' asked Rachel.

'Hang on a minute.' David looked annoyed. She could tell what he was thinking – who's in charge here?

'What's the problem?' she asked coolly. 'Don't you like the fact that I respect my responsibilities a little more than you do?'

David approached her with that same mean, ass-kicking look he had used with Bailey. 'Just remember you're working to our agenda, not yours.'

Rachel faced him off calmly. 'Don't worry, David. If this operation goes tits up, it won't be because of me. Maybe you should look in the mirror and say that last sentence again.'

He left, slamming the door behind him. He was getting quite good at it, she thought sadly.

'Yeeouch! You are one mean lady!' Pepe chuckled.

'I haven't seen him so hot since ... shit, I don't think I've ever seen him so hot as he is for you,' Carlos said approvingly. 'I'd love to see you without that wig.'

'Well, if I get through this, maybe you will,' Rachel said wryly. She slipped her arm through his. 'Come on, boys. Let's go find the lusty Mrs G before she finds her husband.'

They didn't have to look very far. She was still in the foyer, complaining to the unflappable receptionist that the champagne she had ordered was too cold. Rachel decided to get to work right away. She tapped Robyn on the arm.

'Hi there! Remember me? I was at Flick and Justin's a few months back. Fancy seeing you here.' She twittered on. 'Why don't you have a drink with me while they're sorting out your stuff?'

'Stuff?' Robyn looked thoroughly confused, as well as horrified that she might have once spent time with this monstrously common blonde.

'Stuff, you know.' Rachel gestured as if it were obvious. 'There's a great bar down the road, does a luscious Cosmos. Best thing to get you in the holiday mood. We could reminisce about that party. I was ever so grateful to Flick for inviting me. Opened up a whole new world of wonders.' She winked saucily.

Robyn's refusal was on her lips, but then Carlos and Pepe appeared behind Rachel's left shoulder. Instantly she looked interested.

'Oh, I met these two on the way there.' Rachel lowered her voice to a conspiratorial whisper. 'Brothers. Really hot. They'd give that horny husband of yours a run for his money any day. Where is he, anyway? Not that it matters with these two around. They're hung like bulls and go on for hours and hours.' She caught Pepe's eyes and winked again. He flushed with pleasure and cupped his crotch.

Carlos took Robyn's hand and kissed it, introducing himself. Pepe did the same with the other hand. Suddenly, Robyn looked as threatening as a tiger cub.

'Well, a cocktail may be just what I need,' she murmured, allowing the men to lead her away.

In the nick of time, as it turned out. Adrian Grodin padded through the foyer as the boys disappeared out the door. When he saw Rachel his eyes lit up.

'Mademoiselle, you forgot your book.' He held out her copy of *Miami*.

'Thank you, I'm sure,' she said demurely, giving him a coy glance.

'You're welcome. And I was hoping to buy you a drink.'

Now was not the time, she thought, knowing that Robyn would wonder why she had disappeared.

'Ooh, I love your accent,' she said in her best Essex party-girl voice, buying some time. He smiled indulgently, his eyes scanning down her body. Apparently he decided that her voice was a price worth paying for her assets.

'Yours is . . . most interesting. Where are you from?'

'England,' she said, fluttering her long black eyelashes at him.

He smiled condescendingly and started to say he knew that already, but probably decided that it wasn't worth the effort.

'Are you alone here?'

She simpered at him. 'Yeah, I am. But I bet you're not.'

He smiled and offered her a Gitane, but she declined and instead produced a slender cigar, motioning at him to light it. He seemed to take a new interest then, perhaps thinking that this bimbo was not all that she seemed.

'So, what about that drink?' he asked.

She savoured the rich, leathery smoke. 'I'd like that.' She glanced at her watch. 'What about meeting up at seven by the pool? Maybe we could get to know each other.' She held the promise of more in her eyes. He saw it and nodded.

'Maybe. At seven then. Do not forget me.'

'Believe me, I won't,' she replied, blowing him a playful kiss as she ran out of the hotel.

Two hours. That would give her enough time to enjoy for a while the boys working on Robyn, before dressing so irresistibly that Adrian would be a fool not to want her company that evening. That was, if he didn't already have a partner, which was a possibility she had not bargained for. Oh well, she would just have to turn on the charm full bore and hope he fell for it.

The bar and restaurant she had steered Robyn and the boys towards was a safe distance away from the hotel, dark and smoky despite the warmth of the late afternoon. Thumping reggae, heaving bodies slick with sweat, not Robyn's type of thing at all, one would think, but Rachel had made a calculated gamble. After starchy, etiquette-obsessed Paris, Robyn might like to hang loose a little, even if she did not herself know it yet. And the food was consistently excellent, some of the best in Montego Bay. Robyn was already pleased with the boys, who were showering attention on her as if she were the only woman left in the world. Rachel sipped her Cosmopolitan and watched them go to work. They ordered a gargantuan feast of lobster, Tiger Bay prawns and mussels poached in white wine. At first Robyn demurred, saying faintly that she could not eat more than a salad, as it was only five o'clock. Once the food arrived, however, the succulent white meat of the lobster tempted her, and after another glass of Chardonnay the mussels were sliding down her throat with precocious ease.

Rachel nibbled at her food, aware that she might be

expected to eat later. She was enthralled by Carlos and Pepe's methods, constantly refilling Robyn's glass when she wasn't looking.

'You're being very wicked,' Rachel whispered to Carlos.

'I like my women well fed, drunk and compliant,' he replied, his eyes gleaming with anticipation. He leaned closer to her and pressed his lips against her ear. 'I love this job,' he murmured.

'I can tell.' She glanced at her watch again. The party wasn't until nine o'clock, but she needed to leave so she could work on Adrian.

'You don't need me here any more,' she said to Carlos as dessert arrived. It came in the form of a rich chocolate torte and fresh tropical fruit, exquisitely fashioned into the shape of a peacock, each feather being mango, kumquat and kiwi. Robyn, by this time getting inebriated and dizzy with attention, proceeded to gorge herself on cake. Pepe put a black cherry into his mouth and kissed her, transferring the cherry from his mouth to hers while Carlos filled her glass again. Robyn's chiffon dress with the cutaway front didn't look quite as streamlined as before, with all that food and wine inside her. Rachel wondered whether she would actually be able to stand up at all. She was now giggly and silly, exchanging open kisses with Carlos and being fed more fruit from his lips. If only her society friends could see her now, Rachel thought. She bade her farewells and left, though Robyn hardly noticed she had gone.

As she walked back to the hotel, a wicked idea occurred to her. Thinking about it, she had to force herself to affect the casual stroll instead of the purposeful stride that David had criticised her for. Jay's Bar was closed, with a large sign hung on the gate saying 'CLOSED TONIGHT – PRIVATE PARTY'. Behind the white trellis activity was frenzied. Large white tablecloths were spread over ten round tables and one long one at the top end, opposite the bar. Strings of pearly fairy lights were strung around every tree. A stressed individual with a clipboard stood in the middle of it all, barking orders.

When she arrived back at the hotel, she wrote a note on plain paper, in writing totally unlike her own, just in case. The note said, 'Parisian Society Queen Robyn Grodin slums it at Coco de Mer with two horny young studs, and it's happening right now.'

Humming gaily, she went to the bar to see if her paparazzi friend from breakfast was there. He was, all orange tan and double chin, goggling at the tits and ass on display around the pool. He looked very happy when she tapped him on the shoulder and gave him the note she had scribbled.

'A message for you,' she said, and left him to read it. At a discreet distance, she watched him leave and head towards the restaurant, camera on his shoulder.

15

To work, then. What would turn Adrian on and be respectable enough to wear at Lady Bling's party? She looked in her minimal wardrobe. The denim miniskirt was a no-no, the gold bikini and black leather hotpants too trashy. In the end she chose the dress she had bought the previous morning while out with the boys. In white silk, the top had a halter neck and a very plunging neckline, down to the point where wearing a bra was impossible. The skirt was simple, down to her ankles, but slashed almost to her thigh on one side. As Rachel she would never have worn it, but as Kim she thought it totally appropriate. With her tan and her artfully tousled blonde hair, she looked stunning, even by her own admission. The skyscraper Manolo sandals she had brought with her completed her look. There was no way in hell she would wear the hated white stilettos with the nasty little red bows, even if it meant putting the security of England in danger. Finally she wrestled with the transparent cups to put under her breasts to enhance her cleavage. She didn't look in the mirror until both of them were in place, and what she saw made her eyes widen.

'Blimey,' she muttered, ogling her pneumatic chest. She leaned carefully forward. Her cleavage lurched dangerously out of the bodice, but did not tumble out completely, thanks to some tit tape. A few more shakes and a jump up and down, and she was satisfied that, unlike any man she had met recently, the secret cups wouldn't let her down.

In a strange way she was feeling rather excited, she

thought, walking through the hotel and resisting the urge to continuously look down. Her chest seemed to reach the poolside five minutes before she did, and was already talking to Adrian by the time she got there. He looked deliciously cool in cream silk trousers and a white silk shirt, the jacket slung over his shoulder.

'It's the golden girl,' he said cheerfully, snapping his fingers at the bartender. She ordered a Cosmopolitan. He placed his hand on her waist and gave it a squeeze. 'You gave me a problem today, I hope you realise.'

She moved closer to him. 'What kind of problem?'

'The problem a man has when he is wearing very little, and a woman he finds attractive is wearing very little, and they are in a public place. In fact, I have the same problem now.' His gaze dropped to her bosom. 'This is a very beautiful dress you are not wearing, *cherie*. How can you stand so close to me and not realise this problem I have?'

'You sound so severe,' she said coyly, thrusting her pneumatic breasts further out at him. 'What can I do to make you pleased with me again?' She ran her tongue over her glossy lips and moved closer, pressing her hip against what she hoped was his erection.

Right on the button. He caught his breath and a flush crept up over his handsome face as she wriggled ever so subtly against him. He did not move away.

'Maybe you can help me with another problem I have,' he said, slipping his hand around her waist to hold her close against him.

'Oh dear, what's that?'

'I have a party to go to tonight, and no one to go with.'

Surely it wasn't going to be that easy, she thought. 'Oh, that's a shame,' she breathed, and giggled saucily.

'I know. I thought you might like to come.'

'Maybe I don't want to,' she said, pouting prettily at him.

'But I think you will, or I'll have to give you a spank-ing.' He squeezed her bottom so hard and unexpectedly that she let out a yelp of shocked laughter.

'Is that a yes?' he asked.

'To the party invitation or to the spanking?' She laughed.

'Both, if you like. We can leave early and I can take you somewhere quiet. I shall drink coconut milk from those divine breasts and you can eat fresh pineapple from my cock. How does that sound?'

As sales techniques went, it took some beating. Despite all she knew about him, she could feel herself melting under his tempting caramel gaze.

'Are you always this forward?' she couldn't help but ask.

'Why waste time when a beautiful woman is rubbing against me, with the sole intention of making me hard? She is not a woman to be insulted by pointless small talk.' He kissed her naked shoulder and pressed his erec-tion harder against her hip.

'I'd better get ready then,' she murmured.

'Why? You are beautiful as you are.'

She had just remembered she needed to pick up the wire from her room. Without it, David would be blind and deaf to the activities at the party, and she, stupid as she was, had forgotten it, thanks to being too worried about falling out of her dress.

'Thank you, Adrian. I just need to put some perfume on. I will be five minutes. No more.'

'Ah, perfume. French, I hope.'

'Givenchy, Organza,' she replied.

'Excellent! Hurry back, my dear.'

As she slipped the credit-card key in the lock, she heard David's voice.

'You'll never guess what I've just blagged –' She stopped and stared. David was on the bed, butt naked.

Amelia was crouching before him, clutching at the pillows as he screwed her hard from behind. They were frozen in a sordid tableau, staring back at her.

'What the hell are you doing here?' David asked hoarsely.

'What the hell is she doing here?' Rachel almost screamed back at him.

He withdrew and Amelia ran into the bathroom, grabbing at her clothes on the way. She looked genuinely upset.

'I'm really sorry.'

'Don't bother. I only came up here to fix my make-up,' Rachel said coldly. She turned back to David. He was sitting on the bed, covering himself with Rachel's discarded skirt from earlier that evening.

'You're supposed to be with Adrian,' he said.

'And that makes screwing another woman in my bed acceptable, does it?' She hurriedly did what she had to do, spritzing Organza on her wrists and between her breasts, before giving him a healthy blast in the face. He coughed and spluttered.

'Why are you so upset? You were the one rolling about with Carlos and Pepe yesterday.'

'And you were the one giving me bullshit last night! Why this, after that?'

He gave a hollow laugh. 'You work it out.'

'No time, David. Adrian will be wondering where I am.' She hurled his clothes at him with some force. 'Remember how much is riding on this,' she said, throwing his words mockingly back in his face. 'And I don't mean you personally.'

Back at the bar, Adrian's smile lifted her spirits, even though she suddenly remembered that the reason she had gone back up to her room was still sitting on the dressing table. She couldn't go back up there again. All she could do was hope that someone was watching her every move, as David had promised. With an effort she forced the picture of David fucking Amelia to the back of her mind, and accepted Adrian's offer of another cocktail. She drank it more rapidly than was advisable, but at least she felt better afterwards. Then she heard Adrian asking her to go with him to his room.

'Don't worry, *cherie*,' he said as he steered her towards the stairs. 'I have no intention of ruining your lovely dress just yet. I just have something for you that I think you may like. Not to keep, but for tonight only.'

'Sounds interesting,' Rachel said, feeling a tad nervous.

'Do not look concerned. I will not hurt you, yet.' Adrian held a box aloft and opened it with the flourish of a magician. She gasped, and did not need to act at all.

No imposter could match the stunning piece of perfection that nestled in black velvet, luring her to reach out and touch. The necklace was a choker, dripping with tiny chips of diamond and platinum, designed to wear with a dress just like hers. The central point hung down between her breasts, widening in a delta shape to drape elegantly over her collar bones.

'It's beautiful,' she said, as he released the necklace from its box and put it on her. A million pounds' worth of diamonds and platinum. She would never wear the like again.

'It is beautiful on you,' he corrected her, kissing her neck. In the mirror she watched his hands come up and cup her breasts. 'Hmm, *cherie*. You smell and look like a goddess, but if you want to wear this to the party, you have to agree to one thing.'

'What is it?' She didn't want to take the necklace off. It felt so right against her skin. She heard a clink and saw he had some handcuffs. 'It is very valuable and, as I hardly know you, I must insist you wear these. One cuff for you, and one for me. That way you will never be able to leave my side, which is a bonus for me, naturally. Even if you were not wearing the necklace, I would still insist on them.'

She didn't quite know what to say. The thought had also hit her that David would hardly be able to swap the necklaces if she had the real one wrapped around her neck.

What to do then.

'I really don't think I should wear this tonight,' she said, reluctantly.

'But you must,' he replied. 'Jermaine is expecting it. Please, *cherie*, do this for me.' He pulled her close and held up the handcuffs. 'Be my possession for the evening, my play toy.' He kissed her neck. 'I have some excellent cocaine for later, and when you're high I shall lick your pussy so tenderly you will think you have died and gone to heaven, I promise.'

'That sounds good,' she purred, thinking that actually it did sound good, except for the coke. But he wasn't the Adrian she had known. He was darker, more dangerous. She sensed that subversive side to him running underneath the surface, like a riptide in a calm sea. And she remembered his mentor, and Justin, and the way he had spoken to her that night before her life blew up again.

The handcuffs clicked, and they were joined. The chain between them was long enough to allow for ease of movement at least. He smiled slightly, as if he enjoyed being enslaved, and he led her from the room.

They entered a magical kingdom of fairy lights, nubile young women in tiny Brazilian bikinis offering pink champagne and loud, laughing voices. She recognised a few of the guests from the rap world, laden down with gold chains and diamond pendants. At least, she presumed they were diamonds. She doubted whether the dress code would demand anything less. Without exception the girls were beautiful, haughty and proud in tiny scraps of Versace. Rachel felt a tad cheap next to the skinny coffee-skinned girls with their blonde hairpieces and elaborate braids.

She wasn't expected to say anything. She was eye candy, nothing more. No one even asked about the handcuffs. As an artist, she soon gathered that Adrian was generally considered an eccentric. He did not introduce her, and no one asked her name. He handed her a slender flute of champagne and continued his conversation with a large gem dealer from Florida as if she were invisible.

As she looked around she saw Amelia. She was stunning in a white halter dress that looked more like three spiders' webs, two to cover her breasts, one to cover her pubis. Each outward-reaching strand glistened with tiny gems like droplets of dew. She wore a matching close-fitting cap of white silk, also studded with sparkling crystals, and diamonds at her ears and throat. She saw Rachel and went over to her.

'I really am sorry,' she whispered. 'He paid for me, if that makes it any easier.'

'Actually it doesn't,' Rachel replied sharply, feeling alarmingly close to tears.

Amelia took Rachel's hand to lead her away to talk but Rachel motioned frantically to the handcuffs.

'I told you he was perverse,' Amelia whispered. She leaned closer so that only Rachel would hear her next words. 'When you have time, check your bag.' She took a step back as Adrian noticed her presence. Rachel watched as they exchanged false pleasantries, then Amelia hightailed it as fast as she could.

Adrian tucked her cuffed arm under his and led her through the room, purposefully heading towards a short, thickset man who was as dark as bitter chocolate and as wide as the Pacific. He was adorned with platinum chains and diamond rings. The woman with him was slender and graceful, her jewellery understated. She still had the face and figure of a supermodel and, clearly, the trauma of turning forty that day was lost on her. Her black hair had been straightened and hung in a thick shiny curtain down past her shoulders. She appeared more regal than any royalty had a right to look. Her name was Lady, and she was the King of Bling's wife.

This time, Adrian did introduce them. Rachel fought the urge to curtsey. As Rachel Wright, she would have been able to engage in conversation, but as Kim the bimbo, they frightened her to death.

'Kim, huh?' Jermaine said, when she said she was pleased to meet him. 'You should change your hair colour, girl. Give Liz Hurley a run for her money with that accent.'

She had dropped the Essex voice without realising it, but everyone's attention was now on her neck. Jermaine had whipped out a loupe and was examining the longest strand of diamonds. She could smell his fruity aftershave and feel his warm breath tickling her bounteous cleavage. She looked over his heavily gelled head to Lady and grimaced involuntarily. Lady unexpectedly smiled. Jermaine stepped back and nodded.

'Good ice, Grodin. What's the source?'

'Private seller,' Adrian replied smoothly. 'Part of a legacy.'

Rachel was profoundly relieved that they had forgotten about her, but also slightly put out. She was meat, nothing more, just something pretty to display the baubles Jermaine was interested in buying. Lady was far more generous, and obviously practised in the art of conversation. Rachel wished she could relax and talk normally but, even so, she could see the woman thinking that the hair, the voice and the dress didn't quite match the articulate brain underneath.

Eventually Rachel really did need the bathroom. All

that champagne and not much food had worked its way through her system. Adrian unfastened the handcuffs and snapped his fingers at a six-foot-plus kick-boxer and told him to escort Rachel to the bathrooms. Once inside, she had a pee and looked around to see if there were any means of escape. There were none, no opportunities to shimmy out the window in her knickers and the million-dollar necklace. Then she checked her bag. A fat gold vibrator had appeared as if by magic. She took it out, shook it and turned it on. It didn't work. Rapidly she unscrewed it, and found the fake necklace. Now she was in a quandary. Should she swap the necklaces now that Jermaine had cast his eyes over it, or wait in case he wanted to give it a closer look? Before she could make up her mind, the door opened.

'Hey, you OK in here?'

'I'm fine!' Rachel flushed the toilet and hurriedly screwed the vibrator back together. She appeared from the cubicle with a meek smile. The bodyguard looked suspicious. He held out a big beefy hand for her bag. 'I want to check your purse, lady.'

Knowing she had no choice, she handed it over. 'What for?' she asked timidly.

He unzipped the bag, peered around inside it and drew out the vibrator. Then he laughed and put it back, and handed the bag back to her again.

'Jermaine, he don't like drugs at his family parties, but I don't know what his rule is on jilling off in the toilets.' He grinned at her and held the door open. Blushing furiously, Rachel followed him out into the fray again. Adrian was waiting and the handcuffs were replaced. The bodyguard gave Adrian an amused glance as he went back to his position at the door.

What followed was not so much a meal as a journey into sensual pleasure via oral satisfaction. Velvety smoked salmon pâté timbales were served first, sprinkled with a hazelnut-oil dressing and a scattering of rocket leaves. Then a refreshing lime sorbet that fizzed delicately on the tongue, followed by a sumptuous choice of jerk chicken and shrimp, with spiced rice and mango salsa. The tables were round to facilitate ease of conversation, and covered in white ground-length tablecloths. Rachel remembered the top table she had seen before, which was no longer there. Apparently, Lady didn't like the formality of it, so it had been changed to let her be down among her friends and family. Rachel liked her even more for that.

Every piece of cutlery shone as if polished obsessively that afternoon, which it had been, and every piece of crystal sparkled fair to outshine the copious amounts of diamond ice on display. In the background, a five-piece band played Lady's favourite pieces, with smoky saxophone and blues guitar. It was a glittering occasion, brought down to earth by the location and the gutsy food and the colourful staff, all of whom Lady and Jermaine knew by name. Adrian informed her that some of Jermaine's business rivals called him The Tramp, but never to his face. Rachel could understand why. He was fierce, fussy, loud and terrifying, but she could sense a deep-rooted sweetness and righteousness in his personality as well. Adrian, on the other hand, clearly thought him an inferior fool, though he hid his superciliousness behind being a polished European, not used to the lusty ways of the Islanders. That way he believed that his patronising ways and thinly veiled insults could easily be excused, but Rachel wasn't taken in. She could see what a thin line he was treading, and how close he was to falling off.

During the meal Jerry could not take his eyes off Rachel, but his attempts to monopolise her attention were continually foiled by Adrian. The enmity between the two men was potent. Rachel suspected that it was because Adrian was French, and Jerry had always professed to a dislike of 'fancy foreigners'. She felt like a bone being worried between two dogs, and it caused her some amusement. From Jerry's position he could see her left side, with her exposed length of leg and tight haunch in the revealing dress. When the meal ended and the dancing began, Adrian suavely cut in when Jerry attempted to drag her out on to the floor. They danced for a while, their bodies picking up the rich saxophone and using it as a sensual form of foreplay. For the second time in her life she felt as if a man was actually making love to her on a dance floor. Adrian's lips on the base of her throat and the pressure of his hand in the small of her back were turning her body to steam. She saw Jerry watching them, and she smiled. He looked sick and angry, his hands bunched into fists, but there was no way he could make an issue of it. Not with one of Jermaine's business associates. So he had to watch the Frenchman moving in on his bird while he just stood there looking like a complete pussy.

Rachel knew his thoughts as clearly as if she could hear him speaking them. Twenty years had taught her something about him, after all. Adrian's hand was now on her buttock, squeezing it, keeping her locked against him. His erection was massive, bruising her pelvis. Suddenly she didn't want it there, she wanted it inside her, bruising her from the inside out. Adrian was apparently thinking the same thing.

'I think we would enjoy ourselves more if I made love to you.'

'I thought that's what you were doing.'

He ground his hips against hers again. 'You have a lot to learn, my little dove.'

But instead of walking back to the hotel, Adrian steered her off in a different direction.

'We don't want my wife walking in on us. She may want to join in.'

Rachel giggled, but inside she was thinking, how would David find her now?

Adrian walked them further up the strip, where the garish neon palm trees and flashing lights had given way to the older, more genteel buildings of the bygone plantation era. The hotel was a clover-blue colonial, the porch awash with hanging baskets of vivid pink geraniums, and getting a room was no problem. When they got upstairs the cool, crisp white bedsheets had already been turned down for the night, and a handmade white chocolate enclosing a cherry had been put on the pillow in a tiny paper case. Adrian fed the chocolate to Rachel and rang down for some Bollinger.

'We have much to celebrate. Jermaine thinks his client will approve of the necklace.' He made no move to remove the handcuffs. When the champagne came, he made the waiter open the bottle and pour. The young waiter studiously avoided looking at their cuffed hands as he did it, then left as rapidly as he could. Adrian handed her a crystal flute and picked up his own.

'To you, my dear, and the promise of a killing.'

Rachel shuddered at the word 'killing', as she sipped her champagne, aware that she had probably drunk a little too much already. She also had a more pressing problem. How was she going to slip the drug into Adrian's drink when she was still cuffed to him? He leaned over and kissed her neck, a hot, tender kiss full of desire.

'I've been waiting all evening to touch you again, *cherie*,' he said, removing her glass and laying her gently down on the bed. Their cuffed hands were up over her head, so he could lie beside her and press his body on to hers. His other hand stroked her thigh through the deep slit in the dress. Looking down, he admired her tiny panties, a triangle of white lace held together with transparent tape so they would not show under the dress. His fingers were wicked, circling on her flesh, making her body react despite the danger. The champagne and adrenaline had stoked the sexual fire that was raging within her, and now she was ready to use him as he had used her, almost since the first day they met. She responded to his kisses, biting gently at his lower lip and accepting his tongue deep in her mouth as his stealthy fingers slipped down between her legs and under the panties. When he discovered she was velvety and hairless he moaned, ripping the panties off her.

'What a beautiful, silky pussy,' he murmured, shifting down to look at it properly. He spread her legs and opened her up like a delicate fruit, but he did not lick her straight away. His breath playing across her most sensitive of regions was the sweetest torment as his fingers massaged all around her pudenda, pattering against it, kneading it, setting her alight with anticipation. When he did finally use his tongue it was across the fleshy triangle just above her cleft, which until then she had no idea was so sensitive. As he licked and blew across the moistened skin she lifted her hips, wanting him to go lower down.

'I know what you want, but you're not getting it yet,' he said, coming up to kiss her mouth again. His lips were moist and red, inflamed with desire. They left scalding trails as he worked down her throat, stopping to lick at the diamonds there as if they too could be given pleasure. Further down she could feel a very hard lump rubbing against her thigh, restrained in his black trousers, and she realised then that the diamonds were as desirable to him as the woman wearing them. With a trembling hand he unfastened the clasp and moved the necklace down so that the strands lay over one breast, with her rosy nipple just poking through. Then she let out a soft scream as his tongue swept around that nipple, over and over until she was undulating with delight.

'You love your rocks, don't you?' she breathed.

'Hush, my love.' He seemed annoyed that she had interrupted his reverence of the priceless stones mingling with her soft, pink flesh. He took his champagne and trickled some on her nipples and the diamonds, then licked it off again as she gasped at the intense cold, followed by the delight of his hot tongue.

'You like that, *cherie*?' he asked.

'Oh, yes,' she breathed.

He peeled the necklace away from her breast and placed it on her pubis, where it lay like a vastly expensive pair of bikini panties, the longest strands tickling her clitoris. Then he stopped and felt in his pocket. He drew out a small key and, having unfastened his cuff from his wrist, he attached it to the bed instead, so she was still trapped. But her problematic situation was forgotten under the joy of having his tongue inveigle his way between the strands of diamonds into her pussy, thrusting deep as he sucked on her engorged lips and the diamonds at the same time. The hardness of the gems gave her a sensation very near to orgasm, as the other diamonds played over her clitoris with every greedy movement of Adrian's tongue. When he splashed more champagne over her pussy, over the necklace and over the bed, she opened herself up even more and begged him to make her come, but he had other ideas. He moved away and removed his shirt and trousers, but left his tight bikini briefs on, even though his cock was fully erect and painfully trapped. As he kneeled over her she could see it through the transparent silk, engorged and reddened. He adjusted the necklace until it looked the way he wanted it, demurely covering her pubis but with the longest strands of diamonds sneaking like tendrils into her pussy.

'Do not move,' he said sternly. He stared at her for the longest time, his hand on his cock, rubbing it through the silk. She sensed he was building his desire, so that when it was finally unleashed it would blow them both away. She stared at his cock, so massive in those tiny briefs, and her pussy pulsed in appreciation. She dared not talk, because his manner suggested that talk was intrusive. Finally he moved until he was straddling her waist. The briefs he wore were fastened on one side by clips, and the strain of holding his cock in was making them dig painfully into his hip. He continued to rub himself, upping the desperation, while she feasted her eyes on that immense bulge. Then he unclipped the briefs.

Very slowly he peeled them away, and his cock sprang joyfully forwards. The weight of it made it hang down, temptingly, towards her lips. Now his eyes were feverish, his lips moist and overblown, and the tip of his cock gaping and needy. Her mouth came up to suck him in as he moved down to let her, and his grunt of pleasure was drawn out as she took as much as she could of him into her mouth. He tasted hot and musky, just the way a man should taste if he's been waiting a long time. As she continued to flutter her tongue around the tip he rescued the diamond necklace and wrapped it around his shaft, then began to masturbate himself slowly, sensuously.

'How does it feel?' she asked.

'Hard as diamonds,' he replied, taking her free hand and positioning it over the necklace and his cock. He continued to move, effectively fucking the necklace and her hand, while she thought that it must feel very strange, but the power of screwing with such a valuable item probably had the same kick as screwing the expensive wife of a business rival. He came almost immediately, spreading come in pearls around her neck. His orgasm was tightly restrained, as if he were only awaiting a taster of delights to come. Afterwards his cock did not wilt, but seemed to be in a state of readiness for the next round.

He licked the droplets of come from her neck and kissed her again, sharing his sweet-tasting seed.

'Don't say a word,' he said, moving down to give her the attention she had so patiently been waiting for. As she watched in total amazement he rolled up the necklace and proceeded to feed it into her pussy. It felt very strange, but exciting at the same time, as he pushed all of it in, leaving one end dangling out. It tickled her arse, making her quiver. This was a very illicit heaven, she thought, but heaven all the same, having a thief eat her out with such finesse, while stimulating her with champagne and stolen diamonds. He was obviously getting as much pleasure as she was as his tongue worked into her overheated pussy, pushing the diamonds further up inside her. Then she felt it cruise slyly over her clitoris and she moaned, needing more than that. As his tongue flashed over it like quicksilver she gripped the sheet with her free hand and rode every wave as it came, crashing and seething until she was in a whirlpool of erotic sensation, no hope of escaping it, even when he slowly pulled the diamond necklace back out of her pussy, giving her yet another totally new feeling.

'Adrian,' she moaned. 'Oh God. Oh . . .' Her legs spread wide, greedily accepting all he was giving her. And as she swirled back down he pushed inside her, taking in at least one strand of diamonds, while the others mercilessly stimulated her clitoris and kept her coming. His cock and the diamonds pressing against the inner walls of her pussy were aggressive and demanding, forcing her body to accept more sensation than she had ever done before.

Afterwards Adrian was flushed with triumph, his cock as firm as it had been before. He gathered up the necklace and sucked her juices from it as if sucking grapes from a luscious bunch picked straight from the vine, then he placed the necklace back over her pussy, feeding the longest strands into her open, waiting entrance. He took a small box from the bedside table and opened it.

'This is going to be a real delight, my dear,' he said, scooping a healthy amount of white powder with a tiny spoon and placing it on her nipples. Then more on her pussy, which felt strange and fuzzy. Then he took a smaller cone on his fingertip and held it close to her nose.

'Coke. The finest quality. Take it.'

She thought fast. 'You know, it makes me puke, so I won't. I'll have just as much fun without it.'

'But this is the finest, *cherie*. I doubt any of your English nightclubs will have experienced this sort of quality. Take.'

There was no option, not while naked and handcuffed to the bed. 'One then,' she said, and he nodded in agreement, holding the tiny powder mountain to her left nostril.

She gave a tentative sniff, but the fine powder went where it was supposed to go straight away. She waited, but nothing seemed to be happening. She watched with relief as Adrian snorted the powder from her left nipple, then her right, before giving her pussy one long, deep lick to take in the rest. When he looked at her again his eyes had a strange sparkle, and his cock seemed to grow before her very eyes. Suddenly it was huge, a rearing beast that she wanted deep inside her, damaging her. But first he was licking her again, so intensely that her orgasm was hard and sharp and almost immediate, making her clitoris quivery and almost too sensitive to touch.

'Come on, you big fuck,' she growled, throwing her legs wide apart. 'Let me go so I can give you what you want.'

'Anything?' he asked harshly.

'Anything.' She wanted that big prick in every orifice. She wanted three big pricks, all fighting for her, abusing her. She wanted to lose her way in a sea of male meat, bending over for them whenever they wanted it, then opening herself up for the next one, getting showered in come until she slipped and fell and she was swimming in it. And still they could fuck her, until she was one huge pussy for every man in the world to fuck. And they would feed her and keep her fat and stupid, so that she would have no choice but to let them screw her whenever they wanted. Feverishly he uncuffed her and then she was free. As if moving through a sea of semen she slowly rolled over, on to her knees.

She pushed her bottom out at him and Adrian swooped down and slavered over her hole, her little puckered hole that no man had ever been into before.

'I'm an anal virgin. Pop my cherry.' She giggled as he spread her cheeks wide and thrust his tongue up that slim orifice. Then something larger followed. Something blunt and much bigger, followed by a slap on the buttocks and a hard command to relax, which she did, imagining another cock in front of her, ready for her to suck.

'Ooh, baby,' she purred as the big, blunt thing fought the resistance and eased in, deeper and deeper until she felt very full.

'Come on, baby, let me feel your balls as well,' she muttered, realising she had to be stoned to talk like this and let him do this, but it wasn't so bad after all. In the mirror opposite the bed she could see Adrian's perfect buttocks bunching, and his priapic cock sliding in and out of her ass. His balls brushed against her thighs, then began to bang against them as his pumping became more desperate. She arched her back down and thrust out her backside and let him go as deep as he pleased, while she flipped her long blonde hair and looked over her shoulder at him and pouted in a very pornographic way. He took the necklace and wrapped it around his cock again and fucked her through a circle of priceless jewels until she was shrieking softly. His fingers on her clitoris almost sent her through the ceiling. As she came she felt him pulse and pulse with a lion's roar.

For a long moment he just stayed where he was, kneeling up behind her, his cock still deep in her. His head was thrown back and his arms were limp by his sides, and it was one of the most beautiful and erotic pictures she had seen for a long time.

Eventually he pulled out of her and staggered to the bathroom. As soon as she heard him taking a piss she went for her handbag. Carefully focusing on her task, because she knew she was still stoned, she found the powder and tipped it into his champagne, swilling it around to disguise the granules. When he came out she was back on the bed, as languorous and receptive as before. He lay with her and lit a cigarette. They shared it, Rachel looking innocently decadent and fucked-out. Adrian poured more champagne and took his glass. After a couple of sips of hers, Rachel was also desperate for a pee.

When she came back he was reassuringly in the same position, and his glass was almost empty. When he saw her he held out his arms.

'Come to me and let us rest for a while. You have made me dizzy with love.'

She curled up next to him and prepared to wait. Five minutes later, he was asleep. After waiting another long five minutes, she decided he wasn't going to wake up any time soon. She gave him a prod just to make sure, but he did not move.

As quickly as she could with the coke still in her system, she got to work. She opened the vibrator and retrieved the fake necklace. Quickly she swapped it for the sticky, million-dollar diamonds, replaced the end and put it back in her handbag. That had taken less than a minute. She struggled back into her dress, running into the bathroom with the fake necklace to make it look as if she had tried to clean it up. She ran some water in the white marble bowl and dropped the necklace in, then ran out again.

Straight into Adrian.

She had never felt so sick in her life. He did not say anything. He backed her into the bathroom, up against the vanity unit, and snatched the necklace up from the water.

'I was washing it,' she stammered, knowing she sounded and looked as guilty as hell.

'How considerate of you,' he said. 'And I suppose that attempting to drug me was your way of ensuring I had a good night's sleep?' His hand came up and she flinched from it, but he stroked her hair, tenderly, frightening her more than outright violence would have done.

A soft knock on the outside bedroom door saved her, but not for long. He went to open it, and she received her second shock. Jerry walked in, a big fat grin all over his face.

'Hello,' he said, beaming. 'Did you save some for me?'

'Did you make sure you were not followed?' Adrian asked abruptly.

'It's all right, keep your hair on. Jermaine and his missus are all tucked up nice and cosy in bed. Everything's set. No problem.'

'Except this woman was trying to walk out with our diamonds.'

'No!' Jerry looked disappointed, but Rachel could tell it was an act. 'I think she should be punished, don't you?'

'We don't have time,' Adrian said crisply, looking at his Rolex. 'We need to get on with it. It seems a pity to waste good champagne, though.' He poured the remainder of the Bollinger into the flutes, handing one to Rachel and the other to Jerry.

'I could get off in five minutes with her,' Jerry said,

swigging his champagne and unzipping his fly. Rachel downed the remainder of her champagne and tried not to stare, but the sight of Jerry's unimpressive cock and whopping balls sticking out of black dinner-suit trousers was too nasty to avoid. 'Come and wrap your laughing gear around this,' he said lasciviously.

Adrian grimaced with distaste. 'Put it away,' he said irritably. 'This time tomorrow you can bang yourself to death with every whore in the Caribbean. Let's go.'

'Where to?' Rachel asked. It was the first time she had spoken since being discovered.

'A mystery tour,' Adrian said, smiling. 'Do not worry, my little dove. We will take care of you.'

As he put his arm around her she was aware of a very peculiar feeling. The floor seemed to be at a strange angle, no longer parallel to the ceiling. As she watched, it began to move. Adrian took her glass and steered her towards the door. As she tottered along, it felt as if the floor was sinking under her feet. She held on to Adrian, trying to keep upright, but her hand and brain were no longer communicating as well as they should have been. Jerry was by her side, holding her handbag. She realised what had happened. As they went out into the night and weaved towards the car she struggled to escape, but her limbs felt as if they were moving through treacle.

'You drive,' she heard Adrian say to Jerry.

'Why can't I get in the back with her?' Jerry whined.

'Because I've had too much to drink, you idiot! Argue with me and your payment will be halved.'

What payment, she thought muzzily. Adrian slipped into the car next to her and put his arm around her shoulders. The last thing she was aware of were his words.

'You have a good long sleep, my love. Who knows where you will be when you wake up?'

16

The couch felt and smelled like leather. She felt as if she had been thrown on to it, her face mushed up against the cushion, and she realised her wrists were tied. She freed up one nostril so she could breathe and opened one eye, then the other. The room was dark, and two men were talking. She could tell that one of them was Adrian. The other was Jermaine. He wasn't very happy. She closed her eyes again, feigning unconsciousness, and listened.

'The bitch is your mess, Grodin. Why the hell did you bring her here?'

'Where else could I bring her? She was about to walk away with our diamonds!'

'That still don't make it my mess. What the fuck do you want me to do with her?'

'Why don't you tell me? You must be better at this than I am.'

There was a long silence. Rachel froze as footsteps moved closer to her. He glared down at her so intently that she could feel the heat of his stare through her eyelids.

'I resent your implication, Mr Grodin,' he said coldly. 'How long have we been doing business? And you still assume that I can jump tracks whenever it suits me. I operate strictly within the law at all times, but for your sake I'll make an exception. I'll have the gems, and in return you can hightail it off the island, with your bitch, and I don't want to hear, breathe or see you again in Jamaica. Is that understood?'

'Oh, I see, you want the necklace as hush money!

Pardon, monsieur, but it doesn't help my problem. The woman will still talk.'

'That isn't my problem, Mr Grodin. It is yours. Now you can just take it away.'

'I cannot do that, I'm afraid.'

There was a metallic click, and a deep fruity chuckle from Jermaine. 'Man, you are wired. Security is already on its way to dismiss your ass out of this house.'

'Actually not, because before I announced myself I despatched your security guards with a bullet to the back of the head. Now you can show me the contents of your safe.'

The door opened. Rachel heard Jermaine say, 'What the . . .' and another man's voice, plus that of a woman sobbing.

'Hey, what's going on!' A muffled sound, and a roar of pain, followed by a heavy thump. The woman started to scream, but a hard slap turned her noise into choked sobs.

'Don't you touch her, you treacherous son-of-a-bitch!' Jermaine's voice was ragged with agony and rage. He grunted as handcuffs were fastened on his wrists.

Rachel heard Jerry's voice.

'Sorry, mate. I need cold hard cash and lots of it, right now. Mr Grodin needed my expertise and was prepared to pay a lot more than you.'

'Shut up, you fool!' hissed Adrian.

'They'll be dead soon. What's the difference?'

Rachel could hear heavy breathing, like that of a man in pain. She wished she could see what was going on.

'You'll never get away with this,' Jermaine warned.

'On the contrary, your house has been wired to explode fifteen minutes after I set the timing device. It will take a further hour for the police to get here, at least an hour for the fire department to get enough water up here to put out the blaze and weeks for them to identify you by your dental records. In the meantime, I will be gone and no one will be able to touch me.'

'And what about you, you treacherous fuck?' Jermaine said, presumably addressing Jerry.

'I'll be in the Caymans, earning twenty per cent, not that it'll make any difference to you. You'll be toast in half an hour,' Jerry replied carelessly.

Rachel could just see a sliver of Lady Jermaine, sitting bolt upright in an armless chair, looking angry and proud, but her face was wet with tears. Rachel thought fast. Where was the cavalry now? Well, she guessed she was it. Was he bluffing about the explosives? She didn't think so. It was well within Jerry's capabilities, thanks to his army training. Great. She could have told David that his simple plan just wasn't going to work out.

She was shaken violently by the shoulder. Playing dead, she rolled off the couch and sprawled on the floor.

'Still out for it,' Jerry said, kicking her over on to her front. 'It's a shame. She's a fit little dolly.' As she felt him pulling the knot she tensed her wrists, as she had once seen someone do in a film. When he went away, she relaxed, and the bindings were not quite as tight as they should have been.

'You show us the safe now, please,' Adrian said. Together with Jerry he hauled Jermaine to his feet. Groaning with pain, he was dragged from the room.

Rachel immediately started to fight her bindings, which she managed to untie. She kneeled up, hindered by the stupid long dress, and looked at Lady Jermaine, whose face now showed absolute shock.

'What happened?' Rachel kept her voice to an urgent whisper.

'They shot him in the leg!' The tears welled up again. Rachel struggled free and looked around for something sharp to cut Lady's bindings.

'In the desk,' she whispered. Rachel ran to it and found

scissors, then hacked desperately at the bindings. It was punishingly slow work, and she grew angrier and more frustrated with each fibre that refused to budge. Lady pulled against them and worried at them more so that Rachel could get better purchase. With a fearful ear ready for footsteps, they worked silently together, almost holding their breath until the bindings were off.

'Now what?' Lady asked.

Rachel was at the phone. 'The line's been cut,' she said. She looked around for her handbag. It was nowhere to be seen. 'Have you a mobile?'

'In the bedroom, but there's no time!'

The men were coming back. Rachel grabbed a small stone statue. Lady had armed herself with a bronze candlestick. They waited together by the door.

'I'll take the first, you take the second,' Rachel whispered.

Jermaine came in first, followed by Adrian, then Jerry. In the split second that the men noticed the women were no longer where they should be, they struck. Rachel smashed the statue across Adrian's forehead. Jerry's warning shout was cut off by Lady as the candlestick landed on the back of his head. Both men slumped, unconscious, on the floor, the gun skimming away from Adrian's outstretched hand.

'Way to go, girls!' Jermaine said, laughing through his pain. He too was prone on the floor, as he could no longer walk properly.

Rachel felt in Adrian's pocket for the small timing device. He had already set it five minutes earlier.

'Shit! We've got to get out of here.' Rachel felt in Adrian's pockets again for keys to the handcuffs but they weren't there. Feverishly, she felt in Jerry's trousers and found them. Fumbling, desperately aware of the diminishing seconds, she set him free.

'Come on!' she said, as she and Lady grabbed Jermaine

by the shoulders and heaved him to his feet. It was difficult, as he was a big man. Looking back, she could see Jerry stirring and, on the table behind him, her handbag with the priceless diamond necklace.

'Go on,' she said to Lady, and turned back to retrieve the bag. She grabbed it just as Jerry opened his eyes. He made a weak lunge at her ankle, which she avoided easily.

'Kimmy, help us up,' he said feebly.

She peeled off the wig, letting her long dark hair swing free, and smiled triumphantly. As he registered her true identity she kicked him hard in the crotch.

'Fry, you bastard,' she said coldly, and ran from the room.

But he was lumbering to his feet, holding his balls, shouting, 'Come here, you bitch!' Like she was actually going to do as he said. She ran through the house, past the deceased security men and took the stairs two at a time, catching up with Lady, who was at the end of her strength from helping Jermaine. The long, winding staircase down to the courtyard was excruciatingly slow. When they got there, the Bentley was blocked in by the silver Mercedes, which was in turn blocked by the old black Cadillac that Adrian and Jerry had arrived in.

'Try and get to the gate,' Rachel said as she ran to the car, leaving Lady to support Jermaine. It would be too easy for Adrian to have left his keys in it, she thought, although she couldn't recall seeing them. She was right, though. No keys. Lady was struggling with Jermaine, desperately trying to put some distance between them and the house. Rachel dared to look at her watch. If it was accurate, there were only two minutes to go.

She had remembered a trick that Jerry had taught her once, many years ago when he still wanted to impress her. She had tried it since, but had never succeeded in making it work. Now it had to. In her handbag was a tiny penknife and scissors which she always kept for emergencies. With less than ninety seconds on the timer, this classed as one. She had only one chance of getting it right, and she did, thrusting the penknife into the old Caddy's ignition and hearing the sweet sound of the engine roaring into life. She floored it and flew towards the iron gates just as a figure appeared at the bottom of the stairs and started to run towards them.

'Get in!' she screamed at Lady and Jermaine. Lady bundled Jermaine into the back of the car and leaped in as Jerry closed in on them. Rachel didn't wait. She flew towards the gates as a dull thump hit the car, almost lifting the back end. The house suddenly illuminated with light.

'Oh my,' Lady moaned, looking back behind her. Fallout banged against the car roof. A large chunk of mortar landed in front of them just as they reached the gates. Rachel swerved, frantically trying to remember what to do in a car not equipped with ABS. Her training kicked in as the car started to skid and they missed crashing into the concrete gate posts with millimetres to spare. Then they were on the road and away from the inferno that had been Santega Heights. Jermaine and Lady were staring out the back window, their arms around each other.

Rachel felt in her handbag for her mobile. After asking for the number she dialled the police and told them to get to Santega Heights, along with the fire brigade, soonest.

'I hope that son-of-a-bitch fries,' Jermaine said angrily as Lady started to cry. 'Jerry was the one guy I trusted out of all of them.'

'Did you know he was thrown out of the army ten years ago?' Rachel asked.

'Huh, he said he left because the money wasn't good enough.'

'That's what he told me. The truth was he didn't make the grade. But before he left he did a training course on how to deal with explosives. I'm betting that the device used back there was pretty crude, but to a man with the knowledge and the run of the place, it could be pretty easy to wire the place up and wait for the right moment.'

'How do you know all this?' Lady said curiously. Then she realised that Rachel's hair had dramatically changed colour. 'Who are you?'

Rachel kept her eyes on the wheel.

'My name is Rachel Wright. Unfortunately, Jerry is still my husband,' she said. There was a soft moan from the back. 'It's OK, I'm friendly! I came because I wanted to nail the bastard for myself. And Adrian Grodin.' She wished she could see their faces. 'Oh, and that necklace he was so desperate to get back? Relax, it was a fake.'

'You mean he's been dealing me fake goods? No way. I would have picked that up straight off,' Jermaine said, but with a hint of doubt.

'You're right, he wasn't. He was stealing them from British houses and selling them on to you.'

'Oh, sweet Mary. Anything else?' Jermaine groaned.

'Yes. Tell me where the nearest hospital is so we can get you sorted out.'

Flashing lights approached them. Rachel pulled over and let two police cars and a fire truck go past. They were followed by another car, not a police vehicle, with its full beam on. Just as it passed them it braked and turned around. Rachel saw it start to pursue them.

'Oh, no. Now what?' she muttered, pulling away at speed.

Just then her question was answered. A bullet smashed through the rear windscreen, showering Lady and Jermaine with glass. They threw themselves into the rear foot wells and Rachel stepped on the throttle. Desperately she headed towards the glow of distant lights, keeping as low as she could while still being able to see. Another shot, another scream from Lady, and the car began to veer. One of the back tyres had been blown out. Rachel fought for control of the crazily spinning wheel, but this time the car wasn't listening to her. She felt a jolting sideways thump and it tilted crazily, sloughing through the undergrowth to who knew where. She gave up on the wheel and braced herself for the inevitable impact, telling her passengers to do the same.

When it came, it was more like a soft thud into a very large, wet mattress. For a moment she did not realise they had stopped moving, but she heard Jermaine's voice from somewhere above her, calling Lady's name, and the tremulous answer that she was still in one piece.

'But there's water coming in,' she said, with an edge of panic in her voice. Rachel could feel it too, cold and insidious against her legs. She peered cautiously out of the window for their pursuers, but all she could see was stars. The Cadillac was effectively standing on its passenger side, propped into a deep, narrow stream lined with lush ferns. There was the strong smell of petrol fumes, together with the earthier scent of ripped vegetation.

'We've got to get out of here!' Lady sounded almost hysterical now, struggling at the door handle. Then a sound made them all freeze.

'Show me your hands, Grodin.'

Rachel had never felt so relieved in her life. 'David, it's me,' she said, her voice winded out of her by her impact with the seatbelt. Instantly the door was wrenched open.

There was no warm welcome, but a suspicious glance into the car to check whether Adrian was still there. The gun was still in her face. A torch was shone into the back, to reveal Jermaine and Lady, lying in a tangled, shivering heap, water up to their waists.

'Jesus, turn that thing off and get us out!' Jermaine growled.

They were helped out of the car. Carlos and Pepe were there, helping Rachel. The hug she needed from David she got from Carlos.

'I need my handbag,' she said when he set her down carefully on the ground.

'Forget it. We've got to get you all to hospital,' David said curtly.

'Fine! So let someone else find the million-dollar necklace that's inside it!'

Jermaine turned to her as he was being helped into David's car.

'You mean, you've had the real goods all along?'

'We'll explain in the car,' David said, steering them all towards a black Lincoln. 'Where's Grodin now?'

'Being toasted,' Jermaine said. David nodded and got on to his mobile to tell the police to look out for him and Jerry. Then they all travelled in silence back to the hospital in Montego Bay.

Jermaine and Lady were treated like royalty in the quiet white confines of the private clinic David drove them to. Rachel was given the same deferential treatment, after a word from Jermaine to the effect that she had saved their lives. Until then she had not thought of it like that. In fact, she still couldn't think of it like that. She accepted a sedative and slipped into a long, deep, dreamless sleep.

She woke next morning to the sound of breakfast being brought in. The smell of rich Blue Mountain coffee and the exquisitely arranged slivers of fresh fruit laid out on white china reminded her that she was hungry. The doctor came in and pronounced her fit enough to go home the next day. She had escaped with a few cuts and bruises, nothing that a vacation in the sun wouldn't solve, she thought sadly. But her time was up. David had booked them on the London flight early next morning. Job done and on to the next thing. Inside she felt a burning resentment. He had not commented at all on her performance over the last few days, or his own appalling behaviour.

She called Sharma, using Carlos's credit card. He had shrugged and told her to take as long as she wanted, because it was charged to 'the Company'. So she was on the phone for over an hour, and Sharma was hugely enjoying herself at the other end, relaying to Colin the salient points as he lay in bed beside her.

'Oh God, the house blew up! What, you shot Adrian in the leg? No? Oh my God!' Then, 'What do you mean, you're coming home tomorrow? Aren't they giving you a few days to chill out? It's the least they can do!'

'David says we need to come home. There are legal reasons. The charge hasn't been lifted off me for Tagger's murder and officially I could still be charged with obstruction.'

'Bullshit! Give me that guy's number!'

When they said goodbye twenty minutes later, Rachel felt emotionally drained, but far happier having found some level ground again with Sharma. Carlos came in as she was getting stuck into morning coffee.

'I feel a complete fraud, being in here,' she said, sucking cinnamon sugar off her fingers. She had dressed and was sitting by the window, basking in the sun.

'They've got Grodin.' Carlos grinned.

Adrian had been picked up by the police the night before while stumbling in a daze around the ruins of the house, looking for a way out, his pockets stuffed full of Lady Jermaine's jewellery. The previous night, Carlos and Pepe had slipped away from Robyn as she was sleeping off her binge of sex and wine and rich food, leaving the police to arrest her in connection with conspiracy to trade in stolen goods. Added to that, the unflattering pictures of her with two anonymous gigolos were about to hit the British press, and the sharks were gathering for a feast of gargantuan proportions.

Meanwhile, Adrian and Robyn were awaiting deportation back to France, where the authorities and the media were rubbing their hands with gleeful anticipation. Apparently, they had been pulling the same scam in the south of France. While the French police didn't seem too fussed about British aristocracy being ripped off, they did take exception to their own rich and famous being made foolish in the same manner. An agreement had been reached by the top brass of both English and French security services that enquiries would not reach over the Channel, 'to preserve the dignity of all concerned'.

'What about Jerry?' she said fearfully. Adrian had been the murderous one, but Jerry was more dangerous now.

'Don't worry, Rachel. He won't get far. All the airports and harbours have been alerted. When they find him, they'll come down on him like a fucking anvil. They've got enough to nail him for attempted murder.'

Rachel stared curiously. 'How come?'

Carlos grinned. 'That vibe you were given was also a radio transmitter. And if you're wondering why David is so mad at you, I guess it could be because he's feeling kind of inadequate.'

Rachel suddenly remembered her coke-fuelled adventure into anal satisfaction, and she cringed inwardly.

'Hey, call it a perk of the job,' Carlos said cheerfully. 'I think he realises where your loyalties really lie.'

She hoped Carlos was right. After he left she hugged her knees and stared out the window, wishing that David would come and see how she was. The ocean sparkled like diamonds on blue silk, but it was untrue that the sun made everything seem better.

The following morning she went to see Lady.

She was in a large bed, surrounded by mountainous pillows, looking drawn and doe-eyed, but her mouth was firm and her manner matter-of-fact.

'Happy birthday,' Rachel said. 'I wish I had something to bring you.'

'Oh, I think what you did is good enough,' Lady said lightly. They talked for a long time. At Lady's urging, Rachel told her about Interlude, and Jerry, and the problem of Reginald Tagger. Then Lady told her about a new project she was involved with in New York, fundraising among the wealthy to raise awareness of the plight of the children affected by drugs in the Caribbean. Underneath the glitz was a woman in touch with her modest roots and grateful for her own good fortune.

'Where will you live while the house is being rebuilt?' Rachel asked her.

Lady heaved her slim shoulders in a sigh. 'I don't want to go back there. Jermaine is already talking of moving to our apartment in New York. I don't mind for a couple of years. At least I will be closer to my work. But I will have to come back here. This is my home.'

Eventually, Jermaine was wheeled in. He looked resplendent with his bandaged leg and metres of gold chains and platinum rings weighing down each hand.

'They gave me some X-rays. It took ten minutes to get all this shit off!' He laughed. 'What happened to the real necklace?'

'Mr Fielding has it. I don't think he trusts me with it,' Rachel said dryly.

'Huh. He should be giving it to you,' Jermaine muttered.

In more ways than one, Rachel thought wistfully. She stood up to leave.

'I've got to catch my plane. Goodbye,' she said, holding out her hand.

'I can't believe you're going already.' Lady looked disappointed.

'I have to. This wasn't a holiday. Anyway, I've got a business to run at home. It needs me.'

'What do you do?' Jermaine asked curiously.

'I'm a chauffeur,' she said with a final wink as she went out the door.

At the airport, Carlos and Pepe were waiting for her with her papers and her case full of Kim Clarke's clothes.

'You can keep that,' she said, pointing to it. 'I'm never going to wear those clothes again if you paid me. Which you didn't,' she couldn't help adding pointedly, glaring at David.

'We'll miss you, baby,' Pepe said, squeezing her tightly.

'Especially now. I love brunettes,' Carlos purred, rubbing suggestively against her.

'Let's go,' David said shortly. 'Good work, guys.' He shook hands with them and led her firmly away. It was a ten-hour flight back to London, but it would seem like twenty.

A small man approached them. He had the name of a courier company emblazoned on his T-shirt. He handed an envelope to Rachel and waited while she signed for it. She opened it, looking at David. Inside was a note, simply saying, 'Thank you. Jermaine.' There was another piece of paper. She looked at all the noughts, and her name on the top and his signature at the bottom.

'I guess your finances are back in the black,' he said, with a pathetic attempt at humour in his voice.

'I guess so.' She pocketed the precious £500,000 cheque. Suddenly his attitude was no longer her priority. Suddenly she had choices. Choices that for twenty years she had never dreamed of having. She could have an apartment of her own, by the river, where she could retreat to if life became too crazy again. Then another thought struck her. Maybe life would never be this crazy again. This was it, her adventurous blast. Now she was heading back to rainy, grey England and she would have to fight for excitement like everyone else. The thought depressed her, so she cast it aside. She did not speak to David for the whole of the flight. Her mind was too busy on other things, and he had no right into her private musings into the unknown.

Two days later, she was a free member of the public again, all charges dropped. She walked out of Scotland Yard, into Sharma's arms and wept.

'Come on, honey. We're going to the Ivy for lunch,' Sharma said, steering her towards a waiting black stretch limousine. Inside, Colin and Matt were waiting with glasses of champagne. Her family.

After another couple of days a letter fell on to her doormat from Jamaica. The writing was long and sloping, written in fountain pen. She had to read it twice before the contents actually sank in.

Dear Rachel

Words cannot adequately say how impressed I was at your actions last week. It only leaves me to thank you, and to say that your note of thanks to my husband for his small token of gratitude was unnecessary. We are both very grateful.

Of course, all this leaves us without a suitable chauffeur, and it seems providential that you came to our aid when we needed you. Your skill has been proven and I felt very comfortable with you when we talked at the hospital. I would like to offer you the position of chauffeur to myself and, on occasions, to my husband, for the duration of our time in New York, which looks to be for at least two years. This would mean relocating to Manhattan, and travelling with us on a bimonthly basis. Of course, the appropriate relocation expenses would be met, together with the use of an apartment

*in Park Avenue. It can be challenging, as I am sure you
are already aware, but I for one would be delighted to
have someone I liked and trusted to fulfil this role for
me.*

And so it went on. Rachel sensed the unsaid words
between the oddly formal script. What Lady wanted was
a companion, a friend as well as a trusted employee. And
the money was very, very good. She sat, stunned, for an
hour until the phone rang. It was David.

17

An hour later a car arrived to pick her up. On the journey to Scotland Yard she could not help grinning all the way.

She was shown into a dim, empty room very much like the one she had been in a week before, with the Formica table and two plastic chairs. Only this time one of the chairs was already occupied. The figure in it was bloated, unshaven and red-eyed. He looked up and the blood drained from his face.

'Hi, Jez. You look like you've seen a ghost,' she said chirpily in Kim's voice.

Jerry looked away. She guessed he really didn't want to see how satisfied she was at his downfall.

'One of my friends told me you'd come down with a crash. Looks like you have, doesn't it?' she added, rubbing it in with glee.

'Fuck off,' he muttered.

'I intend to, Jerry, but first there's something I want to show you.' She delved in her bag and pulled out the gold vibrator. His eyes bulged and he reddened. He had always felt uncomfortable around 'women's things'. 'And I'm going to use it right now,' she said in a sultry whisper. She picked it up and stroked it thoughtfully. Jerry went redder still. She could tell that he was fighting conflicting emotions, and trying desperately not to show it.

'Does this excite you, Jerry?' she murmured. He looked away, and she knew what the answer was. He was remembering Kim, with the humungous bosoms and smoky promises, and the pain in his balls, together with the shock of finding out that Kim was none other than his estranged wife. It was quite a lot for an underdeveloped brain to take in. She slipped off her shoe and felt for his crotch. In the second before he fell backwards off his chair she discovered that he was hard as a stick of rock.

'It's gratifying to know I still do the business for you, Jerry, but sorry to say you haven't done it for me for a long time. You are shit in bed, which is why I'm so familiar with these little babies. Only this one is special. It's a radio transmitter and it's picked up everything you've said. What was it now? "Don't worry, they'll be toast in half an hour."'

Jerry stared. He forgot to get up from the floor.

'Pretty damned clever, isn't it? But I don't suppose we'll ever see them in any James Bond movies.' She sounded amused, both by that thought and the look of comic horror on Jerry's face. She grinned at him.

'They're going to throw the book at you, you slimy little shit. Not only for attempted murder, but conspiracy to cause explosions, blackmail, attempting to extort money with menaces. Anything else?' she asked of David, who had been waiting discreetly in the corner, waiting for his cue.

'Plenty,' David said succinctly. 'It's out of my bailiwick though. I'll let the little guys deal with you.' He opened the door for Rachel and she turned to go.

Jerry leaped from his chair. 'Wait, babe. I'm sorry, OK? I really am. I was desperate.'

'Desperate enough to kill for money?'

'Yes – no!' he added hurriedly, but it was too late. Rachel smiled at him.

'You'd better hope for life imprisonment, because when you get out you'll have nothing. No home, no fancy car, no adoring little wife. You'll be out on the streets. And if I walk past you, I won't give you a penny.' She gave him a little wave. 'Bye bye.'

She swept out the door, blocking out his pleas for her

to stay and talk. Outside, she took a deep breath and walked out of the police station without a second thought.

David joined her outside. He lit a cigarette and leaned against the wall. 'How does that feel?'

Rachel took the cigarette from him and took a drag. It was nowhere near as pleasant as the small cigars she had liked in Montego Bay. She handed it back, wrinkling her nose.

'Pretty righteous,' she said. And that was all. She had been expecting a cathartic rush of emotion, of a light, floating feeling of joy, but somehow this low-key satisfaction was more solid and long lasting. Now she was aware of David's eyes all over her body. She looked down at the ground, up at the sky, anywhere but at him. Her memory wasn't that short. He had deceived her, and he still couldn't see why she was angry with him. When he bent to kiss her she turned her head away, still smarting from being fooled by all his sweet disguises.

He sharply drew in his breath and backed away. 'The car's here. Lady Longmere wishes to see you this afternoon. I'll pick you up at three.'

'Should I wear the wig?' Rachel asked sarcastically.

'Wear what you like,' he said, and walked smartly back into the grey building, out of sight.

The weather was warm and balmy that afternoon so she wore her stone linen shift, together with a necklace of handmade beads that she had bought in Montego Bay. She kept her hair simple, fastening it back with a tortoiseshell clip. At precisely three o'clock she heard a growly engine outside the front of the house. David rang the doorbell.

'Ready?'

'Yes.' She wasn't looking at his tight-lipped face, but at the Aston Martin behind him. 'Oh my God, it's a Vanquish.' Instantly his mood was forgotten as she ran her hand over one gleaming black flank. David followed her, watching the lust on her face. 'I saw the Bond movie last year but I've never seen one in the metal.' She peered inside the open passenger door. 'How do you get on with the paddle-shift steering?'

'I'm getting used to it.' He obviously wasn't in the mood to talk about his new toy. 'We need to get going.'

The cream interior was like a miniature penthouse. The soft lamb's leather creaked under her bottom. She had to forcibly resist the temptation to run her fingers over the exquisite hand-stitching and plump steering wheel. Instead she looked at David's tense face as he gunned the engine.

'You know what I can't understand?' she said as they roared down the road at Mach speed.

'No. What?'

'How a man can get behind the wheel of a work of art like this, call it his own and still look so goddamned miserable.'

He didn't say anything. They drove five miles in stony silence.

'Is there anything I shouldn't say to the old bag?' she asked as they drove through the village on the outskirts of the Longmere Hall estate.

'Quite frankly, I don't care.'

She had had enough. 'OK, stop the car,' she said firmly.

'We'll be late.'

'I don't care. Just stop the fucking car!'

He pulled over, almost causing her whiplash as they stopped in a gateway to a large ploughed field. For a moment they just stared at each other, before he grabbed her by the throat and kissed her so hard it hurt.

'What's wrong with you?' she asked, licking at her sore bottom lip. 'Tell me before I have to beat it out of you!'

'It's you. Everything. I'm crazy about you and you don't care. You won't talk to me or look at me and I know I don't deserve even a minute of your time but I can't help needing you to. It's all –' he slapped the steering wheel in frustration '– wrong. I don't know how to deal with it.'

There was silence. She read the helplessness in his angry face.

'You could start by saying you're sorry,' she said slowly. 'And then there's a thank you. That's always worth a try. And a little dose of admitting you behaved like a total pig usually goes a long way.'

'I'm sorry. I behaved like a pig. And thank you. You surpassed my expectations.'

'I surpassed your expectations? What kind of talk is that? Where's the man with the diamond earring and the dodgy collection of sex toys?'

'That wasn't me. I was playing a part.' But he said it unconvincingly.

'I don't believe you. I think that was the real you, that for once you could be yourself and not this starchy, up-market prig you've been conditioned to be. In Jamaica you told me all about yourself, remember? I believed you then and I still do now. Forgive the psychoanalysis, but I believe you're only happy when you're someone else, whereas I'm only happy when I'm me.'

He nodded, understanding what she meant. 'Does this mean you prefer the Porsche?'

She burst out laughing. 'Well, there are some aspects of being a starchy, up-market prig that I could get used to.' She reached up and turned his face towards hers. 'You've got a lot of making up to do. Are there any more surprises I should brace myself for before you start?'

He gunned the engine and grinned. It was a fast, loose, dangerous grin, suited to the man she had given him licence to be once more. 'Just one,' he said.

But he would not tell her what it was. This time the atmosphere between them was totally different. He radiated energy, driving with testosterone-charged recklessness. It was as if a large rock had been lifted from his shoulders and she had freed him to be the man he was inside, instead of the one he was obliged to be. As they sped along the country lane she thought, could she really give all this up? Answer, yes, but there was a price to pay. Nothing ever came for free.

The large iron gates slowly and silently opened and he was through, tipping the Aston's speedometer at seventy down the long, straight driveway. They arrived outside the entrance to the house, showering gravel into the stone fountain in the middle of the courtyard. The butler looked amused as he opened the door for Rachel.

'Good afternoon, Mrs Bond,' he said, with a twinkle in his eye. She laughed, breathless with fear and exhilaration. David leaped from the car and ran up the steps as if he owned the place.

Back up a minute. Rachel stared at the house, and the butler, and David waiting for her at the top of the stone stairs.

'Your godmother is in the garden, sir,' the butler said.

'Your godmother?' she repeated, staring at David.

David was grinning at her. 'Who do you think financed your trip to Jamaica? Tony Blair?'

The butler had slipped discreetly away. Rachel continued to stare at David. She didn't know whether to hug him or hit him. He came back down the stairs and took her hand.

'Come on. The old bag doesn't bite.'

Rachel winced. 'Oops, sorry.'

'Don't be. She is an old bag.' David led her through the house to the garden, where afternoon tea was being served. Lady Longmere greeted them and thanked Rachel formally for her assistance in retrieving the diamonds. Justin was there, silent and uncomfortable. It was obvious there was no love lost between him and David. Felicity, his wife, looked lustful when David appeared. It was clear whom she would have preferred to get her claws into. She was Rachel's age, but with the polished air of an accomplished corporate wife. Just remember who screwed up in the first place, Rachel reminded herself with a secret smile.

Tea was a stiff, formal affair. Everyone thought carefully before they spoke, and chewed with their mouths closed and dared not spill tea into their Royal Worcester china saucers. But David kept catching Rachel's eye and trying to make her laugh. Eventually he stood up.

'Rachel is interested in art, so I thought I'd show her the Corot.'

'He says that to all the girls,' Justin muttered.

Rachel looked up and smiled brightly. 'Oh yes, I'd love to see it,' she enthused.

When they were back inside the house David pushed her up against the silk-lined wall and kissed her hard.

'Where is the Corot?' she asked breathlessly.

'Upstairs in the library.' He led her by the hand, up the dark oak staircase lined with paintings of distant ancestors. When they were at the top David grabbed her again. His hands were warm on her waist as he rubbed himself against her again. She held him close, her hands squeezing his buttocks.

'It's a pity Felicity doesn't get the same treatment from Justin.' She laughed. 'Then she wouldn't be so busy panting after you.'

'Don't be fooled. She gets her propers from Justin.' He dropped his voice. 'When she comes she sounds like a moose!' He made a disgusting snorting sound which made her giggle. He led her down another corridor to the bedroom at the end. It was a masculine room, but the bed was smothered with fluffy toys. 'This is Justin's old room. They're both plushy-lovers. Isn't it gross? And check this out.' David grinned, holding up a large, strap-on dildo.

'Is that for him or her?' They laughed together as he tucked it back under the pillow.

'Now the library,' he said.

They stood in front of an uninspiring painting of a grey sky and a grey lake, surrounded by black and green trees. In the middle was a small rowing boat. The rower wore a tiny cap of red.

'Corot's trademark,' David explained.

'Call me a Philistine, but it does nothing for me at all,' Rachel said regretfully.

'It does nothing for me either, but it's worth about a hundred thousand, so I guess we shouldn't be too rude about it. Anyway, I didn't bring you up here to look at a boring old painting.' He leaned back on the desk and drew her to him. 'I work here sometimes when I need to get away from the city. Nice piece of mahogany, as you can see.' He stroked the wood lovingly. 'And finely tooled leather to go with it. Looks a bit empty, though.' His fingertips played across the burgundy leather inlay.

'So it could be improved by some form of expensive executive toy?' Rachel sat on the corner of the desk and posed coyly. 'Maybe something like this?'

'Maybe. Or this.' He pushed her knees apart and sat back in the large leather executive chair, looking up her skirt.

'How about this?' Rachel thrust out her breasts. She flipped her hair over one shoulder and one eye, giving him a sultry look from beneath the silky chestnut curtain.

'Hmmm. Possibly.' David's hand dropped down to his crotch. 'This is beginning to get a bit tight.' He unzipped his trousers and a large, black silk bulge pushed through. 'I've got this fucking cock ring on and now you've made me so hard I can't get it off.'

'Until you get off,' Rachel purred. Over his shoulder she could see the little tea party continuing. The window was open, so they would have to be quiet. She inched her dress up to her waist and watched his face suffuse with lust at the sight of her shaven pudenda under tiny panties, hot pink and formed in the shape of a hibiscus flower.

'Let me smell that,' he said hoarsely, burying his face between her legs. When she felt a sly tongue flicker against the inside of her thigh she bit back a moan.

'What if someone comes?' she whispered.

'That was my intention.' David was pressing neat, nibbling kisses all along her inner thighs. His breath was hot and tickly on her sensitive flesh. She widened her legs involuntarily, needing him to go higher. As he opened her up with his thumbs she watched him, so serious in the huge chair, his tanned throat contrasting darkly with the cream cotton shirt unbuttoned just enough to show a silky patch of hair on his upper chest. His dark-brown hair was crisp and wavy, neatly cut at the back in a navy crop. She had not noticed that before, or maybe he had just had it done. She liked it, anyway.

Her musing was shattered by the long, slow lick to her very centre. She cried out, remembering too late the open window.

'You weren't paying attention,' David said accusingly. 'For that you can bend over and receive a spanking.' He turned her around and pushed her over the desk. She could feel him standing between her spread legs, rubbing his hardness against the crevice of her buttocks. His hands were on her waist, massaging deep into her skin. He was breathing like the middle-aged, randy headmaster of a girls' private school. She felt very lewd and naughty, being watched by the haughty ancestors glaring balefully down from ancient canvas.

He smacked her sharply on one buttock. It made a very loud noise.

'Shut the window,' she hissed at him.

'They won't hear from down there,' he replied,

smacking the other buttock and raising a warm red blush on her tanned skin. He traced the slender white line of her thong bikini with his fingertip and forced her buttocks apart. She felt a cool drop of saliva fall directly on to her rosy hole and she flinched, earning another slap.

'Keep still for Uncle David,' he leered, pushing his finger against the resistant opening. When she felt his cock throb against her pussy lips she opened up, wanting him inside her with growing urgency. His finger inside her arse felt dangerous and wicked, but some inner force kept her moving against it, driving it deep as her pussy yearned for his hot, blunt cock to fill her up.

'Screw me,' she whispered greedily, bearing back down on him so the message was understood. She had to bite her lip when she felt him, so big with his finger still buried deeply inside her. She collapsed on to the desk and abandoned herself to his relentless attack on both her orifices as he thrust his cock into her all the way, again and again. She felt that familiar feeling of being on the edge of a tall cliff, about to step off the edge, when he drew away totally, leaving her with her arse in the air.

'No,' he sneered, 'you can eat me instead.' He sat back in the chair and spread his legs in an aggressively male manner. He palmed his cock lovingly, staring down at her with a cold arrogance that made her shiver with lustful anticipation.

'As you wish,' she said demurely, and peeled the boxers down to expose him fully.

Footsteps outside the door made them jump. With no time to collect herself Rachel dived under the desk, whisking her panties from under David's chair. He moved forwards, trapping her, and began shuffling papers about. Lady Longmere walked in at that moment.

'Where's Rachel?'

'She ... had to make a private call. I believe she's somewhere in the grounds.'

'Justin and Felicity are leaving now. Perhaps you would like to come and say goodbye.'

Rachel couldn't resist the temptation his exposed cock offered to her. She inched forwards and gave his cock a saucy lick. David's voice jumped an octave.

'Sorry, but I don't think I have anything useful to say to Justin right now.'

'Are you well?' Lady Longmere asked curiously.

'I'm fine. I just need to finish this before I take Rachel back home.' He leaned forward to pick up a file, forcing more of his cock into Rachel's wicked mouth. He made a queer whimpering sound which he tried to disguise as a cough.

'You've probably caught one of these revolting bugs from the air conditioning in those wretched aeroplanes. You really do look quite ill.'

David had broken out into a sweat but Lady Longmere refused to leave. She was now fretting over the irritations of finding an alternative gardener, as theirs had slipped a disc while David was in Jamaica. And there was Justin, totally ungrateful for the way David had saved his reputation.

'He's jealous, that's all. You know ... what he's like. I really have to come ... I mean, go in a minute.'

'Bring Rachel to say goodbye before you do. I rather like her, you know.' The calculating tone made Rachel smile around David's cock. He was slumped in the chair, thrusting his pelvis as far as he dared towards her. As Lady Longmere walked out of the room again Rachel pushed her finger up against David's rectum and plunged his whole length into her mouth. Above, she could hear his rasping breath as he started to come. The first pulse was huge and cathartic.

'Fucking bitch!' he hissed, just as Lady Longmere walked back into the room.

'I beg your pardon?'

David was frozen in a grimace of horrified lust as, underneath the table, his cock ruthlessly ruled his whole being. Frantically he shook his head, trying to shed the ragged remains of his orgasm.

'Sorry,' he gasped, as Rachel mercilessly lashed his cock with her tongue. Lady Longmere arched one perfectly plucked eyebrow.

'Don't apologise. You're forty years of age, David. If you want to have a pretty girl give you a blow job under your desk, that is no concern of mine.'

And she walked out.

Later that night, Rachel and David were in the cosier confines of his luxurious apartment, feeling well fed and well fucked. They were sharing a slim, juicy cigar, one of several that Rachel had brought home with her.

'If you're really going to make a habit of these, you need to get a humidor,' he said, inhaling the rich, fragrant smoke. She rolled over and laid her head on his bare stomach. With his free hand he stroked her hair. She decided that now was probably as good a time as any to tell him about her letter from Lady.

'What do you want to do?' he asked finally.

She sighed deeply. 'I don't know whether I want Interlude to continue, now that it can. Seeing Jamaica has made me realise that there is so much I haven't seen. This job would allow me to do that and earn a living at the same time. I'm just not cut out for tax returns and long-term business plans and profit margins. I want to live, David! But . . .' She turned to look at his face. 'I'm not ready for a heavy relationship yet. It's too soon after Jerry. But I know that you're looking for one and . . . I can't have everything, I guess.'

He looked thoughtful. 'Would you settle for a lightweight, fun-filled relationship with someone with whom you can enjoy great sex without guilt, and who is always on the end of a telephone? Someone who will get on a plane and fly five hours for two hours in bed with you? Maybe someone with an apartment in New York and a stately home in England, together with an unlimited private income? And who is willing to wait, because some people are worth waiting for?'

Rachel laughed. 'I would, but that man doesn't exist.'

'He does, for a strictly limited period of two years. After that, I'm public domain and you will have to fight for me.' He covered her mouth with a firm kiss. 'Deal?'

She suddenly felt feather light, as if wings had sprouted from her shoulders and she could fly around the lampshade like Wendy Darling. 'Deal,' she agreed, 'but that doesn't mean I have to choose you or the job at the end of it.'

'On the contrary. I love independent women.'

She pulled him down for another kiss. This time their bodies meshed together, searching for every inch of skin as their tongues entwined for a smoky, fragrant kiss. When he broke away his eyes were hazy with desire. The slow movement of her hips against his had made him rock hard again.

'Think of all the places we could fuck,' she mused. 'Like the back of a yellow cab in Times Square on a Saturday night.'

'Or on the Verrazano Narrows Bridge,' David added.

'Or one of those little rafts moored off the seafront in Montego Bay.'

David shook his head. 'No thrust. Last time I tried it I fell off.'

'Oh, come on, where's your sense of adventure?' She sparkled mischievously at him. 'But first I think we should try it on the London Eye.'

He laughed richly. 'Now you're talking! Can you imagine the scandal if we got caught? It would just about finish my godmother off.'

She nestled close to him again. 'I can see the headlines now. "Racy Spy Shoots Wad On Pod".'

'"London Cops An Eyeful".' David drew on the cigar and blew creamy smoke towards the ceiling before kissing her again. 'You'd better make that call to Jamaica.'

'I think she can wait a couple more hours,' Rachel said, smiling at him. She gave his tumescent cock a frankly sensual glance. 'But I'm damned sure you won't.'

'We'll see. Close your eyes.'

She obeyed, feeling him reach under the pillow. Something cold and heavy was placed over her naked mound, and she felt the delicate touch of some kind of string lightly brushing against her clitoris. Then she felt David's tongue, working exquisitely slowly around her inner thighs, working inexorably towards her sex, which was swollen with yearning for his touch.

'Open them,' he said. She spread her legs wider. 'I meant your eyes, you daft tart.'

She looked down and saw the million-dollar diamond necklace, carefully positioned to accentuate the delta of her sex. He gave her one long, lavish lick from perineum to clitoris, making her pant with pleasure.

'I bet this has never happened to you before,' he said, rearing up above her and burying himself deep in her pussy, carrying strands of the fabulously expensive gems along with his cock so she was literally being fucked with diamonds. He began to move with deeply penetrating, relentless strokes as she clung to his broad back, stimulated beyond reason. This wasn't the time to say she had already been there and done it. Adrian's loving had never made her feel like this. David had given her two years to decide whether she really wanted him or not, but the very fact that he had given her that option had made up her mind already. She surrendered herself to orgasmic joy in the knowledge that this was just the beginning.

Life was sweet. At last.

Visit the Black Lace website at
www.blacklace-books.co.uk

FIND OUT THE LATEST INFORMATION AND TAKE
ADVANTAGE OF OUR FANTASTIC FREE BOOK OFFER!
ALSO VISIT THE SITE FOR . . .

- All Black Lace titles currently available
  and how to order online
- Great new offers
- Writers' guidelines
- Author interviews
- An erotica newsletter
- Features
- Cool links

**BLACK LACE – THE LEADING IMPRINT
OF WOMEN'S SEXY FICTION**

**TAKING YOUR EROTIC READING
PLEASURE TO NEW HORIZONS**

LOOK OUT FOR THE ALL-NEW BLACK LACE BOOKS – AVAILABLE NOW!

All books priced £6.99 in the UK. Please note publication dates apply to the UK only. For other territories, please contact your retailer.

FIGHTING OVER YOU
Laura Hamilton
ISBN O 352 33795 8

Yasmin and U seem like the perfect couple. She's a scriptwriter and he's a magazine editor who has a knack for tapping into the latest trends. One evening, however, U confesses to Yasmin that he's 'having a thing' with a nineteen-year-old violinist – the precocious niece of Yasmin and U's old boss, the formidable Pandora Fairchild. Amelia, the violinist, turns out to be a catalyst for a whole series of erotic experiments that even Yasmin finds intriguing. In a haze of absinthe, lust and wild abandon, all parties find answers to questions about their sexuality they were once too afraid to ask. **Contemporary erotica at its best from the author of the bestselling *Fire and Ice*.**

THE LION LOVER
Mercedes Kelly
ISBN O 352 33162 3

Settling into life in 1930s Kenya, Mathilde Valentine finds herself sent to a harem where the Sultan, his sadistic brother and adolescent son all make sexual demands on her. Meanwhile, Olensky – the rugged game hunter and 'lion lover' – plotS her escape, but will she want to be rescued? **A wonderful exploration of 'White Mischief' goings on in 1930s Africa.**

Coming in July

COUNTRY PLEASURES
Primula Bond
ISBN 0 352 33810 5

Janie and Sally escape to the countryside hoping to get some sun and relaxation. When the weather turns nasty, the two women find themselves confined to their remote cottage with little to do except eat, drink and talk about men. They soon become the focus of attention for the lusty farmers in the area who are well built, down to earth and very different from the boys they have been dating in town. **Lust-filled pursuits in the English countryside.**

THE RELUCTANT PRINCESS
Patty Glenn
ISBN 0 532 33809 1

Martha's a rich valley girl who's living on the wrong side of the tracks and hanging out with Hollywood hustlers. Things were OK when her bodyguard Gus was looking after her, but now he's in hospital Martha's gone back to her bad old ways. When she meets mean, moody and magnificent private investigator Joaquin Lee, the sexual attraction between them is instant and intense. If Martha can keep herself on the straight and narrow for a year, her family will let her have access to her inheritance. Lee reckons he can help out while pocketing a cut for himself. **A dynamic battle of wills between two very stubborn, very sexy characters.**

ARIA APPASSIONATA
Juliet Hastings
ISBN O 352 33056 2

Tess Challoner has made it. She is going to play Carmen in a new production of the opera that promises to be as raunchy and explicit as it is intelligent. But Tess needs to learn a lot about passion and desire before the opening night. Tony Varguez, the handsome but jealous Spanish tenor, takes on the task of her education. When Tess finds herself drawn to a desirable new member of the cast, she knows she's playing with fire. **Life imitating art – with dramatically sexual consequences.**

Coming in August

WILD IN THE COUNTRY
Monica Belle
ISBN O 352 33824 5

When Juliet Eden is sacked for having sex with a sous-chef, she leaves the prestigious London kitchen where she's been working and heads for the country. Alone in her inherited cottage, boredom soon sets in – until she discovers the rural delights of poaching, and of the muscular young gamekeeper who works the estate. When the local landowner falls for her, things are looking better still, but threaten to turn sour when her ex-boss, Gabriel, makes an unexpected appearance. **City vs country in Monica Belle's latest story of rustic retreats and sumptuous feasts!**

THE TUTOR
Portia Da Costa
ISBN O 352 32946 7

When Rosalind Howard becomes Julian Hadey's private librarian, she soon finds herself attracted by his persuasive charms and distinguished appearance. He is an unashamed sensualist who, together with his wife, Celeste, has hatched an intriguing challenge for their new employee. As well as cataloguing their collection of erotica, Rosie is expected to educate Celeste's young and beautiful cousin David in the arts of erotic love. **A long-overdue reprint of this arousing tale of erotic initiation written by a pioneer of women's sex fiction.**

Black Lace Booklist

Information is correct at time of printing. To avoid disappointment check availability before ordering. Go to www.blacklace-books.co.uk. All books are priced £6.99 unless another price is given.

BLACK LACE BOOKS WITH A CONTEMPORARY SETTING

☐ IN THE FLESH Emma Holly	ISBN 0 352 33498 3	£5.99
☐ A PRIVATE VIEW Crystalle Valentino	ISBN 0 352 33308 1	£5.99
☐ SHAMELESS Stella Black	ISBN 0 352 33485 1	£5.99
☐ INTENSE BLUE Lyn Wood	ISBN 0 352 33496 7	£5.99
☐ THE NAKED TRUTH Natasha Rostova	ISBN 0 352 33497 5	£5.99
☐ A SPORTING CHANCE Susie Raymond	ISBN 0 352 33501 7	£5.99
☐ TAKING LIBERTIES Susie Raymond	ISBN 0 352 33357 X	£5.99
☐ A SCANDALOUS AFFAIR Holly Graham	ISBN 0 352 33523 8	£5.99
☐ THE NAKED FLAME Crystalle Valentino	ISBN 0 352 33528 9	£5.99
☐ ON THE EDGE Laura Hamilton	ISBN 0 352 33534 3	£5.99
☐ LURED BY LUST Tania Picarda	ISBN 0 352 33533 5	£5.99
☐ THE HOTTEST PLACE Tabitha Flyte	ISBN 0 352 33536 X	£5.99
☐ THE NINETY DAYS OF GENEVIEVE Lucinda Carrington	ISBN 0 352 33070 8	£5.99
☐ DREAMING SPIRES Juliet Hastings	ISBN 0 352 33584 X	
☐ THE TRANSFORMATION Natasha Rostova	ISBN 0 352 33311 1	
☐ SIN.NET Helena Ravenscroft	ISBN 0 352 33598 X	
☐ TWO WEEKS IN TANGIER Annabel Lee	ISBN 0 352 33599 8	
☐ HIGHLAND FLING Jane Justine	ISBN 0 352 33616 1	
☐ PLAYING HARD Tina Troy	ISBN 0 352 33617 X	
☐ SYMPHONY X Jasmine Stone	ISBN 0 352 33629 3	
☐ STRICTLY CONFIDENTIAL Alison Tyler	ISBN 0 352 33624 2	
☐ SUMMER FEVER Anna Ricci	ISBN 0 352 33625 0	
☐ CONTINUUM Portia Da Costa	ISBN 0 352 33120 8	
☐ OPENING ACTS Suki Cunningham	ISBN 0 352 33630 7	
☐ FULL STEAM AHEAD Tabitha Flyte	ISBN 0 352 33637 4	
☐ A SECRET PLACE Ella Broussard	ISBN 0 352 33307 3	
☐ GAME FOR ANYTHING Lyn Wood	ISBN 0 352 33639 0	